O9-BUA-140

UNEXPECTED

11 MYSTERIOUS STORIES

UNEXPECTED

11 MYSTERIOUS STORIES

EDITED BY

Laura E. Williams

SCHOLASTIC INC.

New York Toronto London Auckland Sydney
Mexico City New Delhi Hong Kong Buenos Aires

If you purchased this book without a cover, you should be aware that this book is stolen property. It was reported as "unsold and destroyed" to the publisher, and neither the author nor the publisher has received any payment for this "stripped book."

No part of this publication may be reproduced, stored in a retrieval system, or transmitted in any form or by any means, electronic, mechanical, photocopying, recording, or otherwise, without written permission of the publisher. For information regarding permission, write to Scholastic Inc., Attention: Permissions Department, 557 Broadway, New York, NY 10012.

"Introduction" and "The Telltale Croak" copyright © 2005 by Laura E. Williams
"Loser" copyright © 2005 by Peter Lerangis
"Little Time" copyright © 2005 by Gail Carson Levine
"Max, the Hand, and Me" copyright © 2005 by Heidi E. Y. Stemple and Jane Yolen
"Baby from Outer Space" copyright © 2005 by Norma Fox Mazer
"Who Broke Harry's Head?" copyright © 2005 by Graham Salisbury
"The Troddler" copyright © 2005 by Bruce Coville
"Infinity Jinx" copyright © 2005 by Margaret Peterson Haddix
"Marked for Death" copyright © 2005 by Will Weaver
"Dear, Dear Kitty" copyright © 2005 by Marion Dane Bauer
"Sleuth 2500" copyright © 2005 by Dian Curtis Regan

All rights reserved. Published by Scholastic Inc. SCHOLASTIC, APPLE PAPERBACKS, and associated logos are trademarks and/or registered trademarks of Scholastic Inc.

ISBN 0-439-45585-5

12 11 10 9 8 7 6 5 4 3   5 6 7 8 9 10/0

Printed in the U.S.A.

First printing, November 2005

CONTENTS

Introduction

~~~~~~~~~~~

Laura E. Williams

IT'S EASY TO BELIEVE THE WORLD IS MERELY WHAT YOU SEE, feel, hear, taste, and smell. But what goes on just outside the realm of your five senses? Do you have that sixth sense (or seventh or eighth . . .) that takes you beyond the everyday world?

Imagine if you woke up tomorrow to discover yourself lost inside this warped dimension, so similar to yesterday's world and yet so different. Now imagine it is not, in fact, your imagination. It's an alternate reality. What sort of twisted truths might greet you there?

Picture this: A frog calls you a murderer. You discover love and happiness in a realm of miniatures. A girl tells you she's a detective from the future. Your sister's rocking horse has been murdered. You find an eerie mansion filled with long-lost treasures. . . .

Not to mention the smelly trolls who invaded your home and kidnapped your mom.

A word of advice: Don't fear the unexpected. It's already here. Turn the page and see.

UNEXPECTED

11 MYSTERIOUS STORIES

Loser

Peter Lerangis

I, NORMAN FERDNIK, THE SMARTEST EIGHTH-GRADER IN the history of Beeler County, have a confession to make: I am not perfect.

I know. You're shocked. You're saying to yourself, "What? The Norman Ferdnik whose math average has been 101.7% (because of extra credit) since October 17 of second grade? Who was selected 'Beeler's Last Great Hope' in the *Daily Bugler* this year? Who composed a concerto for orchestra and nose flute, discovered a previously unknown species of stag beetle, and won a patent for his Name-Squawker Lost-Keychain Finder?"

Yes, yes, yes, yes, and yes.

But the truth is, I wasn't always this way. Many of you have forgotten, but I was once a Loser.

Now, most people hear the word Loser and they picture one kind of kid. It's not a pretty picture. But there are many different types of Losers. Me? I'm a Loser of Things. You name it, I lose it. Well, I *was* that way, back in the time before Beef Pounder, the house on Hemlock and Wormwood, and the day I thought I would die.

But I'm getting ahead of myself.

UNEXPECTED

I trace the Making of Norman the Loser to the beginning of seventh grade.

That was over a year ago, back when we first moved to Beeler County. Boy, was I mad. I really liked our old home in East Foboff, and I didn't want to move. So I started Losing Things on purpose — which technically isn't really Losing, it's Hiding. For example, I once hid the marble figurine called "Angelic Schoolchild" that my grandma gave me. It was worth about a thousand dollars, according to a Sunday newspaper magazine ad. I figured that if we couldn't find it, we couldn't move from the house.

Well, my dad was onto me. To him, Hiding Things is a habit worse than stealing, lying, getting lost, or trusting people. In fact, his motto is Trust No One, Especially People in Soap Operas. Dad takes soap operas very seriously. When we finally did move, he insisted on following the van in our car. He was sure the moving men would get lost, take our stuff halfway around the country, and charge us by the hour. The van drivers weren't too pleased. (Mostly, I think, they were embarrassed to be followed by Dad's beat-up old Augenschmerz sedan. It was made in some country that fell in a 1987 uprising, and if you've ever seen an Augenschmerz . . . well, you wouldn't want to be followed by it, either.) Needless to say, everyone was grumpy, even my little sister, Mars, who had no reason to be. So to cheer myself up, I took my iPod from my backpack.

Only it wasn't an iPod at all. It was a box of frozen blueberry waffles.

"What are you doing with a box of frozen blueberry waffles?" asked my dad.

"I thought I packed my iPod," I replied.

We stopped the car. The van sped off, which of course made Dad furious. We checked the trunk of the car. We even went back to the house. The new owners, Mr. and Mrs. Pettigrew, had already given my bedroom to their four sheepdogs: Strudl, Knudl, Rudl, and George. They were busy tearing up the room. My iPod was nowhere to be found.

As we walked back to the car, my dad grumbled angrily. But my mom just put her arm around my shoulders and said exactly the thing I expected. "Oh, well. I guess Ferguson took it."

I smiled. That's Mom's saying from her childhood. Back then, whenever anyone lost something, my grandma would say Ferguson took it. Ferguson is an imaginary spirit. It's supposed to be a joke.

"Ha-ha," said my dad.

"Waaah," said Mars.

Little did I know, that was the beginning of the end.

Now, don't get me wrong. From the start, I loved Beeler County. There is nothing quite like those parched, flat, brown plains stretching out to nowhere. And from the start, I was intrigued by this local legend of a mansion on a hill haunted by dancing buffaloes. But let me be frank. It's hard to be different here. It's bad enough that I'm both smart and fat — my IQ and weight run neck and neck — but add to that the fact that I was a Person Who Loses Things, and forget it. Dead in the water. I was punched, poked, pushed, knocked down, called names, wedgied, and noogied a total of 4,729 times. And that was just in seventh grade.

I should explain something else about Beeler County. Colorful nicknames are big here. Right away I met Pete "Pimple" Popper, Hanna "Hammerhead" Sharkey, and John "Loud" Belcher. One kid, Kevin Korn, who has a full head of white hair, is called "Pops." On the first day, I was assigned a seat next to Percy "Raw Beef" Pounder ("Beef" for short), who earned his name from the rough way he treated kids, making them feel like, well, raw beef.

It was Beef who thought of my nickname. It happened the first day in school. My homeroom teacher, Mrs. Skaggs, introduced me to the class and asked me to stand up. The desks were kind of small, so I got stuck. I tried to get loose. I lurched upward, again and again, but that just made things worse. My desk and I just bounced together, traveling across the aisle.

Well, everybody was staring at me as if I were some wayward sea elephant. That's when Beef pointed to my left foot and called out, "Hey, what happened to your sock?"

I looked down. My right ankle showed a yellow smiley-face sock, but my left ankle was bare. I shrugged. "Guess I lost it."

"Yeah, I guess you're a real LOSER!" Beef shouted, cracking up at his own cleverness.

From that day on, I was known as Loser.

I didn't accept the name without a fight. Right there in that classroom, I made a vow to Remember Everything, Forever and Ever and Unto the Ages. The next day I made a list before I left the house. That made my dad happy. His favorite saying is, "Lists are your best friend." My list read: WATCH, NOTEBOOKS, TWO SHOES AND SOCKS, PENCILS, BACKPACK, LUNCH, GLASSES, HAVE A NICE DAY ☺.

Imagine my surprise in gym class, when I discovered the one thing I hadn't packed.

"Where are your gym shorts?" were the welcoming words of my new gym teacher, Mr. Trapezus, as I took my place in line wearing khaki pants. Mr. Trapezus was a Navy S.E.A.L. He's very competitive. To him, physical fitness is a religion.

"Uh — Ferguson took them?" I squeaked. It was the first thing that popped into my head. It was also about the dumbest thing I could have said.

"Fifty push-ups," said Mr. Trapezus. "In your underwear."

Now, I promise you, up until then I had never, ever forgotten something as important as underwear. I hadn't even thought to put it on my list.

I should have.

I will spare you the gory details. Perhaps you heard about them on the nightly news. It was awful. Even Mr. Trapezus was laughing — until Beef started laughing louder than him and was forced to do fifty push-ups as punishment.

"You die, Loser," Beef murmured to me after class. "That's a promise."

I tied a string around my finger during the next period. The string was a reminder to "Be Nice to Beef." But I lost the string during social studies.

Now, believe me, I spent entire nights trying to figure out what had caused my problem. Maybe it was the stress of the move. Maybe it was the adjustment to the new school, or the climate, or just plain fear of Beef. My parents tried to understand. They sent me to a priest, a psychotherapist, a hypnotist, a nutritionist, and a spiritual advisor named Dewdrop who spent an hour with me in silence, nodding as if I were telling a string of mildly amusing jokes.

None of it worked.

Every day, it seemed, I lost something new: a hairbrush, a compass, a notebook, a watch, a tuba.

At that last revelation, I thought my band teacher, Mr. Demiquaver, was going to faint. "What kind of kid loses a *tuba*?" he said.

I explained it all in great detail. It's not as strange as it sounds. See, one day I brought it home to practice, but

Mars said it hurt her ears. So I practiced in the back-yard, but the neighbors complained. So I went to the park, but the ducks started to quack. So I decided to take a walk with my tuba. That's when I found Worm-wood Street. It was all dark and overgrown with pine trees, and it led up a long, winding hill — which was weird, considering that Beeler County is about as flat as a whoopee cushion at rest. I began to climb. As the in-cline got steeper, I began huffing and puffing. Soon I could see my breath. I was shivering. And as I reached the top of the hill, at the corner of Wormwood and Hemlock, a thick mist rolled in. *A rolling mist, in Beeler?* I turned to run, but that's when I spotted the mansion on the corner. It was all gray and dark in the setting sun. The windows seemed nearly black with grime. I knew what this place was. I'd heard all about it. I'm not usually scared of anything — especially houses alleg-edly haunted by dancing buffaloes — but this made my skin crawl. And when the wind suddenly began to howl, I ran for my life.

When I returned to the park, I had no tuba. I tried to go back and look for it, but I couldn't find Wormwood Street at all.

Mr. Demiquaver was not impressed. "Maybe a buffalo danced away with it," he said.

I had to pay the school back. My dad was furious. Over the following weeks, he began docking my allow-ance. When I ran out of allowance, I had to write him

IOUs and promise to pay interest from future allowances. When my debt reached $1,719.83, he just threw up his hands and yelled at me.

I have to hand it to Mom. She always knew how to deal with Dad in situations like that. Whenever he got mad she would just quietly pop a soap opera tape into the VCR. In minutes Dad would be on the couch, blubbering like a baby, and muttering over and over, "You just can't trust anyone. . . ."

"Ferguson's at it again, isn't he?" Mom would whisper to me with a little laugh. "Hey, don't worry, you'll grow out of this."

She definitely made me feel better. But I could see the concern on her face. Night after night, I would hope and pray she was right about outgrowing it.

Then the next day would roll around, and I'd lose something else.

As for Beef, he did not live up to his promise. I did not die. But he did devote himself, heart and soul, to making my life miserable on a daily basis. And because he treated me so badly, other kids followed his example.

One day I found the contents of my locker covered with shaving cream. Another day I pulled a dissected frog out of my lunch bag. I discovered seaweed in my science textbook and gum in my pencil case. I grew accustomed to checking the back of my shirt for taped signs that said I AM A LOSER — KICK ME! in various hand-writings.

Teachers tried to help me. Most of them were nicer than Mr. Trapezus. They would yell at my tormentors. But I could tell that even they wanted me to shape up. I could see it in their droopy, exasperated glances.

I was scared. I was having awful nightmares. In them, I'd be losing my final exams or showing up at school naked. I'd see all my stuff guarded by an ogre with body odor and yellow teeth. Soon everything I owned, everything I made, scared me out of my mind because I knew I would lose it someday. I grew so afraid of losing things, I began losing them even more: a basketball, a pound of pork roast, one black dress shoe, and more dollar bills, DVDs, and CDs than I could count.

I had to take my mind off the problem. So I did the only thing I could do. I threw myself into my work. My grades, which were already pretty good, got even better.

"Congratulations, Ferdnik," said my English teacher, Mr. Exlibris, as he handed back our midterm book reports one day. "Your report on *Sorrows of a Seventh-Grade Nothing* is only missing one page. Luckily I have gotten very good at correctly predicting what has been written on your lost pages. So I have given you an A+, both for the work you have done and for the surprising insights contained on the page I haven't yet read."

Wow. That really made my day. I was feeling great until 3:25, when school let out. That's when Beef cornered me outside the front door. I tried to get away, but it was starting to rain, and I slipped and fell.

Beef lifted me up and slammed me against the right rear fender of the school bus. "I handed in *all* of my book report," he said through teeth gritted with anger.

He thrust his report into my hand. In red ink across the top, Mr. Exlibris had written D — SEE ME AFTER SCHOOL. "It's only one paragraph long," I said.

"That's not the point! It's complete, isn't it? And yours isn't. Face it, Ferdnik, it ain't fair!"

Beef had this speech problem. He spat when he said the letter *F*. And his mouth was level with my eyes. Temporarily blinded, I turned my head sideways and replied, "So, did you see him?"

"And have to do more work? Forget it!" Beef spat. "Fortunately I've finally found effortless and effective relief to forfend my failure. Follow me, Ferdnik?"

Beef was doing this on purpose. His face was twisted into a grotesque, distorted mask of derision that on anyone else would have passed as a smile. I reached for my folding umbrella, until I remembered I had lost it. So I just shielded my eyes. "What are you talking about?"

"What I'm talking about is a deal. Our take-home final is worth fifty percent of the final grade. You write me a fine final and find freedom from fear."

I couldn't believe what he was spraying. "But it's due Monday! And we've had weeks to work on it —"

Beef grabbed me by the shirt and dragged me away from the school. We headed for the duck pond. I thought he would throw me in, but he didn't. He kept going, following a path behind a grove of old trees.

And then we were climbing a hill.

The trees grew high and thick, and the air grew cooler. At the top of the hill, on a block with no other houses, was the old mansion I had seen the day I lost my tuba. The branches on the trees in front were bare, save for a few tattered plastic bags that whipped and crackled in the wind. The lawn was parched and brown, swirling with eddies of dust.

In the front window, I thought I saw a dark form stop and move away quickly.

"The corner of Wormwood and Hemlock," said Beef, his voice nearly a whisper. "Like it?"

I looked over my shoulder. There was no breeze at all across the street. "Does anyone l-l-live here?" I squeaked.

"Not any*one*." I couldn't be sure, but Beef seemed to be shaking. "Any*thing*. See, even the neighborhood dogs won't come near this place. The electric company won't either, so it's always dark inside. But something lives here. Every night, the trash on the lawn is picked up. You can see a candle burning and hear banging noises. And I know what's in there, too."

"Dancing buffaloes?" I asked.

"Don't be stupid." Beef's face got all pinched and sour-looking, as if he'd bitten into a rotten lemon. I assumed this was his serious expression. "Tell me, Ferdnik — besides me, what's your worst fear?"

I thought for a moment. "Losing things."

Beef groaned. "You can do better than that."

"What's yours?" I asked.

"The monkeys," Beef said in a soft voice. "Those flying monkeys in *The Wizard of Oz*. The ones that pick you up by the shoulders with their sharp, sharp claws. My mom always told me they were fake. But I knew she was wrong. At night, when I couldn't get to sleep, I would see them sometimes, flying over Beeler. They'd squeak and giggle, and their claws would glint in the moonlight. Just seeing them made my shoulders ache. *That's* who lives in there. A whole family of them. They're real, Ferdnik. But they're night creatures, and they sleep during the day. So no one ever sees them — unless a person is dumb enough to try to break in. And then, their wrath is fierce."

A looney. A total nutcase. A spitting, bullying, underachieving nutcase. I was discovering Beef's hidden qualities by the minute.

I tried to edge away, but he pulled me back. "You think I'm a sissy, don't you?"

"I — I didn't say that!" I protested.

"Kevin Korn — *he* was the sissy! He was afraid of *ev-*

erything when we were kids. He saw monsters around every corner — weird ones that made no sense. It wasn't *my* fault that he broke into this house! He just wanted to prove how brave he was. What kind of moron does that?"

"Kevin Korn?" I said. "You mean Pops? The quiet kid with the white hair? *He* went into the house?"

"Before that night, his hair was brown," Beef replied. "Afterward, no one saw him for days. His parents called the police, but even they were too scared to investigate. They'd pretend they couldn't get a warrant. When Kevin finally did show up at his own house, white as a ghost, he couldn't remember a thing. But every night for months, he screamed in his sleep about a dancing creature with the head of a buffalo and the body of a cobra. It was the same stupid monster he used to make up when he was a little boy. That's when the rumor started. After that, I went to see for myself. And I found out that Kevin had seen wrong. Way wrong."

"How can a person mistake dancing buffaloes for flying monkeys?" I asked.

"The house does awful things to people," said Beef, a slow, malevolent grin spreading across his face. "Unbelievably awful things. Say no to my deal, Loser, and you're taking a trip inside there to find out, feet first. Say yes, and you'll fare just fine, my forgetful friend."

It was blackmail. It was immoral. It was inhuman.

But what could I do? I mean, I didn't really believe in monsters, flying or dancing. But the sight of the house made me prickle all over. I didn't want to go in there, no matter what.

"Deal," I said.

THE TAKE-HOME FINAL WAS HARD ENOUGH — WRITE A STORY using the characters from five of the books we had read in class, set in ancient Egypt with accurate historical detail. But now I had to write two of them, and make them different — if I valued my life.

I worked all Friday night and Saturday to finish my own final. I started Beef's early Sunday morning.

"My, you're working hard," said my mom, looking into my room.

"He's hardly working," said Mars.

"Make a copy of every page, dear!" yelled my dad from the living room, his voice choked with emotion over an episode of *The Years of Our Restless Lives*. "Make two copies, in case he loses one! Copy the entire hard drive, in case he loses that!"

Fear drove me onward. I pulled characters from every book I'd ever read. I shaped them into a story with great suspense and crackling dialogue. I packed the plot with details about ancient Egyptian religious customs, history, and agriculture. I even threw in a few hieroglyphics. This was not easy to make realistic, considering that some of my characters had to have names like Harriet the Spy and Dumbledore. But I did it. I did it brilliantly.

And at 11:00 P.M. on Sunday, I called Beef on the phone to tell him I was done.

"Done with what?" was his reply.

"The take-home!" I said.

"Oh, yeah, I forgot about that! I've been busy. First the beach — you know, riding the waves and having a barbecue — then home to play video games and make ice-cream sundaes . . ."

"I'll read it to you," I said, trying to keep my cool. "In case you have any suggestions."

I didn't get very far. He interrupted me halfway through the second paragraph. "Loser, that is the most boring thing I ever heard. It *has* to be an A+. Just hand it in. Then tomorrow night you can start working on my social studies long-term."

"*Social studies?* That wasn't part of the deal —"

"Gotta go, *Extreme Wrestling Nation* is about to start. Oh, and one other thing. About that English report? Make sure it's in my handwriting."

"What? I can't do that at this hour!"

Beef cackled with glee. "I think you would look really cool with white hair, Ferdnik. . . ."

I jammed the phone down. His own handwriting? Who did he think he was?

I printed out the report. It was ten pages, single-spaced. Then I looked at Beef's book report, which he had never taken back from me. He had the worst hand-writing I'd ever seen; even worse than my sister's, which gave me an idea.

"Mars?" I called out. "Would you copy a report for me and keep it a total secret, if I gave you ten dollars and an ice-cream cone every week until June?"

"Mo-o-o-om, Loser's trying to bribe me to do his homework again!"

I slammed the bedroom door. Nobody cuts a Loser any slack.

I ended up writing the whole thing with my left hand. The words were atrocious, all shaky and off the lines, with backward letters. It was perfect.

At about 1:30 A.M., I finished. I collected the pages and went right to bed.

The next morning, my mom woke me up with a re-port in her hands, all bound in a clear plastic cover. "It's all complete. I put an extra copy in your backpack, an-other in the trunk of the car, and one in my study for safekeeping."

My heart nearly jumped out of my body. Was she holding Beef's report? I would have to tell her the truth! "Give me that!" I grabbed the report and saw right away that it wasn't Beef's at all. She had bound the right one. "Uh, great, Mom. Sorry, I'm just feeling a little tense. It looks great. Thanks."

"Good luck," she replied with a warm smile. "Hey, Ferguson isn't touching this one."

I hugged her tight.

Instead of taking the bus to school, I used my bike. It was a long ride, but I needed to clear my head. As I pedaled, I felt a mixture of relief and dread. One Beef report down, another to go. I made a vow. I would do his social studies report, but that was it. No more. I was not going to be his doormat, no matter what.

Beef was waiting in front of the school. "Got it?"

"Yes," I replied.

"Yes, *what*?"

I looked into his eyes and tried to control a feeling of disgust. "Yes . . . sir?"

"That's better. Now give it over."

I pulled off my backpack. I set it down, opened it, and carefully looked through.

"Come on, Loser, come on," Beef said.

I pulled aside my science textbook, my library book, my loose-leaf notebook, my nicely bound English report, my homework folder.

It wasn't there.

Beef's report wasn't there.

"Um . . ." I said. "Uh . . ."

"Don't tell me." Beef's face was turning the color of his nickname. He reached down and grabbed my arm. "You read it to me over the phone. I know you wrote it! Listen, Ferdnik, you're on the verge of big trouble. Because if I don't hand this in, I flunk. Do you hear me? Flunk, flunk, flunk. F, F, F!"

I wiped my face off. I thought I had brought sunglasses for an occasion such as this, but I must have lost them, too. "Maybe it fell out along the way," I said, climbing back on my bike. "Maybe I left it at home!"

"Fine." Beef plopped himself down on my bike's bar — the long one that extends from the seat to the handlebars. He was not going to let me go alone. "Fly, Ferdnik. And find it. Or forfeit your future."

Beef must have had something spicy for breakfast, because my eyes stung as I began to pedal. Due to Beef's girth, my legs jutted out on either side. We wobbled down the street. If you think it's easy riding a bike with a 150-pound, saliva-spewing bully on your bar, then you're from another planet.

I took the exact same path I had taken to school, carefully checking the roads, the sidewalks, the lawns. I made it all the way home, then went inside and looked in every possible place.

"It's gone," I said meekly as I walked out.

Beef was strangely calm. He just nodded. "No problem, Loser," he said, sitting on the bike seat. "You must be tired. This time, let me give you a ride."

I gulped. We traded places. I sat on the bar, holding tight to the handlebars.

Beef had a terrible sense of balance. We nearly fell over seven times. But he kept going, through the center of town and down an old rutted path that was so bumpy I couldn't even see straight.

I finally fell off into a pile of leaves at the intersection of two roads. Beef yanked me onto my feet. "Move," he said, pushing me hard.

The road was steeply inclined. I nearly fell again, but before Beef gave me another shove, I looked up at the street sign.

WORMWOOD, it read.

MY BACK WAS BRUISED BY THE TIME WE REACHED THE TOP OF the hill. It was still bright and early in the morning, but the old mansion was dim and gray in a thick mist.

Beef pushed me through the front gate. It swung on a rusty hinge, creaking. "Am I jogging your memory, Ferdnik?"

"I promise I'll make you another report," I said. "I'll do your math final, too!"

"A little late for that." Beef placed two hands on my chest and put all his weight into them. I tumbled backward over the uprooted cobblestones of the walkway and fell, hitting my head on a step of the wooden porch.

The edge of the step broke into crumbly pieces, rotten and mildewed. "Beef, please, let's work this out."

"Yeah, work *this* out!" Beef charged toward me like a linebacker. Or at least I think that's what a linebacker does. I did the first thing that came to mind. I ducked.

Beef went flying over my head. He landed on the top of the porch with a dull thud. Beneath him, the boards buckled but didn't break.

I tried to bolt, but my foot was stuck between two cobblestones.

Beef rose above me. "Ferdnik, you are fish fodder," he spat, balling his fists.

Crrrrreak.

We both stopped moving.

The sound had come from in front of the house. The gate.

I peered in that direction. The mist had thickened even more, but I could see a darkening in the center of it — a figure, moving closer. Whoever lived here had come home!

I quickly worked my foot out of the cobblestones.

"Oh, no," Beef whispered. *"No!"*

I didn't even look. I had to think fast. The place was surrounded by a fence — and I couldn't even see it. Trying to escape would have been foolish, so I bolted into the house. The door was ajar, but I slammed it shut behind me.

Beef was still outside.

"DON'T!" he shrieked, banging on the door. "DON'T LEAVE ME!"

The knob was an old, metal latch. I tried to pull it open, but it was rusted and my hands were shaking — and the constant pounding from the other side didn't help.

Then the pounding stopped. I heard footsteps along the porch. Shadows flitted across the grimy, broken windows, but I couldn't make them out. I heard an un-earthly noise that might or might not have been Beef.

I ran. I hate to admit it, but I ran through the parlor, deeper into the house. The room was covered with dust. A mounted moose-head and a grandfather clock, stuck at midnight, stared down at the surroundings like two lost old souls. Just beneath them were an ancient sofa with ripped tassels, a large oriental rug drained of any color, and a tea table listing to one side from the accumulation of grime. At the other end was a wide oak stairway that led upward.

I darted up to the second floor, finding myself in a long hallway that seemed to stretch out far longer than the house was. There must have been a dozen doors along the walls, all closed.

Thump.

On the floor below, someone — some*thing* — had stepped into the house.

I pulled on the first knob I saw, on a door to the left. The door swung open to a windowless room. In the dim light of the hallway I could make out shelves and shelves of stuff, stacked floor to ceiling, all neatly arranged. There was just enough room for me. I stepped in and shut the door behind me, as quietly as I could.

The room was pitch-dark, save for the ring of light around the door. I gulped to catch my breath. My pulse was thunderous in my own ears, and I worried it could be heard downstairs.

I heard thumping, bumping, scratching, and the sound of muffled voices. Or maybe it was just one voice. It was impossible to tell.

Slowly my eyes began to adjust to the dark. My back ached, so I unhooked my backpack and lowered it quietly to the floor. I felt around the shelves. In the fleeting moment I'd seen the room, I could have sworn I had spotted a flashlight. It looked just like one I'd lost, with a long, solid, metal shank. I could use it to find my way around the house, then sneak up behind whoever was down there and clobber him before he could do any harm to Beef — not that Beef *deserved* to be rescued, but if I didn't do something I couldn't live with the guilt.

Yes. There it was. My fingers closed around the flashlight, and I took it off the shelf. It felt heavy and solid, reassuringly familiar. It even had a chip near the lens, at about the same place where I had dropped it when I was five. I pushed the button. A light clicked on, illuminating the room for a moment and then dimming.

That was like my flashlight, too. I always managed to leave it on too long, so the batteries were constantly in a state of near-death.

It wasn't going to do me any good. I pressed my ear to the door and listened. The sounds downstairs had stopped, but I thought I could hear something more distant — footsteps crunching the dry leaves on the lawn.

I pushed the door open a crack.

The hallway was empty. Behind me now, the little room glowed with dull reflected light. My eyes caught the only motion in the room, a sweeping second hand of a watch, sitting on a bottom shelf. I picked it up and examined it carefully. It, too, was exactly like the one I had lost. And it still told perfect time.

I placed it on my wrist.

Then I saw the hairbrush. And the compass. And a marble composition notebook with some familiar-looking writing on it: NORMAN FERDNIK. DO NOT STEAL. THIS MEANS YOU, MARS!

"I don't believe this," I whispered. It was the note-book I had lost at the beginning of the school year.

I looked closely at the flashlight. I saw a long, dry blob of Wite-Out, exactly where I had dripped it one night while doing homework. The flashlight was mine, too! And so was the watch.

I staggered backward. My foot banged against something big propped against the wall. It clattered to the floor with a loud *CLANG*, bringing a heap of stuff down around it.

Even in the dark, I recognized the shape of a fallen tuba.

I backed out of the room, feeling cold and prickly, slowly surveying the shelves. It was all there: one black shoe; a pound of pork roast, still tightly shrink-wrapped; my gym shorts; three neat piles of dollar bills, DVDs, and CDs. Stuff I hadn't seen in ages.

"BEEEEEF!" I called out at the top of my lungs.

I turned around, ready to bolt, but only managed one step before running into a large, dark figure.

I jumped back, clutching the door to keep myself from falling. But the door swung outward, taking me with it. The figure lunged forward, and I screamed.

A hand grabbed my wrist, tightly. "Oopsy," came the soft voice of a man. "Losing our balance, are we?"

The man's face caught the glow of the light from downstairs. He had round, red cheeks and only two small tufts of gray hair on the sides of his head. He wore a tuxedo, and white gloves that felt soft and cottony around my wrist. "So glad you could come, Norman," he said. "I've been hoping to see you."

"How do you know my name?" I cried out. "Who are you?"

"I'm an old friend of the family's." The man smiled as if he'd known me all my life.

I scrambled to my feet. "I've never seen you before. How did all my things get here?"

"You lost them," the man said, as if that explained everything. "But now you're here, tra-la! So go ahead, Norman. Step lively. Take it all away!"

I began to shake. The idea of taking my stuff — of having it all back again, as if nothing had been lost at all — well, it should have made me happy. But it didn't. I was a nervous wreck. "I — can't."

"Of course you can!" the man said. "You should be

proud of yourself. You've done what you came here to do. Not everyone can face his greatest fear."

"My greatest fear? *You?*"

The man laughed. "Not *me*. Your *things*. Losing them, that is. So . . . zip-zip-zip, away it all goes!"

I stood there like a plank.

The man was right. I had been afraid of Losing Things. Petrified. And now, here I was, face-to-face with all of it, free to bring it home. Free!

But I couldn't.

I was Norman Ferdnik of Beeler County, and Norman Ferdnik Lost Things. It was a simple truth, like the sun rising in the east, the birds singing in spring, my sister smelling like cherry Jolly Ranchers. Okay, I didn't love my own particular truth, but it wasn't so bad, really. At least everyone knew what to expect.

"I'm — I'm scared," I whispered, backing away.

"Ah, well, it's your choice — you're a big boy now," the man said, reaching into his jacket pocket. "If you ever need me . . ."

He pulled out what looked like a business card, but I was already booking. I grabbed the wooden post at the head of the stairs and vaulted down. I raced through the parlor, kicking up dust, and reached for the front door. But as I grabbed the latch, I felt a breeze at my back and realized I'd lost my backpack!

No. I hadn't *lost* it. I'd left it on the floor of the room.

Click. I sprung the latch. One pull, and I would be out of there.

But how could I go back to school without my take-home final? Not to mention my books and pencils and notes and homework. Nothing to turn in. A report card with big fat F's — F, F, F, across the board. Losing Things was one thing. Being a loser was something else.

I was not a loser.

I released the latch. With a feeling of dread, I faced the stairs. And slowly, I began to climb.

When I reached the top, the old man was gone. He'd left the room open, though, and as I stepped inside, it seemed different somehow. Brighter, maybe? I wasn't sure. I took a good look at all the junk. A lot of it was useless, but I would be happy to have some of it back.

I picked up my gym shorts and my dress shoe. I examined the pork roast. It was still frozen.

I began loading things, one by one, into the bell of the tuba.

And that was when I noticed the little business card, tucked into the crook of the tuba's spit valve. The old man had left it for me.

I pulled out the card and held it to the light. On it was printed just one word:

FERGUSON

EPILOGUE

YOU'RE PROBABLY WONDERING ABOUT BEEF. WELL, HE DIDN'T show up at his house at all on that fateful day. His parents were going crazy, calling the police and the fire department. But I wasn't worried too much. I figured he was hiding out somewhere near the duck pond, and I'd go look for him later. It was too much fun watching my dad pull all my lost stuff out of the tuba. With each item he subtracted a sum of money from the amount I owed him. He was like a little kid at Christmas.

In all the confusion, I realized I had forgotten to look for one important thing in the old house — Beef's paper! I made a silent promise to go back and look for it. Maybe he could get an extension.

When we got the call from the Pounders that night, just after dinner, we raced over.

I was not prepared for what I saw. Beef's face was drained of color. His hair was pulled back and messed up, as if he'd been in a windstorm. I asked him questions, but he seemed not to hear a word.

The family doctor bustled in a moment later. He began examining Beef, looking in his eyes, checking his pulse, testing his reflexes. The diagnosis was posttraumatic stress brought about by a visual or environmental shock of a possibly imaginary nature, accompanied by a few unexplained and probably accidental skin lesions in areas surrounding the clavicle.

Over time, Beef slowly recovered. He was a changed

kid. He never teased another soul in school. He defended defenseless kids and protected anyone under attack.

Me? I changed, too. I never lost another thing. Without that pressure, I became the perfect young man you know today. My dad calmed down. He even sold the Augenschmerz for a ten-year-old Ford. Mars — well, she still tries to make my life awful, but I just ignore her. My mom has never again mentioned Ferguson. And neither have I.

Three months ago, the house on Hemlock and Wormwood was destroyed to build condos. No one mentioned a thing about any inhabitants, or anything else found inside.

As for Beef's skin lesions, well, they healed fine. But to this day you can still see the scars. I've asked him about them, but he just changes the subject.

It is weird, though, that there's one on each shoulder. And if you ask me, they don't look unexplained or accidental at all. They look exactly like claw marks.

Loser

Author's Note

The author wishes to apologize for misunderstanding his writing assignment for this book. Although he was told rather clearly to write something *mysterious*, he heard the word *serious*, which explains his autobiographical essay, "Loser." Some of the names have been changed to protect the identities of those who have gone on to prominent careers in politics, the music industry, and crime. Otherwise, Peter insists that every single detail of the story is true. [Note from editor: We suspect he may have actually heard the word *delirious*.]

PETER LERANGIS grew up in the village of Freeport, New York, where he often found his way home successfully after school. Nowadays he lives in New York City with his wife and two sons, who find him lovable but odd — but most important, they find him. He only rarely leaves his office and almost *never* loses anything, although recently he did lose the last eighteen years of his writing, but that was the fault of a nasty hard drive. With a Number 2 pencil, he has been writing a series called Spy X, but his publisher hopes to convince him to buy another computer soon.

Little Time

⮰⮰⮰

Gail Carson Levine

I WAKE UP. THE CLOCK RADIO SAYS IT'S ONE O'CLOCK. One A.M., Friday morning, the last weekday of spring break. I hear my parents' voices downstairs. Neither of them got home before I went to bed.

They hardly ever do. Mom runs fund-raising for Northeast Hospital, and Dad is an environmental lawyer. They're very busy. The only time they spend with me is Quality Time.

According to their child-rearing books, Quality Time is when their attention is supposed to be completely on me. Nothing else should matter and nothing else should intrude.

But Mom and Dad are always sneaking peeks at their watches, and Quality Time never goes into Overtime, not even by a single minute.

They take turns on Quality Time duty, which always happens for an hour on Sunday mornings. Mom or Dad, whichever it is that day, asks me about school, about my friends, about sports, about piano lessons.

I tell the truth about piano lessons. I say I hate them. I say I'm not musical. I say they're wasting their money. It makes no difference. Piano lessons continue. They say I'll thank them someday.

I tell them everything else is fine. When I'm done saying that, fifty Quality Minutes are left, and they crawl by. Sometimes we talk about where to go on vacation or what to do for my birthday or what clothes I need. We've even talked about the weather.

I never tell them that everything else is as bad as piano. I hate the new school more than I hate piano lessons. J. J. Zeck Middle School. Isn't that an awful name? Zeck, fleck, gleck, shmeck. Yuck.

English used to be my favorite subject, but my English teacher only cares about grammar. My French teacher has it in for me. We're playing volleyball in Phys. Ed., and I can't get the ball over the net on my serve. Everybody on my team despises me.

I'm starving. I get up and go downstairs to the kitchen. Mom and Dad are in the den, but I don't go in, because they may tell me not to eat in the middle of the night.

I take a bag of chocolate chip cookies out of the cabinet. I'm pouring a glass of milk when I hear Dad say my name.

I put my glass down carefully and tiptoe out of the kitchen. I stand outside the den and try not to breathe.

"Jeff, I can't do it this Sunday," Mom is saying. "Can you do Quality Time with Erica?"

"No way. I'm meeting Steven. I can't cancel."

Mom groans. "I won't get anything done. And it's so boring."

Dad says, "It could be worse. Jack's daughter's bulimic. He spends forever with the school counselors, a psych —"

"Jack's no kind of parent. Not like us."

"Right," Dad says. He doesn't say anything for a few seconds. Then he adds, "Still, I never thought we could have a boring child."

I sneak back to the kitchen and grab my milk and cookies. My hands are shaking. I pray I don't drop the glass. They *can't* know I'm down here.

I'm crying. Maybe I'm boring, but I'm one of the few people on earth who can cry without making a sound.

Upstairs, I spill the milk out in the bathroom and leave the cookies on my desk. I'll throw up if I try to eat.

Do Mom and Dad love me? They hate to spend time with me. They think I'm boring. Duh. Of course, they don't love me.

Eventually I fall asleep. In the morning I wake up early. I hear Mom and Dad downstairs, so I stay in bed. I don't want to bore them with my presence.

I wonder if they'd still think I'm boring if I told them the truth about school.

Hi, Mom. My French teacher hates me.

Boring.

Hi, Dad. I stink at volleyball.

Boring.

The good things aren't especially exciting, either.

Hi, Mom. I got a hundred on my history test.

Boring.

Hi, Dad. I'm reading on the twelfth-grade level.

Boring.

What interests me most — science fiction and fantasy books — wouldn't interest them. Dad only reads books about the Civil War, and Mom only reads mysteries.

I start crying again. I can't help it. I wish Sarah were still here. She was our housekeeper from the time I was two till last year, when she moved to Florida to take care of her mother. When she left, she said, "Your parents don't know what they have, Erica. They have no idea what they're missing."

At first we e-mailed each other every day, but then her mom got sicker, and more and more time went by between my e-mails and Sarah's answers. Now I haven't heard from her for months.

I could call her, but I don't want to bother her. I also don't want to say out loud that my parents think I'm boring. I'm embarrassed to say the words. Parents are supposed to think their kids are beautiful and smart and fascinating, even if nobody else does.

I cry harder. I hear Mom pull out of the driveway, and five minutes later I hear Dad leave, too.

If Sarah were here she'd worm it all out of me. I miss her so much.

In a while I stop crying and notice that I'm hungry. I smile. Sarah always said that whatever you eat after you cry has no calories.

In the kitchen, Mrs. Eller, our current housekeeper,

gives me cereal and goes upstairs to clean. Sarah would have poured herself a cup of coffee and kept me company.

After breakfast I read my book, *NuEra*. It's hard to read for the first couple of pages, because my throat keeps getting lumpy. But I make myself keep going, and soon I get lost in the class struggle on the planet Partesis. I love sci-fi and fantasy because they're really about us here on earth, but disguised so we can see ourselves in a new way. The authors ask: *What if? What if a society dealt this way with poverty or that way with war?*

After lunch, I put *NuEra* in my backpack, tell Mrs. Eller I'm leaving, and go.

We moved here two months ago, and I've been spending spring break exploring. I love to walk, love the rhythm, love the way my body feels.

But today I think walking is boring.

I try something Sarah taught me. I focus on my breathing, and that helps. I notice that it's a gorgeous day, warm with a soft breeze.

Late yesterday I found a new place to explore. I head that way now. About a quarter of a mile from home I turn onto a dirt road. I walk along next to a wooden fence. After a few minutes I come to an open gate.

Beyond the gate I see a field sloping down to a lake where two swans and a family of ducks are paddling. Three huge evergreens face me across the water. The trees next to them are misted a faint green.

It's so pretty it hurts.

A sign on the gate reads: WEST SALEM OPEN LAND FOUN-DATION. It says you can hike, ride horses, walk dogs. But you can't litter, camp, or drive a motorized vehicle. I don't see any people, horses, or dogs. There's just the scenery and me.

I follow a path halfway around the lake and stop by a giant pussy willow, the biggest I've ever seen. It's in full fuzzy bloom, and it's awesome.

I keep going. The path leaves the lake and veers across a field to another wooden fence, this one topped by barbed wire. There are woods on the other side of the fence. When I reach the gate, it's open. An old wooden sign reads:

WHEELER FARM

1772

A smaller metal sign says: CAUTION! ELECTRIFIED FENCE. And a third sign says: HIDDEN VILLAGE. An arrow points to a narrow path through the trees. I can't resist. I go through the gate and follow the path. This is becoming an adventure.

An adventure isn't boring.

After a few minutes the trees end. In front of me is a boarded-up barn. A farmhouse is half a field away. No one is in sight. I walk around the barn. At the back a door is open about six inches. I'm pretty sure I'm tres-passing, but I push it open anyway.

"Ohmigosh," I say out loud.

UNEXPECTED

A dollhouse village fills the barn. I see the street in front of me and, beyond the street, rooftops, a clock tower, and what looks like a factory building, taller than the tower. It's what I'd see if I were on a hill, looking down on a real village.

It's bright as day in here. There are fluorescent lights as well as skylights in the barn roof.

The village is built on a platform at knee-height. It starts a foot or so from where I am, leaving an aisle that seems to go all around the edge of the barn. Aisles also cut into the village at the end of every block.

It's warm in here, and the lilies are in bloom in the yard of the house in front of me.

Dummy, I think. Those aren't real lilies.

I peek in a window on the second floor. It's an office. There's a tiny bookcase filled with even tinier books. There are file cabinets. There's a monitor, a CPU, and a keyboard on a desk. The keyboard is just like Mom's, a funny-looking ergonomic one.

I look into a first-floor window. A male doll sits at a dining-room table, holding a book in front of him. His other hand grasps the handle of a coffee mug.

A wisp of steam rises from the mug.

How do they do that?

I tell the doll, "Take your coffee into the office and get to work."

There are no people-dolls in the other windows, but a dog-doll is sleeping on the living-room rug.

Little Time

I hear a real dog barking. It isn't loud. It must come from somewhere outside.

More barking. I'm wrong — it's in here. And it doesn't sound exactly like a dog. Do they pipe in sounds to make everything more real? I look for speakers but don't see any.

I step to the street corner and go into an aisle, which is barely wide enough to walk through. Several bridges cross it — for the dolls, I guess. The first bridge is hinged on one end and clamped in place on the other. I fumble with the clamp before I see a button. I press it, and the bridge rises. After I pass through, the bridge lowers itself.

Wow.

The barking has stopped, but now I hear a splash. It's coming from my right. I turn into the next aisle.

I'm on a street with shops. There's a butcher, a baker, but no candlestick maker. The hardware store window is full of different kinds of lawn mowers.

A crow caws. I look up, but I don't see any birds.

A lion roars.

I realize what the barking was before: a seal. There must be a zoo somewhere.

This is so cool!

I stand on my tiptoes and see a break in the roofs. In a few steps I see the zoo. And the lion. With a flick of its tail it saunters into a cave that's built into a zoo building.

"Come back, lion," I say.

The lion reminds me of the motorized people and animals in store windows at Christmas. Only they move jerkily, and this lion moves like velvet.

Microchips, I think. Has to be, but it's still unbelievable.

The zoo takes up three blocks. There's a monkey house, a bird house, a reptile house, and a pool for seals. All the animals seem to be inside for now.

I hear a new bark. A dog stands on the sidewalk outside the zoo, barking at me.

It has a curly poodle coat, but it's not a poodle. One ear sticks up and the other folds over. Its tail is short and perky. The whole dog is about an inch tall.

I pick it up as gently as I can and place it on my palm. It doesn't seem frightened. It barks again and wags its tail at the same time.

I've wanted a dog for years, but Mom is afraid of dogs, and Dad says a pet doesn't fit in with their lifestyle — their thrilling lifestyle.

Well, this dog-doll is too little to scare anyone, and it won't need to be walked.

It's licking my palm with such a tiny tongue that I have to concentrate to feel it.

I have to find someone. I want to buy the dog. I leave the barn and walk towards the farmhouse. A woman is sitting on the porch, reading. As I get close I see what she's reading — *NuEra*, the same book I'm reading. Amazing.

She looks up. She's a freckly woman, no bigger than I am, and no more than ten years older.

I walk up the porch steps, aware that I shouldn't have gone into the barn. "Um . . ." I say and stop. I'm having trouble keeping my dog hand steady. I don't want it to lose its balance. It's up on its hind legs, wagging its tail like crazy at the woman.

"Um . . ." I really am boring.

"That's Hilton," she says. She pushes back her long hair. "Did you find him on the street? He's always getting out."

I guess it's okay that I went into the barn. I say, "I'm reading that book."

"Do you like it?"

"Yeah." I try to think of the next thing to say, and finally it comes. "Do you?"

"Uh-huh, especially the way it leads up to the war. What are you up to?"

"Marla just left the Dusties for her cousin's farm."

The Dusties are the industrialists, and they're fighting the Hoedowns, the farmers.

"Wait till you see what happens next." She waves her hand at the barn. "How do you like the village?"

"It's incredible. Especially the lion and Hilton."

The dog is sitting now, facing me and cocking its head. I've never seen anything so cute.

"I want to know" — I raise my hand a little — "if I can buy it."

She shakes her head. "We sell the houses and the villages, but we don't sell the critters."

"Oh." I shouldn't have asked. I should have just taken the dog.

She says, "But you can stay a while, and you can come back and play with him."

I'll come every day.

It's trying to dig a hole in my hand, which tickles.

"He likes you. He doesn't relax so quickly with everyone."

I can't help feeling pleased. I'm crazy to be glad a doll likes me. She's crazy to say it. But she's in the dollhouse business, so she has an excuse.

She says her name is Tamara Wheeler.

"Hi, Ms. Wheeler. I'm Erica."

"Call me Tamara. I'll walk you back to the barn." She stands. She's wearing a long peasant skirt. It's a retro look.

On the way she asks if I read a lot of science fiction and fantasy.

"Yeah, lots. The ones I like best are about alternate worlds."

"Did you read the one — I don't remember the title — about the telepaths who can't hide anything from each other?"

I shake my head. She says the book is about self-acceptance. We've reached the barn door. I ask her what her favorite fantasy is. She names a book called *The Long Forever*, which I've never heard of.

Turns out we've read a lot of the same books, but we also don't know some of each other's favorites. She pulls a pad and pen out of the pocket of her denim jacket. She writes a list of books for herself and a list for me. Hilton stretches out and goes to sleep on my palm.

By the time we're done talking, it's starting to get dark and I have to go home.

Tamara takes Hilton. She says, "Come up to the house tomorrow, and I'll let you into the barn. We usually keep it locked."

That night, Dad doesn't get home till after I've gone to bed, but Mom is home around eight-thirty. Boring old me is in the living room, reading with the TV on.

She kisses me hello, pours herself a glass of wine, and takes it into her office.

I leave for the farm early Saturday morning. Tamara lets me into the barn and shows me Hilton's house, which is on the corner of Halcyon Street and Century Avenue.

"Whistle and he'll come out. I have to go." She starts for the door, calling behind her, "I'll come back later."

I whistle, and Hilton comes through the dog-doll door that's built into the people-doll door.

His tail is wagging like crazy again. I wish I were tiny, too, so I could really play with him.

UNEXPECTED

I notice that I'm thinking of Hilton as a *him*, not an *it*.

He lifts his leg and pees on a bush. He starts circling and poops next to the yard's white picket fence.

I grin. It's pretty funny that they made a dog that poops. I wonder if the male doll in the dining room poops, too.

Something smells. It's faint, but stinky.

That's weird. I can see creating a dog-doll that poops, but I can't see making the poop stink.

I fish in my backpack for the sandwich Mrs. Eller made for me. I unwrap it and break off a crumb of bread, which I drop into the yard. For Hilton it's about dog-biscuit size, and he gobbles it up. Then he sits and looks up at me hopefully. I give him another crumb.

He cocks his head, as if he's listening. He goes back through his doggie door.

I wonder why. The shades are all drawn on the front windows, so I can't see in. I turn the corner. The shades are drawn on the side windows, too.

Snap! A shade in an upstairs window is spinning around its roller. It's the bathroom window. A male doll in a plaid bathrobe stands at the sink. I see in the mirror that half his face is lathered, and the other half has been shaved.

His right arm moves. It lifts a razor and begins to shave the lathered side of his face. A pinprick of red appears. He's cut himself.

42

Before I can think about this, his eyes in the mirror meet mine.

He's not a doll.

I back away from the house and crash into the platform across the street. I'm gasping for breath. I have to get out of here.

I'm almost the whole village away from the barn door, and the aisles are too narrow to run through. I scoot along sideways, as fast as I can. The bridges take forever to go up.

At last I reach the door and rush out. I run, imagining that the villagers — and Tamara — are laughing their heads off at me.

I don't stop running till I'm through the Wheeler Farm gate and all the way back to the lake. I collapse on the grass to catch my breath.

Gradually I stop panting, and even more gradually my heart stops hammering. I start blaming myself for running. I step into a fantasy as intriguing as the books I love, and I run away. Boring!

I could go back. But I don't move.

If I had spoken to the man, would his little ears have heard more than a roar? Could I have heard him? Would he speak English? Had Hilton and the man been normal size once? If yes, what made them shrink?

My heart starts pounding again. Was I exposed to whatever it was?

"Erica!"

It's Tamara, running towards me. I jump up and run the other way.

Then I stop. I yell to her, "Am I shrinking, too?"

"No. Wait for me." She reaches me. "You're not shrinking. You're fine."

"Then what's going on?" I'm shouting. "Are they holograms? A big joke?"

"I'm sorry. We didn't mean for you to find out like that."

But they did mean for me to find out.

Find out the dolls are real? Or find out something else?

"I was on my way to the barn to explain. I thought you'd be ready to believe after you were with Hilton a while."

I sit down again.

She sits, too. "The story goes back a long ways, back to Joshua Wheeler, grandson of Miles Wheeler who founded this farm. Joshua was an explorer."

My hands are icy. I clasp them and stare down at them.

"In 1833, Joshua went to Africa on an expedition, and he took with him his wolfhound Albert, who weighed 132 pounds. Joshua was twenty-six years old, and Albert was three."

I wonder why the dog's age and weight matter.

"In the desert Joshua found a new species of spider.

He collected a few specimens and brought them back to camp, where Albert ate one of them."

I feel Tamara's eyes on me, but I don't look up.

"By morning the dog had shrunk to the size of a cocker spaniel."

From eating a spider?

"Aside from his new size, Albert wasn't hurt. Joshua collected more spiders and came home. On the farm, he fed spiders to a chicken, a sheep, and a horse. They all shrank. At that point, Joshua lost interest. He had no need for smaller farm animals, and the spiders' effect seemed a useless curiosity.

"Then, in 1838, there was a flood. Except for Albert, all the shrunken animals were lost. The spiders survived. Albert lived for thirty more years."

I look up.

She's staring out over the lake. "Joshua had started breeding and experimenting with the spiders as soon as he connected Albert's long life to them. He isolated the venom and tried it on dozens —"

Ohmigosh! How much spider juice has Tamara had? She's very short for an adult. Not a midget, but short.

"How old are you?" I say.

She meets my eye. "You guessed. I'm fifty-five. I didn't take much serum, and if I don't take more, I'll start showing my age soon, but next year I'm going to join the village."

By shrinking to doll size.

"We still don't know if the shrinking causes the longevity, or if they're separate effects."

Why is she telling me all this?

But I don't ask that because I'm scared of the answer. "How come I never heard about the villagers and the animals? They should be famous."

"We've kept it quiet. Lots of people buy the dollhouses, but they never see anything alive."

"Don't people come to the barn? There's the sign, 'Hidden Village' . . ."

"We put the sign up for you. And the gate's usually locked."

Now I ask, "Why?" My heart is thumping again. They did this for *me*? Boring Erica?

"We don't have enough kids. The village in the barn has none. So we look for the right kind of kids."

Ones whose parents won't miss them.

I'm going to cry in front of her. I clench my fists and overcome the tears. But what I have to do next is harder. I have to say it out loud. I have to know.

"I'm the right kind because my parents won't care much if I'm gone?"

Funny, I feel a little better for saying it. Less ashamed.

She meets my eyes and smiles sadly. "That is one reason, but there are other kids whose parents wouldn't miss them. We want you because you're bright . . ."

Big deal.

"And because of the books you read. You have an imagination, and you believe in the future. We also picked you because your parents are out in the world doing things, and we think you'll be the same way. We're studying . . ."

But I'd be leaving the world by shrinking, not going out into it. No, I would be going out into it — into an alternate world of science fiction and fantasy. If I shrink I can try things out, try to solve problems. For starters, tiny people wouldn't hurt the planet as much as big people do. We could get all the power we need just from the wind. I could try out other ideas, too, solutions I've read about. It could be a new beginning for humans.

Then I flash to Sarah, hugging me when she left, hugging me so hard it hurt. Even though she hasn't stayed in touch lately, she wouldn't want me to vanish.

Tamara is still talking, and I haven't heard any of it.

I interrupt. "What would you do with me if I joined?"

"Nothing we don't do to ourselves. We're studying longevity. We're studying the immune system, because we never get sick. Besides that, you can pick a project. Everybody's working on something."

"Can I get big again?"

"We haven't figured that out yet." She smiles, looking pleased and excited. "We will, though. We have plenty of time."

A thought stuns me. "Is Joshua still alive?"

Her smile fades. "He died three years ago. But he didn't inject himself till he turned sixty. If you join us, we don't know how long you'll live. Hundreds of years. Possibly thousands."

I stand up. I can't stay still anymore. "I have to think."

"Okay." She grins. "We can wait." She stands up, too, and pulls a business card out of the back pocket of her jeans. "Call me if you want to do it."

I take the card and go. When I reach the dirt road I turn the wrong way. I'm not ready to go home yet.

The daffodils along the fence are almost in bloom. If they were injected with the serum, would it take eighty years for the flowers to come out? Would the flowers last two hundred years? That would be nice. Or would I be sick of daffodils?

I don't know what I should do. It would be a lot easier if I could change my mind after I shrank.

Isn't Tamara worried I'll tell someone? Why should she be? They're known as dollhouse makers. The little people and animals can hide. Hiding from giants must be easy. And nobody would believe me that there are real, five-inch-tall people. Little people. Like elves.

I can become an elf. When I was younger, I would have given anything for that. I wouldn't have hesitated.

I stop walking. Tomorrow is Quality Time.

Not necessarily. I can go back to Tamara right now

and never have to do Quality Time again, or see J. J. Zeck Middle School, or play volleyball, or take piano lessons.

I start for home. I have to do Quality Time. If I go, I don't want to feel as though I ran away.

I think again about telling Mom what's really going on with me at school. But none of it's interesting unless you think I'm interesting. That thought brings the lump back to my throat.

I could tell her I know their opinion of me. But what would be the point? She'd say I heard wrong, or she'd say they didn't mean what it sounded like.

When I get home I call Sarah in Florida.

She seems really glad to hear my voice. "Erica? Erica! You sound like yourself."

She does too. It's so good to hear her.

She says, "I've been promising myself to write or call you for weeks. Hang on a minute."

I wait. If I join the village, I'll e-mail Sarah from there, whether I'm supposed to or not.

She's back. "Mom knocked over her water glass. I can't stay on the phone long. Somebody from the hospice is coming."

"How is she?"

"Awful. And it's so slow." Her voice cracks. "Never get Alzheimer's, Erica."

"I'm sorry it's so bad." I rush on. I don't want her to have to hang up before I say what I need to. "I have this opportunity. It's amazing, but I haven't decided if I'm going to take it or not. I can't tell you what it is, but it's amazing. You may hear otherwise, but remember, I'm okay. I'm —"

"You're scaring me. What's —"

I hear a doorbell through the phone.

"What's going on, Erica?"

"I really can't say." I hear the doorbell again.

"I have to get that. Don't do anything crazy. I'll call you —"

"I love you."

"I have to go. I love you, too."

She hangs up. I smile at the phone.

I wonder if the village could take Sarah, after her mother dies.

IN THE MORNING I WAIT IN MY ROOM FOR MOM. I FEEL LIKE there's a fist in my stomach, squeezing. I still don't know what I'm going to do.

Mom knocks and opens the door a crack. "Can I come in?"

I stand and open the door.

She's wearing slacks, not her Quality Time ironed jeans. "Honey? Can I sit down?" She sits at my desk.

I stay standing, feeling awkward.

"Honey, I know this is our time to be together, and I've never missed our Quality Time before . . . but, sweetie, it's crazy at the office with the cancer wing opening." She takes a deep breath. "Could we skip, just this week? If everything's all right with you. Is everything all right?"

What do I say? "You can skip. Everything's all right." In a way, it's true. "Better than everything was yesterday."

She looks puzzled for a second. Then I see her decide not to worry about it. She stands. "Thanks, sweetie. We'll do it next week, then." She starts for the door.

"Mom?"

She turns.

"When I was a baby, what did you and Dad hope I'd be when I grew up?"

She glances at her watch. "We only wanted what we want now, for you to be happy."

"What makes you happy, Mom?"

"Daddy, you. I have to go, honey." She leaves.

I sit down on the bed. She lied.

But the door opens again. "Sweetheart, it's work. Work makes me happy. I hope it'll make you happy, too, someday. We can talk about it next week."

I don't think so, Mom. I smile at the closing door. She gave me something. She really did.

I pick up the phone and dial Tamara.

Author's Note

I gave this story starter to the kids in the writing workshop I teach: Erica is going to sleep over at her friend Josie's house. When Erica gets there, Josie says she's going to show Erica her collection of shrunken animal heads.

Now I always do the exercises along with the kids. This time, when I began writing, I forgot immediately that the shrunken things were supposed to be animal heads and they became entire shrunken animals. I worked on the story during the workshop for a few weeks, and then I was invited to submit a story fo this anthology. I had never written a mysterious story before, but it seemed to me that the shrunken-animal tale might fit the bill.

So I kept writing. I reached page seventeen, and the story was only half done, and the anthology guidelines said that it shouldn't be much more than twenty pages long. I had to perform radical surgery, and I deleted Josie. I was left with a story that had neither Josie nor shrunken animal heads, and this is it!

GAIL CARSON LEVINE mostly writes fairy tales. Her first book, *Ella Enchanted*, won a Newbery Honor award in 1998. Her most recent book is a fantasy called *Fairy Dust and the Quest for the Egg*. Her favorite of her books is her historical novel, *Dave at Night*, which is loosely based on her father's childhood. Gail's been writing since 1987. She lives with her husband David and their Airedale, Baxter, in a two-hundred-year-old farmhouse in New York's Hudson Valley.

Max, the Hand, and Me

Heidi E. Y. Stemple and Jane Yolen

THE SUN WAS JUST COMING UP OVER THE OCEAN WHEN MAX, my lovable but none-too-bright sheep dog, dragged his tongue across my face to wake me for his morning walk. He's my most reliable alarm clock — wetter, but less annoying than a *beep-beep-beep*.

Today I really didn't mind. It was the first day of spring break. School had been out for three days now, but much of that time had been consumed in the drive from Minnesota — where we live — to my grandpop's beach house in Myrtle Beach. It's a long drive, but since we left in the snow and I was about to go outside in shorts, it's totally worth it.

We'd arrived last night and now it was officially vacation, and this was the beach.

BEACH! I yelled in my head — no need to wake up Mom and Grandpop — as Max and I bounded down the stairs and out onto the sand.

It was still very early. We had the beach to ourselves except for one old guy with skin so tan and wrinkled, I figured he must live outdoors. I watched him for a minute to "assess the danger level," as Mom calls it. He was picking up cans, examining them carefully as if he expected them to have diamonds inside, before toting

54

them back to a shopping cart he'd parked on the wooden walkway that leads up and over the dune to the street. He was minding his own business, so we headed out to the water.

I had hoped the ocean would be bathtub-hot, but it was only lukewarm. Still, that was much warmer than the iced-over lakes at home. Max and I ran in and out of the little waves that lapped at our feet. It actually wasn't really hot out yet, but as my Uncle Adam, who lives even farther north than we do — in Fargo — says about this kind of chill, "We barbecue naked in this weather." My Uncle Adam is a funny guy.

So that's how the whole thing started, and why I was on the beach that morning, with Max off his leash because the beach was practically empty. No one there to complain, you see. And suddenly he started barking. Not that "Timmy's-stuck-in-the-well" bark that Lassie used to do on old-time TV, but real loud barks I was sure would wake up all the people living in the expensive stilt houses up and down the beach. Mom would not be thrilled if Max and I woke up all of Grandpop's neighbors on the first day we were here.

Off I trotted to the water's edge to see what Max was barking about.

That's when I saw it, down the beach a bit: a hand sticking out of the sand, as if someone had been buried and was digging his way out.

I rushed over to help, thinking I was probably too

late. Way too late. Thinking that it would be gross, a dead body. And thinking that it would be cool, too. In a gross sort of way.

Max was there ahead of me and got to the hand first.

And I thought: *He'll help me dig the person out and maybe we'll be in time. And maybe we'll be heroes.*

He put his mouth around the hand and pulled it out. Just the hand. No body. And he started back towards me, as if bringing me the greatest present in the world.

I'm not proud to admit that I ran back to Grandpop's screeching like a little girl. But, well, I did.

I slammed through the back door at full speed. My mom was crossing the kitchen towards me when Max galloped in through the open door behind me, sandy hand still in his mouth. He looked triumphant, like this was the gory prize he had just won in some kind of medieval game.

Boy, that stopped Mom dead in her tracks. Had I looked at her — I didn't, of course, because I was too busy looking at the hand — I'd probably have seen she'd lost all the color in her face. Mom is good in a crisis, but this went way beyond what she was prepared to handle first thing in the morning after driving more than a thousand miles.

Excited to give the prize to his ever-loving master, Max did exactly what I'd taught him as a puppy. He dropped the hand at my feet.

You know how important moments always happen in

slow-motion in the movies? Well, this happened like that. I watched the hand drop. Mom watched the hand drop. Slowly, slowly it fell to the floor.

We both cringed and waited for the unmistakable sound of flesh hitting tile — *splat*.

But *splat* never happened. Instead, the hand sounded like that plate I dropped while taking it out of the dishwasher last month: *crasshhhhh*.

Still convinced this was an actual hand of an actual dead person (it's hard to change mind-tracks that quickly), I wondered briefly if that's what rigor mortis did to a body.

As usual, I was light-years behind Mom. She was already shooshing Max away and reaching for a broom.

By the time I had regained my composure, Mom had the entire mess swept into a Ziploc bag. The hand only had one finger left — the first finger. Mr. Pointer. It seemed to be pointing up at the kitchen table.

I looked.

There sat the unread newspaper.

On the front page was an article with a headline compelling me to read further:

Visiting Celeb Loses Hand, Foot, and Jewels in Heist

Late last night, country crooner Bobby Clidesdale was asleep in his hotel suite at the Seasider Reef Resort when thieves broke into his dressing room at the Myrtle

Beach Alabama Theater, where he is slated to perform this weekend.

"The perpetrators seemed to know exactly what they were looking for," reported the spokeswoman for the Sheriff's Dept. "They bypassed many expensive pieces of musical equipment and went straight for the jewelry."

Mr. Clidesdale's jewelry, pieces he wears during his stage show, are kept on a specially designed mannequin. Most pieces of the badly damaged mannequin were recovered, but still missing is one bare foot and one bejeweled hand.

"One hand!" I yelled. Then I kept reading. Aloud.

Also missing are four rings, worth over $2.5 million, according to a spokesperson for Mr. Clidesdale. A reward is being offered for any information leading to the capture of the thief or thieves.

Mr. Clidesdale, distraught over the events of the evening, could only say, "I can't go on without my jewels. They belonged to my dearly departed Mama—God rest her soul."

Anyone with any information is asked to call the Horry County Sheriff's Office.

I looked down at the floor at the pile of fingers my mom had swept up. The one-fingered hand was now pointing at me. Nothing jewel-like was visible. I got down on my hands and knees and got a closer look. I stuck my own finger in the dust and chunks and did a little dig. No rings.

Disappointed, I looked up at my mom, who was about to give me the "now go wash your hands" speech. I didn't give her time.

"What do we do now?" I asked. "I mean, this has to be the missing hand. Maybe we can get the reward. Do we contact the sheriff — or Bobby Clidesdale?"

What a question! Mom was wild about Clidesdale, though I thought he was goofy, with his hair combed so high it looked like a hat. Besides the stupid hair, he sings these drippy love songs about trucks and truck stops and lost loves. Those songs are so full of whining, he should get a yearlong time-out! That's what Uncle Adam says.

Mom got dreamy-eyed.

"Okay," I said. "We go right to the singer."

"We?" Mom may adore this guy, but she's not the adventurous type. She would have happily turned something like this over to the "appropriate authorities" if I let her. I couldn't let that happen. There was, after all, pride at stake here. And bragging rights back home. And — oh, yeah — a reward, too!

"We!" I said. Sometimes with a mom you have to be firm.

I yanked Mom out the door, grabbing the car keys, my backpack, her purse, and the bag-o'-hand. She protested all the way, but didn't drag her feet. She was thinking of goofy Clidesdale, I bet.

It is just a couple of miles up Ocean Boulevard, but that drive always takes so long. There are hundreds of traffic lights, and people drive really slow to gawk at girls in bikinis. And, Grandpop told me, if it's Biker Week, the drive takes even longer.

At the first light, Mom foofed her hair. At another, she managed to dig some lipstick out of the bottom of her purse. She colored in her lips at the last light before we turned.

We pulled into the Seasider Reef Resort (the tackiest hotel on the beach, if you ask me, and impossible to say ten times fast). There were a whole lot of mom-aged women milling around in the lobby. They weren't dressed like moms, though. They were dressed like teenagers — the kind on the boulevard.

Yikes! My mom liked this Clidesdale guy, too, but I was sure glad I got her out of the house before she had time to dress like that.

The police were there, too, in a sea of blue uniforms. I bet even on Biker Week you don't see this many in one place.

My original plan was to go right up the elevator to Bobby Clidesdale's room and talk to him, but clearly that was not going to work. And, unless I had a busboy costume, a room-service tray, and a passkey, I wasn't going to sneak by that many cops. I mean, this wasn't Hollywood, and me, I was just a kid.

So I walked right up to the Sheriff's Deputy, who was standing in front of the elevator. I'm a direct-approach kind of guy.

"Excuse me, Officer. Can I go upstairs?"

All I got in return was a long look down a long nose. Apparently, I wasn't even worth words.

It was Mom's turn.

"Hello, Officer. What we meant to say was, we have something that belongs to Mr. Clidesdale and we were wondering if we could return it to him in person."

That got his attention. I obviously have a lot to learn about talking to grown-ups.

Now it was my turn. I was holding the bag — so to speak. I unzipped my knapsack and pulled out the gallon-sized Ziploc freezer bag containing the remains of the ringless, slobbered-on, now one-fingered manne-quin hand.

That got us up the elevator, personally escorted by Sheriff Long Nose. No one spoke on the way to the top floor. I watched the numbers light up floor by floor until, when PH lit, the door slid open. Once we were upstairs, he nodded to another Sheriff's Officer, whose incredible size all but obscured the door. Officer Large moved to the side and Officer Long Nose knocked on the door; three long knocks, two short. Then he twisted the door handle, and we all crowded in.

THE FIRST THING THAT HIT ME WAS THE SMELL. IT REMINDED me of a funeral parlor. Only, no one was dead here. Just mounds and mounds of flowers. The smells came in waves. First a heavy rose and gardenia smell. Then something else, even more perfumy. I was sure glad I'd taken my allergy meds, or I would have been sneezing up a storm.

A lavender robe hung across a chair and another, the color of an eggplant with light green embroidery, over a couch. A third — the color of Max's sick-up the time he got into Mom's art supplies and ate all the tubes of red, white, and blue acrylic paint — was hanging over a screen. I wondered why one guy would need three robes. But then, he was a famous singer, and probably rich, so I guess he got to collect whatever he wanted.

Seven pairs of high-heeled boots stood in a perfect row beside the couch, all in seven different shades of soft purple leather. I mean — who knew purple had so many shades?

I noticed, off to my right, a fish tank the size of Grand-pop's big-screen TV. The fish weren't huge, but they were fancy. Three were neon yellow with blue stripes. One was so see-through I could see its bones. There were a dozen Day-Glo-blue fish, each with a yellow stripe running the length of its body. The bottom rocks were glittery shades of purple. I'd seen tanks like these, but only in aquariums, not in hotel rooms. I wondered if it came with the room or whether Bobby Clidesdale brought it with him everywhere he went.

"Mom . . ." I started to ask her the fish tank question when she interrupted.

"Isn't it wonderful, Jamie?" she gushed, her eyelids fluttering.

Sheriff Long Nose had clearly had enough of ladies gushing and fluttering. "Mr. Clidesdale," he called, "we have some folks with information. Important information."

His voice grabbed my attention away from those mesmerizing fish.

"Maybe," I whispered so the sheriff could hear me, "reward-type information."

"Be right there," came this moony, moany voice.

I looked over at Mom, afraid she might faint or something.

From behind the screen came Clidesdale. He was wearing another robe, this one almost full-length and almost silver, but unmistakably still purple. Tied tightly around his slender waist was a plum-colored belt. Dark grape socks peeked out of the robe's bottom.

He wasn't ugly, I'll give him that, with clear blue eyes and a deep dimple in his wide chin. Deeper even than Uncle Adam's. He had a dark tan — well, I'm from Minnesota, so everyone here looks tan to me — but his color was almost gold. Uncle Adam would have gagged. He says that much tan is a recipe for cancer.

But that hair! I almost giggled. The only other hair I've ever seen like that is on my math teacher, Mrs. Waggel, who is about 107 years old. Only Bobby Clidesdale's hair was black and shiny, and Mrs. Waggel's hair is blue.

From across the room, Clidesdale seemed tall, whether it was because old guys always look tall to me, or the extra inches that hair gave him, I don't know. But as he walked towards us, I realized he was short. Almost as short as me. And I'm only twelve.

Before Mom could speak, or groan his name, or do something equally embarrassing, I held up the freezer bag. "I found this," I said. "On the beach."

The golden color drained from Bobby Clidesdale's face and his eyes got almost as big as his hair.

"But no rings," he asked — or said, I wasn't sure which.

By then my mom had regained enough composure to say, "No, Bobby," like she knew him. "No rings. I'm sorry."

Then, I swear, the guy started to cry.

Well, I looked to the ceiling, and I looked to the floor. I looked every which way but at him. I mean, Uncle Adam says a man has to be sensitive and all, but he doesn't mean crying out loud.

When Clidesdale finally regained his composure, he signed a picture for Mom and took two concert tickets from a bowl on the coffee table and placed them in her hand, which he held a little too long. She didn't seem to notice, but I did. Just as I was about to protest, he reached into his robe pocket and pulled out a crisp new twenty-dollar bill, which he handed to me. He sure knew the way to both our hearts.

Then, after thanking us for being so kind and being such big fans, he nodded to Officer Long Nose, who immediately ushered us out the door.

THE NEXT MORNING MY WET ALARM CLOCK WOKE ME AGAIN. Eager to find something just as exciting as the hand, Max was ready to go outside for his walk. I can't say I was as ready. After all, our last run on the beach had sent me screaming like a coward all the way home and I really had no great desire to repeat that experience. But Max needed a walk. As I didn't wish to seem like a bad dog-owner or — worse yet — a wimp, I climbed out of bed and headed downstairs and to the beach.

That same tan and wrinkly guy was out collecting cans again, though this time he was just north of Grand-pop's house. So I went south. Max didn't have the same idea. He headed *towards* Mr. Wrinkly. I swear, he's not usually so social in the mornings. Must be the naked barbecue weather. After all, he's a Minnesota dog.

So off Max went to have an early morning conversa-

65

tion with the old guy, or sniff session, or whatever dogs do with strangers. He got to Mr. Wrinkly before the old guy reached the shopping cart. Max isn't dangerous. He's been known to be annoying, but never harmful, so I took my time catching up to him. Besides, Mr. Wrinkly was already rubbing Max's tummy. And Max was in doggie heaven, rolling in the sand with all four legs in the air and making those funny happy-puppy moans. What a ham!

I knew my mom would kill me if she saw me chatting with a stranger on the beach (especially one who didn't look like he did much washing — ever), so I kind of hung back. I looked up at the sky, out at the water, and back towards Grandpop's house. I was stalling, not wanting to ruin Max's moment of pleasure, but not in any hurry to break the "stranger danger" rule that had been drummed into my head since kindergarten.

"Nice dawg you got he-ah," drawled the old man to me.

Oh-oh, I could barely understand him, what with his southern drawl and lack of teeth, and now I was going to *have* to talk to him. I supposed in a pinch, Max would protect me, but he was what Uncle Adam called "all bark and no bite."

I took a couple of tentative steps towards Max and Mr. Wrinkly, scooting up off the sand and onto the walkway. Close up, I could see that his hair was bleached white by the sun, or age, or both. It was peeking out from under a golf hat, which probably had never seen a day of golf.

"Yup," I said lamely, "he's a great dog."

"I usen to have ma-self a dawg liken this one," the man told me. "But that was . . ."

He kept talking, but I no longer heard his strange mumbling. I couldn't keep my eyes off his cart. In the middle of the pile of old soda and beer cans stood one bare, detached, flesh-colored mannequin foot.

I am proud to report that I did not run off screaming like a baby again. Not that I didn't want to. But I kept thinking: *If this guy is the jewel thief, what else is he willing to do to cover up his crime? Kidnapping, perhaps? Murder?*

Suddenly I wasn't at all sure that Max would protect me. He didn't look like he even remembered who I was — squirming around on his back and making stupid doggie-delight sounds. And I thought dogs were supposed to be loyal!

It was time to get out of there — gracefully — using all my well-honed conversational skills. I get them from Uncle Adam, Mom says. Only this time they were neither honed nor conversational.

"Well," I started, "I've got to go home. With my dog. Because, um, I think I can, like, hear my mom sort of, like, calling me." I could feel my face flush with the lie.

"Then you and yer dawg just run long nah. He-ah? And y'all be-in careful nah. Strange goin's on round he-ah. Strange goin's on indeed . . ."

I wasn't one hundred percent sure I understood what Mr. Wrinkly said. But, no matter, I was going to get out of there — if I could just get Max to come with me.

I said stuff like, "Oh, Max is, um, always like, well, like this." And "Come on, Max, please, 'cause Mom's sort of expecting us." And it took some whining and whimpering on Max's part. But finally, he grudgingly agreed to accompany me back to Grandpop's.

WE DIDN'T EXACTLY RUN HOME, BUT WE DIDN'T EXACTLY walk, either. When we got to Grandpop's, I took a deep, relieved breath as the door slammed shut behind me.

Grabbing the phone, I began to dial 911, but paused between one 1 and the other to gulp down an entire Yoo-hoo from the fridge. Nothing like chocolate to steel the nerves.

Wait!

The Yoo-hoo, being brain food, made me realize that I had no proof, no actual clues leading in Mr. Wrinkly's direction. Well, the hand, sure. And the foot. But if possession of a missing mannequin appendage was proof of guilt, then Max and I would have been in jail by now. After all, we'd briefly had hold of the hand.

What was it the old guy said?

Strange goin's on round he-ah.

Strange things are going on around here.

What strange things?

Maybe he didn't *do* something. Maybe he *knew* something!

"Come on, Max!" I shouted. "Let's go back and see your friend!"

OF COURSE MAX LED THE WAY. NOW WE HAD A COMMON purpose: find his newest best friend and my key witness. At least I hoped he was my witness. There was still a possibility that he was the jewel thief. I didn't want to think about that.

Max ran south. Max ran north. Mr. Wrinkly was no longer on this stretch of beach. And as good as Max is at finding stinky old stuff, he was getting nowhere fast. And I was getting exhausted faster.

OK. Time to stop thinking like the hunter and start thinking like the hunted. Where would I go if I were an old, wrinkled guy with a shopping cart filled with cans and a foot?

I thought: *Smelling the way I do, I'd go take a bath.*

Then I thought: *I'm thinking like myself, not like the old man.* So I began again.

"I'm an old man," I said aloud. "Been up since dawn. Been dragging my cart around combing the beach. I got lots of stuff. Cans and a foot. And now . . ."

And now I'd go find something to eat! That's what I'd do! Of course.

But I didn't know where he lived. In fact, I didn't

know if he even had a home. For all I knew, he lived in the park, or on the beach, or in a Dumpster. And if he had no home, he probably didn't have a job. How would he afford something to eat, even at McDonald's?

I slapped my head with the palm of my hand. Of course — the cans! The cans were the key! He had to sell the cans for recycling! Well, that or sell the rings. But I had to believe he didn't have the rings, or he was back to being the suspect.

I liked him better as the witness since he'd be less likely to murder me to cover his crime.

BACK AGAIN AT GRANDPOP'S HOUSE, I LOOKED UP RECYCLING places in the Yellow Pages. I called all three. Too far away. I mean, the nice lady on the phone at the closest place told me it would take almost 45 minutes with a car. I didn't think our old guy had a car. What's worse, by then, I was once again convinced he might be the ring thief. It made more sense, explaining why he disappeared so quickly when I spotted the foot. And it put me back in danger.

I hate it when I can't make up my mind.

So I chose. He's not a witness, he's the jewel thief.

I found the police number, not 911, the other one, and dialed.

"Horry County Sheriff's Office."

In the time it took for him to say that, I changed my mind again. I wasn't going to turn Mr. Wrinkly in for possession of a fake foot. I was going to have to find him.

"Hello. I'm looking for a guy from the beach," I started, but the cop on the other end didn't let me finish.

"Would you like to fill out a missing person report, kid? This isn't a locator service unless someone's been missing for 48 hours."

"No, sir, I am looking for a possible witness to a crime," I said. "He's a real tan, wrinkly old guy who pushes a shopping cart with cans in it around the beach."

That got a chuckle.

"A witness, huh? Would you like to tell me to what crime? Though, it sounds like you're talking about Old Homeless Harry. I'd check down at the Mission."

"Thank you, sir," I said, not wanting to give him any other information. I didn't know. Maybe I wanted the glory and the reward if this turned out to be good information, or maybe I didn't want to look stupid if this turned out to be, well . . . stupid. "I'm sure it's nothing, but I'll call if it's something," I said.

MOM WAS NOT THRILLED ABOUT TAKING ME DOWN TO THE Mission. But then she thought about it.

"We're doing this for Bobby Clidesdale." Her voice went mushy and her eyes began to glisten.

"Yeah," I said, remembering how good-looking

she thought he was. I guess that counted for something. Plus, he gave me twenty dollars. In my book that counted for everything.

Then she seemed to shake herself all over. "Of course, it might all be a waste of time." Mom hates a waste of time. "So give me a minute to go clean out Grandpop's old clothes and blankets from the closet. We can donate them to the Mission while we're there."

Nothing like a good deed, I thought. *Except — maybe — a reward.*

WHEN WE PULLED UP TO THE MISSION, THREE HOMELESS guys (none of them Harry) walked smiling to our car. They seemed all set to greet us until they saw Max. Then they each took a couple steps back away from the car. Max might be a pussycat, but you wouldn't know that by just looking at him. He's big.

"This is Max," my mom said as she opened her car door. "He's harmless. Unless . . . Jamie here is in trouble." This is a lie but not a big one. We don't really know because I've never needed Max to help me out, but it's always nice — if a bit embarrassing — to have your mom throw in a little maternal warning.

One of the guys reached out a hand to Max, who, of course, gave it a big wet slobber.

"Tough guy," he said, and grinned. "All tongue and no teeth."

I had to remember to tell that one to Uncle Adam!

We followed them into the Mission. I had Max on his leash and Mom was empty-handed since the guys were all too polite to let her carry any of the boxes herself.

Inside, a friendly man at the front desk knew exactly who we were describing. Harry, he told us, could probably be found by the Seasider Reef Resort. Whenever there were celebrities in town, he kept a close eye on the Dumpsters.

The Seasider Reef Resort. That's where Bobby Clidesdale hung out.

"Mom?" I said.

She got glittery-eyed again and smiled as she touched her hair, which was sprayed and curled out the kazoo. I instantly knew where we were headed next, right after she gave away all the old clothes.

Sure enough, Harry was pushing his cart out on the beach just south of the Seasider, right near the Dumpsters. Max practically yanked my hand off trying to get to him, so I let go.

When Mom and I caught up with them Max was on the ground, upside down, leash still dangling from his collar, getting his belly rubbed. He's easy.

"Hiya, Harry," I greeted the old man.

"Should ha no-un," Harry said. "Y'all be coming 'bout that there foot in ma cart."

"Yes, Harry! The foot!" I was excited and beginning to understand him, at least a little. He was going to tell me about the foot!

"Should ha no-un. Foot not in he-ah no mo-ha." Sure enough, I looked down and the foot was gone. But that didn't matter. I wanted to know how the foot got there in the first place, not how it got out.

"Where'd you find the foot, Harry?" I asked.

"That there-in foot be fah too big for them dare girlie shoes."

Harry seemed to have said his piece. Because without even a good-bye to Max, he turned and pushed his cart away.

"Harry!" I yelled after him. "Where did you *find* the foot?" But he just threw up a hand as if to say, "No more questions," or perhaps just a wave. *What a waste*, I thought. *No use trying to get any more information from him*.

"What now, Jamie?" Mom asked. Her mouth spoke the words but she was gazing longingly up at the top floor of Bobby Clidesdale's hotel.

"Gonna see the man himself," I told her. "Love in a purple robe. We can tell him about the foot. Maybe he'll know what old Harry means. Every clue counts and all that. Come on." Of course, I was thinking I might get another twenty out of it, but didn't say that as I grabbed her wrist.

I didn't have to drag her.

*   *   *

OFFICER LONG NOSE DIDN'T EXACTLY SMILE AT US, BUT HE didn't exactly give us a hard time, either, since he recognized Mom.

"More clues," Mom said.

He nodded. After escorting us up, he did the knocking routine and then let us right in.

Max whined.

"Behave yourself," I said, giving his collar a good warning tug.

Bobby Clidesdale was lounging on an oversized burgundy chair. He was wearing purple leather pants today, under his tightly tied violet robe. His hair was teased up even higher than last time and he wore a pair of those silly high-heeled boots. He was wearing a lot — and I mean a *lot* — of makeup; even more than Mom. He was talking to a reporter who was so completely absorbed by the singer's words, he didn't even notice our entrance.

"The show," Bobby Clidesdale cooed, in a lyrical voice like he was singing instead of merely talking, "must go on. Mama's rings, God rest her soul, or no Mama's rings." He had all of our attention now. I actually found myself trying to mimic his hand gestures. He looked pretty cool.

Undeterred by the presence of the reporter, Mom sat down on the edge of Clidesdale's chair.

"Of course there is insurance," Bobby C. was saying,

"but it means nothing. Mama's rings were everything."
My mom patted his leg and made goo-goo eyes at him.
I was so disgusted at her behavior, so un-mom-like, that
I rolled my eyes almost to the back of my head. I must
have dropped Max's leash because, a moment later, I
could hear the unmistakable sounds of toilet water being lapped up in the bathroom.

Oops! Obviously, Bobby C.'s dear Mama had never
taught him toilet seat manners like my mom had. Cover
down after you go! Also, obviously, neither Bobby nor
Mama Clidesdale ever owned a big dog.

Since everyone was fawning over the singer and I
couldn't possibly get his attention and claim more reward money for my foot information — I walked over
to the fish tank. Geez! I wondered again if Bobby C. had
brought that thing with him or if it had come with the
room. The fish weren't purple but the rocks were.
Chances seemed split even that it stayed here. Maybe
the fish were the hotel's and the tank his. Duh! I hit my
head with the heel of my hand. That just didn't make
any sense. But if he carried the fish tank wherever he
went, he'd need a big staff just to lug the thing around,
or maybe just Officer Large. I giggled out loud thinking
about the big cop carrying the monstrosity on his back.

All of a sudden, Max was next to me. I must have forgotten to feed him lunch because he decided he was
hungry and what he wanted was seafood. He got up on
his hind legs.

"No, Max!" I yelled, but it was too late.

Max dunked his head into the tank.

Bobby Clidesdale and Mom jumped to their feet.

The huge tank started to tip.

Sheriff Long Nose lurched towards us.

Slow motion.

Broken glass, water, fish, and rocks crashed onto the penthouse carpet in one great big wave.

"Surf's up," I cried, trying to make light of it. But I knew it was a total disaster.

Max and Mom both tried to get the fish. Luckily, Mom was faster. She shoveled as many as she could into water glasses from the coffee table, all the while apologizing to Bobby C., who flapped at her with both hands like a duck trying to take off in a fast wind.

Boy, I thought, *am I in trouble*. I figured I was going to be grounded till I was 42 or married, whichever came first. Certainly I could forget about any reward! I didn't dare look up at Mom, so I kept looking down at my feet.

Small, wet, purple high-heeled boots stepped into my view.

Small shoes.

Girlie boots.

Too small for that foot!

The mannequin foot!

Old Harry must have meant the mannequin foot was bigger than Clidesdale's foot and his girlie shoes.

UNEXPECTED

I guessed that when old Homeless Harry was checking Dumpsters for cans, he must have seen Bobby C. dumping the stolen goods. But — I thought with sudden clarity — if Clidesdale was the robber of his own jewelry, he wouldn't have dumped the jewels, only the mannequin — to make it *look* like a robbery.

So the jewels weren't stolen. He still had them somewhere.

Only where would he have stashed them?

Then I saw something at my feet. Just a twinkle at first. In the purple rocks spilled out of the fish tank.

"Mom!" I shouted. "Your dreamboat there stole his own jewelry!"

"Jamie!" Mom yelled, flashing me what Uncle Adam calls "The Look of Death." I couldn't tell if she was mad or mortified, but she held tight to the glass of fish in one hand.

Clidesdale patted her other hand, cooed something, and put his small purple boot in the middle of the fish tank mess, which seemed odd to me, but not to my mom.

The reporter, though, looked a bit interested.

"I can prove it!" I cried, reaching down towards the twinkling stone.

That's when Bobby Clidesdale dropped Mom's hand and grabbed me, shouting, "Stupid boy. Stupid, stupid, stupid boy!" He raised a hand to flap at me, only this time the hand was closed into a fist.

There was no more slow motion. Teeth bared and gnashing, hackles raised, a howling Max pounced on Clidesdale, who hit the wet hotel carpet with a thud. His purple robe fell off his shoulders, exposing a strangely white chest that didn't match the golden tan of his arms and face. The sleek, high hair slid off his head to one side. Max let out one long, low growl and planted his front paws firmly on the man's skinny chest. I couldn't help but wonder what Max's toilet breath smelled like.

Alerted by the commotion, gun drawn, Officer Large barreled into the room to join Officer Long Nose.

"What's going on here?" they asked together.

Mom and the reporter pointed at Clidesdale on the floor.

"He did it!" the reporter said.

"And my brave boy figured it out." Mom's eyes were suddenly clear and shining, and then a little teary, too.

I reached down to the sparkle and handed Officer Long Nose one previously missing gold band with three large amethysts surrounded by about a bazillion diamonds.

"Do we still get the reward?" I asked.

AS THEY CARTED BOBBY CLIDESDALE OFF, OFFICER LONG Nose said to me over his shoulder, "It was all for the insurance money. I guess the guy's not worth what he used to be."

Mom mumbled something in agreement.

"And I would have gotten away with it, too," Bobby Clidesdale whined to the two cops, "if it hadn't been for that stupid meddling kid and his stinky dog!"

"Who's he calling stinky, Max?" I said, looking at my dog as he dripped water onto the floor.

Max's tail thumped on the wet rug.

"Not Max," said Mom. "He's a hero." She smiled at me. "You, too."

I guessed that was going to have to be my reward.

Until, of course, the next day, when the article in the *Sun News* came out. We sure made some impression on that reporter. We even got a full-color picture — on the front page! Uncle Adam was going to love this! He'd probably say, "You're not any richer, but you're a hero." And maybe I am.

Well, me and Max.

Max, the Hand, and Me

Authors' Notes

Heidi: I received an e-mail one day from my mother asking if I wanted to work on a mystery story with her. I said yes and wrote the first page, leaving off at the line, "That's when I saw it." There wasn't much of a story yet — I was just setting it up. Later that day, she sent a paragraph back letting me know that the thing that Jamie saw was a hand. I decided it wasn't real, so I wrote Max picking it up and brought the whole story into the kitchen where Max drops the hand. The story was beginning to emerge.

This is my favorite way to write with my mom — back and forth over e-mail. It is a game we call "Stump the Collaborator." Right now I live in South Carolina and she lives in Massachusetts, so this type of writing is necessary.

Jane: When Heidi moved with her family back to Massachusetts — a month after she wrote the above, but three years gone by the time you read this — we had to work out a new method of working, one that made sure we didn't kill each other in the process! (That's a joke.) I love working with her, watching how differently we both circle an idea and invariably come to the same conclusions. "Like mother, like daughter" may be a cliché, but when it comes to our work, it is certainly true.

JANE YOLEN and **HEIDI E. Y. STEMPLE** are a mother-and-daughter team who have published eight children's books and one adult book together, plus a number of short stories and six more children's books about to come out. Alone, Jane — who has been called the Hans Christian Andersen of America — has written over 270 books, and Heidi has had short fiction and poetry published in anthologies and magazines.

Baby from Outer Space

⌒⌒⌒

Norma Fox Mazer

I ALWAYS WANTED A BABY SISTER. I KNOW IT'S NOT MACHO for a guy to say this, but from the time I was little, I would pretend that I had a sister. She sat next to me at the table and I fed her bits of my food. She had parts in all my games, and I told her stories at night. Even when I got older, I'd make up stories with her in them, mostly about me saving her from danger. Say the house was on fire. I'd run in to rescue her. I'd be coughing and choking, but I'd crawl through the smoke and flames, and I'd find her and carry her out. Everyone would be cheering, Mom would be crying, and Dad would pat me on the back a thousand times and tell me I was a terrific son.

I was an only kid, and Mom and Dad pretty much gave me whatever I needed (Dad) or wanted (Mom), but they drew the line at having another kid.

"I'd like another baby, sure," Mom said, if I mentioned it, "but, no, Greg. Forget it. It's not going to be. Sorry, sweetheart, we all have to learn to live with things not being exactly the way we want them."

If Dad was around, he and Mom would exchange their secret let's-not-tell-the-kid look. When I was little, I didn't get it, but by the time I was twelve, which is the year I'm going to tell you about, I knew what The Look meant. They were waiting for me to grow up . . . so they could break up. I tried not to think about it too much. They didn't have big, loud, screaming fights like some parents. I mean, it wasn't a war. It was more like a never-ending battle — they hardly ever agreed on anything.

In a way, knowing that my parents weren't all that happy with each other made me want a little sister even more. Someone who would look up to me, who would depend on me to tell her stuff — true stuff about other kids, and school, and life, and all that. Mom and Dad were adults, they were pretty old, going on forty, and they wouldn't understand her the way I could. Besides, they would be wanting her to grow up, too, so they could get away from each other.

I'd want her forever. I'd never get tired of her, and I would definitely try to be the best big brother anywhere in, well, the universe. She could share my room, and I'd tell her stories, teach her to read and write her name, and when she got old enough I'd show her all the computer stuff I knew. Mom and Dad, the ex-high-school track stars, could take care of the jock stuff. Maybe they'd have better luck with her than with me. I was definitely not jock material. Of course, as I got older, I sort of put this imagining-a-little-sister stuff away into the back of my mind. I got realistic. I didn't ever expect it to happen.

One February morning, we were all in the kitchen to-gether. Dad was sitting across from me, drinking coffee and reading the financial page. Mom was leaning on the counter, drinking cocoa and reading the front page. I don't know how they managed to read and bicker, but they did. Dad said this, Mom said that. Whatever. Same old, same old.

I was studying my favorite comic strip, checking out the artwork, and trying to tune out the parental units, but then they got to the stage where they call each other Mr. Galluci and Mrs. Galluci. That was it. I looked up and said, "Would you guys please give it a rest?"

For about a peaceful minute, neither of them said anything. Then Mom let out a cry, and Dad said, "What now?" and I banged my head on the table.

"Oh, I can't believe this," Mom said. "Listen to this!" She began reading.

Infant Found by Worker

Herald News Special Report

by Anita Chan and Heather Desai

An abandoned female infant was found yesterday morning in a Dumpster on Delray Street by James Ibraham, a Sanitation Department employee. Police Chief Raymond Bangers is asking anyone who has information to contact him. The infant was naked except for a green swimming cap and white-framed sunglasses.

Patricia Mailer, a spokeswoman for the

Monroe County Child Welfare Department, offered an explanation for the child's bizarre outfit. "Infants are sometimes abandoned by mothers who are young, poor, and panicked. The infant's outfit, to me, means the mother loved her baby and was trying to show that love in some special way. Why else go to the trouble of finding sunglasses that tiny? That couldn't have been easy."

The temperature was 22° F this morning when Mr. Ibraham discovered the child in the Dumpster. "I heard these funny twittering noises, like a bird," Mr. Ibraham said, "and I checked in the Dumpster, thinking somebody might have shoved in one of their pets they didn't want anymore. Because people do that. But instead I see a little baby looking up at the sky. Just lying there, calm as you please. She looked right at me, like she was pleased that I'd heard her calls and rescued her. She knew she could trust me."

Dr. Leona Schwartz, a pediatrician who examined the child, says the infant appears healthy and unharmed by the traumatic experience. Dr. Schwartz estimates her age at no more than ten days. The infant apparently suffered no ill effects from the extreme cold. Dr. Schwartz added that babies this

young are not ready for cognitive reasoning,
and what they see is no more than a blur.

Mom spread the paper out on the table to show us a picture of Mr. Ibraham holding the baby. It was one of those blurry news photos, but you could see that Mr. Ibraham had a big smile.

"This is so sad." Mom leaned over and touched the baby. "I want to do something for this little thing," she said. "Poor little mite."

"Send a check," Dad said.

"Vince, money does not solve every problem."

"It doesn't hurt."

"Vince! Okay, okay, excuse me, I know, you're an accountant, and money is important to you —"

"I think it's important to you, too, Nance, from what —"

"Not the way it is to you. I believe —"

"I know what you believe —"

"You're interrupt —"

"Guys!" I yelled. "Mom and Dad!"

They both stopped and looked at me.

"Could you knock it off? Please!"

"Okay, sorry," Dad said. He half stood up, looked at me across the table, and changed the subject, which was a relief. "Tell me you're not wearing that vest to school, son," he said.

I looked down at my vest — red-and-green plaid with

a yellow stripe. "Dad, all the guys are wearing these vests."

Dad looked upset by this news. He dropped to the floor and ripped off twenty-five push-ups.

Mom winked at me. "Cool," she mouthed, looking at my vest and putting her thumb and forefinger together.

Dad stood up, straightened his tie, gave a last sad look at my vest, and went off to work. When I left for school a few minutes later, Mom was stretching out. She usually went for a three-mile run before leaving for the medical office where she was a receptionist. It was still a normal day.

By the time I came home after school, everything in my life — everything in all our lives — had begun to change.

Mom met me at the door.

"Did the office close early?" I asked. "Is it a holiday or something?"

"Nope!" She gave me a mysterious smile. "Greg, come upstairs. What do you want more than anything in the world?"

I dropped my knapsack and raced upstairs. Outside her bedroom, Mom stopped and gave me that mysterious look again, then slowly opened the door.

On the bed, surrounded by pillows, was the baby whose picture I had seen in the newspaper that morning. There was no doubting it. She was wearing a yellow nightgown, and just as in her picture, she also had on a green swimming cap. A pair of miniature, white-framed sunglasses were lying next to her.

I put a finger on her little flat nose. "Hi, there," I said.

She looked at me with green, fish-shaped eyes, really looked at me, as if she were examining me.

"So what do you think?" I said. "Do I pass the test?"

She stared up at me, and her eyes did this . . . *thing*. They seemed to gather light and grow bigger, and I couldn't stop looking into them. It was like being caught in a spell. Then she stuck her thumb in her mouth and slurped at it.

"Like her?" Mom said.

"Yeah. For sure!" I gave the baby a quick inspection to make sure all the details were in place. "*You* pass," I told her. "Flying colors."

She kicked her legs out from under the nightgown, revealing stout little toes that she kept flexing like fingers.

I noticed that the swimming cap was exactly the same color green as her eyes. I mean, *exactly* the same color. "What's with the swimming cap, Mom?"

"She won't let me take it off," Mom said, with a kind of helpless laugh. "I got the sunglasses off her, but the cap — no way. She's got a will of her own." Mom bent over the baby. "Yes, you have a strong personality, don't you?" she cooed. "Greg, isn't she marvelous? Don't you just love her to pieces already?"

"So what's the story, Mom? She's visiting us?"

"Not visiting, Greg. She's ours. You're looking at your new little sister."

"Mom! Are you joking?"

"No, I am not."

"*Cool!* How'd you get her?"

"You won't believe this, honey. I almost don't believe it myself. This whole day has been so strange. I didn't go in to work this morning. I mean, I started to, and then I turned the car around and, instead, I drove downtown to the Social Services Office. I found someone official-looking to talk to, and I told him I wanted to take the Dumpster baby home with me and care for her."

"Mom, you are awesome."

"I don't even know *why* I did it. I swear, something just made me do it. . . ."

I took the baby's warm foot in my hand. "Hey, little sister, you're what I've been waiting for, for a long time."

"I almost don't believe she's here," Mom said. She bent over and kissed the baby. "At first, it was: 'No, no, no. No way, you can't do that. It takes time. You have to apply. You have to be investigated.' There are papers and forms . . . and who knows what? A whole huge bunch of official stuff! It was going to take forever. Then, the head of the office shows up, this terrific, smart woman who talks to me and makes an on-the-spot decision that I'm trustworthy, that they can handle the details, the inspection, the what-have-you later, and meanwhile, the baby will be taken care of, which is the really important thing."

Mom swiped her hands together. "And that was it. Done. Look at her eyes, Greg. Aren't they gorgeous? I've never seen eyes that color, like green sea-glass —"

"More like traffic lights," I said. "What's her name?"

"I haven't decided yet."

"I'll call her Baby." I stroked Baby's cheek — soft and yet firm. Baby grabbed my finger. She had hands like tiny stuffed gloves, and her grip was strong. "Mom, Baby's shaking hands with me."

"Infants always grab. It's a reflex, honey."

"No, I don't think it's just reflex. She's really shaking it. See?"

"It's instinct, Greg. Something from our way-way-back primal ancestors. Probably a survival thing."

"Whatever," I said. "Hey, Little Traffic-light Eyes, can I take that swimming cap off? Just for a little while to show big brother your pretty head?"

Baby nodded. Okay, Mom would probably call that a reflex, too, but it was just like the handshake. I knew it was the real thing. She shook my hand, and she nodded. She gave me permission to take off the swimming cap.

"Wow," Mom said, as I slowly peeled the cap off. "Good going, honey! I couldn't get that off her for love or money."

Baby's head was bald and perfectly egg-shaped. "Going to give me a smile?" I asked her. "I'll take your picture if you smile."

"It's way too soon for her to smile, Greg," Mom said.

I got my camera from my room. Baby smiled, and I clicked off a bunch of shots.

When Dad came home, Mom met him at the door, too, and brought him upstairs. By that time, Baby was wearing the swimming cap and the sunglasses again. Dad looked at Baby for a long time, while Mom and I and Baby all looked at Dad. "Extraordinary," he said at last.

"Yes, she is," Mom said, picking up Baby. "This is an extraordinary little sweetheart."

"I meant you, Nancy." Dad loosened his tie. "You never did anything like this before. Bringing a strange baby into the house? And not even giving me a chance to say anything? What in the world were you thinking — ?"

"Vince, I had to do it," Mom broke in. "Like I told Greg, I felt almost sick. I couldn't think of anything else. It was like she was inside me, right *here* —" Mom tapped herself on the chest. "It was just as if she were telling me I had to rescue her."

"Telling yourself, you mean," Dad said.

"No, I don't mean that." Mom held Baby out towards Dad. "Vince, hold her, just for a min —"

"No, no, that's okay." Dad backed towards the door.

"Tired. Need a shower. Maybe later. When are you going to return her?"

"Not," Mom said.

Baby gurgled and squeaked and almost seemed to lean out of Mom's arms towards Dad. "Look, Dad," I said. "She wants you to hold her."

Dad sighed and held out his arms, and Mom handed over Baby. Maybe Mom and I were hovering, because Dad said, "Don't worry, you two, I'm not going to drop her." He patted Baby's back.

"I know you won't," Mom said. "I know you're a good father, Vince."

Dad raised his eyebrows.

"You *are*," Mom said. "And that has nothing to do with —" They exchanged a glance, the famous let's-not-tell-the-kid look.

For a few minutes, we all just stood around looking at Baby. "I'm totally in love with this child," Mom said.

"When are you going to return her?" Dad said again.

"She's ours, Dad," I said. "She's staying."

"I thought she was, just, well, on loan?" Dad said.

Baby's head flopped onto Dad's shoulder, and she made a bunch of those funny squeaks, which sounded to me exactly like, *No way!*

IN THE MORNING, WHEN I WENT DOWN TO THE KITCHEN, Mom was sitting at the table with Baby in her arms.

"Greg, I haven't gotten to your breakfast," she said. "I've been trying to feed this child for an hour. She just won't take the bottle. I don't know what to do! She must be starving."

Mom ran the nipple over Baby's mouth, but Baby turned her head and the nipple landed in her ear. "Again!" Mom moaned, yanking the bottle out. "I don't know who's more nervous and upset — Baby or me."

"Want me to give it a try?" I asked.

"Yes. Anything!" Mom said.

I sat down and took Baby on my lap. She looked up at me with those green traffic-light eyes. "Listen, kid," I said, "you've got to drink this stuff. It makes you healthy and strong." I held up the bottle. Half the milk was gone. It must have spilled. "And it goes in your mouth, not your ear. *Capiche?*"

She squeaked, and believe it or don't believe it, but I heard her say, *Oh, so that's it. Mouth, not ear.*

Well, not say it, but *think* it. Okay, I know. A ten-day-old baby can't speak, not to mention think in complete sentences, but how about this? When I held the bottle to her mouth again, she took it. No head-swishing. No detours. No ears. She opened up, took the nipple, and started sucking.

From then on, we had no trouble feeding Baby, and her ears were used for hearing, although not exclusively. It was Dad who first noticed that when Baby was feeling especially loving, she rubbed her ear against our faces. *Ear love*, Mom called it.

So now I had a baby sister and, right away, it was like Mom and Dad had dipped into my brain and seen the things I'd imagined. They moved her crib into my room, and Dad said, "You're in charge here, Greg." He put his hand on my shoulder. "You watch over her. We're depending on you."

"I'll take care of her," I said. "She's safe with me, Dad." I stood straight and saluted like a soldier going off on a dangerous mission. I sure didn't know what I was getting myself into. As Mom said, Baby was "a little, tiny, big, huge handful."

She was actually the first baby I'd ever been near, so I thought that everything she did was what babies normally did. "No way," Mom said, when, less than three weeks after we got her, Baby was crawling and out of her playpen. "It's unbelievable at her age."

Unbelievable or not, Baby was on the loose and on the go for hours on end. She never napped, ever, and you seldom caught her asleep. No matter what time I woke up, middle of the night or dawn, I'd hear Baby in her crib, muttering and twittering away to herself.

"What a little bird. She has to be watched twenty-four-seven," Mom said. "Good thing I didn't give them a date when I'd come back to work!" She had left her job the day after we got Baby. "And no regrets," Mom said.

"None, none, none!" She scooped up Baby and kissed her twenty-five times. Baby giggled and gave Mom ear love in return.

"Greg, take this little imp's picture. Doesn't she look killer-cute in these overalls?"

"I already took her picture today, Mom."

"Take it again."

Photographing Baby, keeping a record, was definitely my job. Taking care of Baby — most of the time, anyway — was definitely Mom's job. Earning money was now Dad's job.

Baby seemed to think she had a job, too — exploring the house. She roamed through every room, climbed bookshelves, opened doors and drawers, dashed on her hands and knees from couch to closet to chair and back to couch. There wasn't an inch she missed. One of her specialties was crawling in reverse. She'd giggle and paddle backward even faster, it seemed, than the normal way. I could never figure out how she managed that. Sometimes she even went up and down the stairs, backwards and beaming. She was mad about *any* movement. She adored going in the car, the stroller, the Snugli, the basket on Mom's bike, or a knapsack on Dad's back.

One day, Dad came home from work, stood in the doorway and called, "Where's my little perpetual motion machine?" Right away, there was Baby, crawling so fast, it looked like she hardly touched the floor, and running after her was Mom.

"I must have jogged ten miles in the house today," she said.

Dad laughed and scooped up Baby, and then we all stood there, talking about the new cute and clever things she had done that day. I think that was when it hit me that our family had changed, that everything had sort of smoothed out. Maybe because Mom and Dad didn't have time to bicker anymore.

"Hey, guys," Mom said at breakfast. "A name for Baby came to me in a dream last night. Herozonia Lettucia."

"What's wrong with Baby?" I said.

Dad just snorted. "Nancy, you're not serious."

"I am," Mom said.

"Herozonia? Lettuce? You can't stick that on her, Mom!"

"Lettucia," Mom said. *"Le-tich-e-a."*

"Mom, they'll call her Saladhead!"

"It'll be all right," Mom said. She was firm and serene. Herozonia Lettucia was going to be — was *meant* to be, she said — Baby's proper name.

Maybe so, but to me, she was Baby: Baby then, Baby now, Baby always, and as I came to believe, Baby from outer space.

But I'm getting ahead of my story.

ONE AFTERNOON WHEN SHE WAS FOUR MONTHS OLD, BABY scooted over to me, looked up, and said, "Greg," clear as a bell. It completely slayed me.

"Your name is her first word?" Mom said. "That's such an honor, Greg! Babies say 'Mama' first. I mean, all over the world, they do this. The 'M' sound is hardwired into us. No matter what language you go to, you hear it. Mom, mama, mami, mommy, ma."

The next day, she started calling Mom "Maatoo" and Dad "Daatoo," and after that, she added new words every day.

"How old was I when I started talking?" I asked Mom.

"Oh, about fifteen months." Mom patted my hand. "That's normal, honey, especially for boys. Girl babies start talking earlier, but I've never heard of a baby talking *this* early. Herozonia is incredibly precocious."

My little sister was something else! A day didn't pass without her doing some new, funny, or, as Mom said, "amazing, astounding" thing. One day, she gave up crawling and started walking. I mean, it was like she made up her mind this was the time to do it — and she did it.

"She just stood up and went bipedal," Dad said.

If we thought Baby was cute before, it was nothing compared to now. She had a bowlegged, hurry-up, strutty stride. It just amazed me to see her racing around the house, telling herself what she was seeing, what the couch felt like, who was on TV, what she smelled cooking. Yak, yak, yak. It was nonstop talking.

Sometimes, though, she would go back to gurgling and babbling her bird sounds. Mom called that "Herozonia Speak."

"That's a lot of hokeypokey, right, my little nightingale?" Dad swung Baby into the air. "You can do better than that. Say 'comfy cushioned chair' for Daddy."

We were always trying to get her to say stuff. It knocked us out to hear her wrap her tongue around big words, but unless she was in the mood, she'd just clamp her mouth shut, wrinkle up that little flat nose, and stonewall us, which she was doing now to Dad.

"Okay, that's too easy for you," Dad said, giving her another toss into the air. "So how about 'rectangular recliner couch recently received'?"

Baby gurgled and babbled something or other in her private Herozonia Speak language, which always sounded like something we *should* understand.

"Still too easy. Okay. Say, 'Bed, place to recline and invite great god of sleep, old snoozy Somnolentis'."

"Dad, she doesn't feel like it right now," I said. "Right, Baby?"

"Wrong, Greggy," Baby said, and out came, "Rectangular recliner couch recently received. Place to invite great god, snoozy Somnolentis."

ONE EVENING I WAS PLAYING WITH BABY, THROWING HER UP to the ceiling, then catching her low, almost to the floor.

"More," she yelled. "Toss me more, Greggy!" Her green eyes glinting with glee, she seemed to hang in the air for an extra second or two, as if she were balanced on an invisible wire.

"You're a weird little kid," I told her, catching her. "Where'd you come from, anyway?"

She went still in my arms and fixed on me with one of her deep, serious looks. And then — I don't know any way to say this, except to say it: *I saw her hurtling through space.* I saw her curled up in a cozy fetal position, swimming cap and sunglasses in place, thumb in her mouth, plunging toward Earth. I know that I saw this only because she let me — let me see, not *where* she'd come from, but *how* she came here.

I saw it as clearly as if I were watching a movie. No, not a movie. Something real. So real. That's when it came to me that my little sister was a baby from outer space. Yeah, I wondered if I was losing it. I told myself I was waaaay off base. I tried to sleep the thought away, but when I woke up, it was still there.

I tried to talk about it with Mom and Dad, but they didn't get it. I don't think they wanted to get it. It was too weird. Mom quickly went into how she worried that Baby's biological mom would show up and want to take her away from us. And Dad just fazed out, saying he was tired and had to take a nap.

But were my sister's origins really that hard to believe? Check out the evidence. Infants have been found in garbage cans and plastic bags and all sorts of terrible places, but how many of them were found wearing a green swimming cap and white, perfectly fitting sunglasses? Isn't that the least bit unusual? How she survived the trip must have something to do with some natural properties from her solar system or universe or — *whatever*.

Here's another thing. In a follow-up newspaper story on abandoned infants, the reporter noted that the vast majority of infants are abandoned in hospitals. Only a tiny fraction are found in this manner where, the story noted, the mother seems to have, in a manner of speaking, "disappeared from the face of the Earth."

Disappeared from the face of the Earth? I don't think so. What I think is that there was no mother to be found on this planet. Was it even a *mother* who gave birth to Baby? We don't know how they do it in other places. Maybe it was a father. Maybe she grew in their version of a petri dish or under some special breeding light that's still undiscovered on Earth.

Who cares? The main thing was, we had Baby, and now Mom and Dad were always thinking of things for us to do as a family. One hot day that summer, we drove to a new amusement park. When Baby saw the sign reading SPACE LAND AMUSEMENT PARK, she almost jumped out of her car seat. "Woooweegee!" she cried, which was her favorite expression. She pointed to the sign. "Greg, look! It says 'space land'."

"What, you're reading now?" I asked. She just giggled. "Hey, guys." I tapped Mom and Dad on the shoulder. "Baby can read."

"Oh, right," Mom said. "Didn't I tell you?"

The space part of Space Land Amusement Park turned out to be a room with a bunch of pictures of stars, planets, and astronauts, plus a so-so video presentation. Baby put her head on Dad's shoulder and yawned.

"Kid's knocked out by the trip," Dad said.

Maybe. Or maybe it was just plain old boring to her. Nothing was happening, and Baby was hooked on speed and movement, which was probably in her DNA, or whatever they called it where she came from. I figured it was like snowboarding. Either you loved to live on the edge, or you didn't.

I didn't. My sister did. She went for anything high, fast, and terrifying, and when she saw the roller coaster, she woke right up. Her eyes flashed green, and she said, "I'll go there with Greg! Okay, everybody?"

The roller coaster whipped around a curve, crashed straight down, and made a double-S turn. "I don't think so, Baby," I said.

"I'll go there with you," she repeated.

"No, Baby."

"Yes, Greg." And then she added, "Greg, brother. *Please*?"

That did it. We bought tickets. We got on the roller coaster. Mom said, "Hold on tight to Herozonia, Greg. Don't let go."

I nodded, but who held on to who is debatable. At the top of the cycle, we hung suspended over nothing, the seat tilting perpendicular to the earth. I didn't move, not a muscle, not a twitch. It was the only way I could get through the torture. Next to me, Baby was shrieking. "Don't worry, Sis," I mumbled. "Brother's here."

"Don't worry, Bro," she chortled. "Baby's here." She was happy. Thrilled. Grooving on the ride, loving every nauseating, whipping, sliding, sickening moment.

Back on solid ground, I staggered a few steps, fell to my knees, and threw up. Baby stood by me, patting my head. "Poor big brother," she crooned, "poor Greggy."

TOWARDS THE END OF THE SUMMER, MOM REALLY GOT INTO the worry thing about Baby's bio-mom. "I'm going to get Herozonia a guard dog," she said. "I wake up in the middle of the night thinking about losing her, and I can't stand it."

"Mom, it's not going to happen," I said. "I guarantee you, Mom, no one is going to come after my little sister."

Mom looked at me like I was over the edge, but come on. What were the chances of Baby's parents (or parent, or whoever, or *whatever*) making a trip to Earth to find her? A billion to one? A billion-billion to one? Or would a trillion-billion to one be closer?

UNEXPECTED

Two days later Mom brought home a dog from the animal shelter — just for watching Baby. "I've named her Blossom, in honor of my best friend from grade school," she said. Baby took to Blossom right away, but Blossom didn't catch on that she was meant to be with Baby *all the time*. She liked hanging around Mom and the refrigerator or taking long naps. Not good. After we had her about a week, Mom said she was going to have to take her back to the animal shelter. "She's just not doing her job for Herozonia."

We were eating supper. "No," Baby said. She always sat on a pile of cushions on top of two phone books on a chair. Her chin just cleared the top of the table, but she could pound her little fists when she wanted to make a point. She was pounding her little fists now. "No, Maatoo! I want Blossom."

"Sweetheart, I'm really sorry," Mom said, "but we need a responsible dog. Don't worry about it, we'll get you another really nice dog."

Baby looked as crushed as she ever looked, but later, when I went into our room, I found her and Blossom sitting on the floor, facing each other. Baby was sucking her thumb, her green eyes fixed on Blossom, who was sitting straight up, her ears pointed forward, with a faint, high-pitched whine issuing from her throat.

"That's one smart canine," Dad said a few days later, watching Blossom following Baby around. "She really shaped up. Almost as if she knew she had to, or else."

"She did know," I said. "Baby told her."

Dad smiled briefly and opened his newspaper. "Good imagination, son. Careful, though. You don't want other people to think you're, you know, *weird*."

"Right," I said.

From then on, Blossom was always by my sister's side, and Baby could do anything to her — yank her ears, grab her tail, flop down on top of her and take a nap, even bite her, which I saw her do more than once — and Blossom allowed it and kept a brave grin on her muzzle.

THAT FALL, A WHOLE LOT OF COOL STUFF HAPPENED IN OUR family. The first thing was Mom showing up with a mouthful of colorful plastic. "Braces. I've wanted straight teeth since I was your age, Greg." She stooped over to kiss Baby, who was building some complicated LEGO structure.

"I didn't know you were going to do this," Dad said.

Mom smiled. "I always thought I was too old. Braces, when you're forty? Then I talked to Herozonia, and she, you know, gave me the courage."

"You talked to the *baby*?" Dad said.

Mom gave Dad a little arm squeeze. "Don't be hurt. I promise I'll talk to you, too, the next time something is on my mind. Okay? And you have to promise, too."

"Okay," Dad said. "I promise."

Then they kissed each other. It was kind of nice and

sort of embarrassing. I just kept my eyes on Baby. She was still completely focused on her weird LEGO structure. The look on her face reminded me of how I'd seen her sitting on Mom's lap one day last week. It had looked like a normal mother-and-daughter cuddle, but there was something different about it. It was sort of the Baby and Blossom thing all over again. That same alert stillness. Baby's eyes filled with the same light. Mom's eyes fixed on Baby's face, as if she were listening very, very hard, as if maybe Baby was saying, *So what if you are forty? Go for it!*

THEN, THE NEXT BIG THING HAPPENED. DAD ANNOUNCED that he was going back to school, so he could become a science teacher. "Something I've always wanted to do."

"Really?" I said. "How come I never knew that?"

"Couldn't earn a living and go to college at the same time, son. Had to be practical. That's what I thought."

"How are we going to live if you're in school?"

Dad and Mom shot each other a look. Not The Look. A different one.

"I'm going back to work," Mom said. She gave me a big braceful smile. "Your dad will arrange his classes so he can be home most of the time with Herozonia, and we'll get her into a preschool for the other times."

"Great," I said. I was a little bit shell-shocked with all the changes going on in our family, but I was cool with them.

Baby was bird-singing to herself, sitting on the floor and reading a book of fairy tales. She was partial to them. She glanced up at me and gave me one of her green-eyed, intense looks. Sure, she'd looked at me like that before, but this time, it was as if I had been yanked through a wall of water into another element. The air sparkled with minute points of light, and I heard Baby's thoughts: *Those talks with Maatoo and Daatoo were excellent. Poor things, they were somewhat perplexed, until I got near them and —*

I knelt down next to Baby. "I heard that," I said. She blinked at me innocently with her little fish eyes, stuck her thumb in her mouth, crawled into my lap, and rubbed her ear against my cheek.

"I love you, too," I said. "You want to say any more about the parents? I'm listening."

She leaned against me, sucking her thumb with little snorty, slobbery sounds. Right. When she was ready to talk, she would talk. When not, she wouldn't. Like Mom had said when we first got her, so many months before, she had a will of her own.

THERE'S NOT A WHOLE LOT MORE TO TELL BEFORE THE FINAL event, which I wish I didn't have to tell.

It happened in January, eleven months and eleven days from the morning we had read about Baby in the newspaper. We woke up and found her gone; Baby and Blossom both.

Maybe you think I went nuts and Mom was all weepy and hysterical? No, it was Dad who raced around the house, calling Baby's name and looking into every closet and cupboard. "Call 911," he yelled. "Greg! Call 911. She's gone!"

"Vince," Mom said. "Vince, there's nothing to do. She told me she was going."

Dad grabbed my shoulder. "Son! Help me out here. Please!"

That's when I lost it and started bawling with Dad. We were a mess for a while. Mom sat down in the middle and put her arms around us. She leaned in close to Dad and whispered into his ear. I thought maybe she'd whisper to me, too, but she didn't. I think Baby must have told her I'd understand.

And I do. But, no, I don't. Not really. I mean, I get it that Baby went back to *wherever*. I get it that she probably had to. I get it that she must have been ready to leave or needed to leave, but the truth is, somewhere inside me, I don't *really* get it. Not any of it. And I never will. We loved her so much. Couldn't she have stayed with us? Even a little longer?

As a birthday present for me, Mom framed a picture she took of me and Baby. We're outside the house, and the sun is shining on Mom's flower garden, and I'm holding Baby and pretty much grinning like a fool. Baby's dressed in jeans and a tiny T-shirt with my school logo on it. She's also wearing her green swimming cap and white sunglasses. It's a riot, but for a long time I couldn't even look at that picture.

Then, a few months after she left us, I picked it up and got to remembering stuff about Baby. After a while, I put the picture back on my bureau, and as I went to straighten it, I saw Baby move. I saw her, in the picture, shift in my arms.

"Baby?" I said, and she gave me a tiny smile, so tiny I might have made it up.

Whenever I look at that picture now — and I do every day — she gives me that little smile. I think she's letting me know that she's watching — watching me, watching all of us, from wherever she is. I like to believe it's someplace with others like her. They're talking in those bird sounds, quick and twittering. They're moving, rushing backwards for the sheer joy of it. Or leaping into the air, probably from something a whole lot better than a couch. And Baby's happy there, I know that for sure. Happiness was hers: She brought happiness to us. She brought it with her.

In case you're wondering, we did call the police. We had to, but of course we couldn't say what we knew about Baby. Nobody would have believed us. The newspaper reporter wrote, *The child seems to have disappeared from the face of the Earth.*

From the face of the Earth. Those same words again. Do we all know more than we know we know?

That's just one of my questions. Was it purely accidental that Baby came to us? Or was it planned somewhere, someplace so far away we can't even comprehend the distance? She came like a gift to our family, and then she left. That's all we really know.

Yes, I'd like to know the answers to all of my questions. Sure, I would. And, yes, I want to see Baby again. But what it comes down to, finally, is that we had her, we loved her, she loved us, and now she's gone. . . .

She's gone. And somehow it's okay.

Baby from Outer Space

Author's Note

Among the hundreds of family photos stuffed into boxes, envelopes, and drawers in our house, there's one of my younger sister, at around age three, standing on a dock near a lake. She's wearing a little pair of bathing trunks, a swimming cap, and oversized white sunglasses. She's jaunty and adorable, a grin on her face, her hands on her hips. I've always loved that picture — so much of her character shows already.

One day, looking at the picture with my middle daughter, Susan, she said, "Aunt Linda looks like a baby from outer space." I immediately went to my desk and scribbled: "baby from outer space . . . . a novel?" I often wrote down things Susan said. From the time she was a small child, she had a unique, quirky, and wonderfully fresh take on the world.

I wrote four chapters of what I intended to be a short novel, and then I got stuck. I didn't know where I was going with the story, so I made a lot of notes and put the partial manuscript aside.

Twelve years passed. I never forgot the story, but I never got back to it, either.

Then I was asked to write a story for this anthology, and it occurred to me that, if not a novel, my "baby from outer space" idea might make a good short story. It was only after I finished the story that I realized that in its deepest meaning — that is, emotionally — I had been writing about my beloved Susan, whom we lost in 2001 to brain cancer.

Susan lives on with us in our memories; in our family pictures; and in her paintings and drawings, which are everywhere in our house and in the homes of her sisters and brother. And now, in some sense, she will live on, too, in this story.

NORMA FOX MAZER is the author of twenty-six novels for children and young adults, plus two collections of short stories. She has edited an anthology of women's poetry and contributed articles, essays, and short stories to numerous journals and anthologies. Many of her books have been on the ALA Best Books for Young Adults, Notable Books, and Best of the Best lists. Among her awards are a Newbery Honor, a National Book Award finalist, the California Young Reader Medal, a Christopher Medal, an Edgar, two Lewis Carroll Shelf Awards, and two Iowa Teen Fiction Awards. Many of her books have been published in England and Australia and translated into French, German, Dutch, Danish, Spanish, Swedish, Norwegian, and Japanese. Her novel *Girlhearts* was a finalist for the *Los Angeles Times* Book Award and named a Notable Book of the Year by *Smithsonian* magazine. Her most recent novel is called *What I Believe*.

Who Broke Harry's Head?

◌◌◌

Graham Salisbury

A WEEK OR SO BEFORE THE MURDER, I CAME HOME FROM hanging around Kailua Beach Park with my friend, Willy, and noticed a nervous yellow parakeet wobbling on a swing in a bamboo cage.

It wasn't our bird, I knew that much, because one of Mom's pet peeves was pets. The closest thing to an animal ever allowed in our house was Harry, my little sister Darci's rocking horse, which used to be mine. My dad made it for me just before he moved out. But pets weren't welcome in our house, Mom said. In fact, the last time I asked her if I could get a dog, she said, "Forget it, just forget it. I'm the one who will have to feed it, and pick ticks off it, and burrs, and then take it to the vet for shots, and I don't need another thing to worry about around this place. It's hard enough as it is. No dogs, no cats, no rats, mice, gerbils, rabbits, fish, or birds. No pets."

So what was with the parakeet?

Stella, our live-in babysitter, was sitting on the living room floor playing Memory with Darci. The birdcage was just behind them, hanging from a tall wrought-iron stand near the big plate-glass window that looked out onto our front yard. The parakeet bobbed its head and blinked its papaya-seed eyes at me.

"Where'd that bird come from?" I asked.

"None of your beeswax," Stella said, not bothering to look up.

Stella was sixteen and borderline cranky. She was sitting back on her bare feet, her long, smooth legs bent under her. Her jeans were frayed where she'd cut them off, just below the bottom of the pockets. A pale blue tube top, no wider than a Band-Aid, peeked out under long, silky blond hair that fell over her face and shoulders like a curtain.

I could hear Mom banging around in the kitchen. Why wasn't she out here complaining about the parakeet?

"Well, whose is it, then?" I said. "Mom said we can't have pets. So what's it doing here?"

Stella glanced up and studied me. She shook her head. "Always trying to stir things up, aren't you?"

"What?"

She smirked. "You're so transparent. Listen, if you have to know, your mother said I could keep it, and if you touch it, you're a dead little ducky, Joe-Babes."

"Joey."

"Whatever."

Stella went back to Memory.

If Mom was letting her keep a parakeet, then maybe I should ask about the dog again, because if anyone got to get a pet around here, it should be me, not Stella.

"Where'd you get it?" I asked.

"Clarence gave it to her . . . that's her boyfriend," Darci said, looking up with a grin in her eyes. Her curly brown hair was pinched back into two tight pigtails that were tied off with crisp yellow ribbons. Stella's work.

"Clarence?" I said. "You have a boyfriend named Clarence?"

Stella looked up again, this time sweeping her hair behind her ear with a finger and stabbing me with one of her stiletto squints.

"Stella," Mom sang from the kitchen. "Will you please-pretty-please get Darci in the tub? Ledward is coming over tonight, and I want her fed and ready for bed before he gets here. Can you get that started? Thaaank you."

Stella rolled her eyes and got up, waving for Darci to follow her. Ledward, who was Mom's boyfriend, came over every Friday, Saturday, and Sunday night. Stella avoided him, because she could hardly understand his pidgin English.

On her way to the bathroom Stella kissed her hand and brushed it across my cheek.

I jerked away, and rubbed it off. "Cut it out, Stella!"

"Oh . . . I'm sorry," she said. "For a second there I thought you were a nice person."

WHEN LEDWARD CAME OVER TO TAKE MOM OUT, THEY GOT into an argument about which movie they would see.

UNEXPECTED

Ledward was this huge Hawaiian guy, and not somebody you'd intentionally go out and pick a fight with. But Mom did it all the time. And she didn't even come up to his shoulder.

I was just around the corner in the kitchen and could hear their voices heating up out in the living room. I crept closer, but they must have known I was there, because they went out to the backyard where they could talk in private.

I peeked out the window.

Ledward's arms were spread wide, looking as if he were protesting something Mom had said. She stood with her back to him, right next to Darci's horse, Harry, who she was rocking absently with one foot. Ledward got tired of that and kicked Harry over. Mom picked Harry back up and started rocking him again.

Ledward scowled and paced and rubbed the back of his neck. Then he softened and came up and put his arms around Mom from behind. She put her hands on his and that was that.

Five minutes later they drove off on their date. Stella and I watched them leave from the front window. Stella frowned and shook her head.

"What?" I said.

She scoffed, and walked away.

Stella named her parakeet Little Richard.

The bird was actually kind of fun to have around the

house. Darci even neglected Harry for a while. When Stella wasn't home, she sometimes stuck her finger in the cage, whispering, "Here, Little Richie," hoping he would hop on.

But Darci soon went back to Harry, singing softly while she groomed him with an old worn-out shoe brush that Ledward had given her. She fed Harry cereal, too — Kix — but she called them oats.

When I tried playing with Little Richard he pecked me with his pointy beak and squawked as if my hand were a cat licking his lips. It was funny. Or maybe he was just mad because I'd interrupted his constant gnawing on the bamboo bars that held him in. That bird definitely wanted out, and with Stella as his boss, who could blame him?

Sometimes, though, Little Richard hopped right up on my finger. I liked that feeling, the scratchy lightness of his prickly feet.

Still, it wasn't fair. If anyone got to get a pet, it should have been me.

MY BEDROOM WAS KIND OF JUNK.

It was made out of half the garage, and at night when I lay in bed I could smell gas from the car. But I could also sneak out whenever I wanted to. It was so easy that I hardly ever did it.

But since my room was part of the garage, and the garage faced the street, I could see whoever drove up. I

117

could just lie on my bunk and look out and watch whatever went on out there.

And that's where I was the first time Clarence came over to get Stella. He drove up about five o'clock for a Saturday night date. He parked, turned off the engine, and honked.

Blat!

Then stayed in his car, a small red Nissan about a hundred years old. The door on the driver's side was dented, and the radio antenna was rusty and bent.

I eased closer to the window, trying to get a good look at him, but the windshield was painted with the white reflection of clouds. All I could see was his beefy tattooed arm hanging out the window. He held a cigarette between his thumb and first finger, and with his second finger, kept flicking ashes off the burning tip. Every now and then he'd pull his arm back into the car. Then it would come out again, followed by a stream of smoke.

Blat! Blat!

Why didn't he just go bang on the front door? Mom wasn't even home.

Blaaat!

He slapped the side of his car, hard. Maybe that's how the dents got there.

Blaaaaaaaaaaaat!

Stella finally came running out, all happy and gooey and so un-Stella-like it was sickening. She got in and slid over to nest right up against him.

Who Broke Harry's Head?

Clarence started the car and jolted it out into the street. As they sped away and the cloud reflections raced off the windows, I could see Stella stretching up to the rearview mirror to dab lipstick onto her smoochy lips.

THE NEXT DAY, SUNDAY, I DRAGGED MYSELF OUT OF BED AND staggered into the kitchen, hungry as a dump dog. It was almost noon. Darci was out in the backyard riding Harry and singing "Old MacDonald Had a Farm."

I grabbed the milk out of the fridge, then got a bowl and a box of Kix and a spoon. I had to shove a stack of old newspapers to the back of the counter just to set my bowl down. A sour odor rose from the sink where a pile of greasy dishes were stacked. Or maybe it was the over-stuffed trashcan that smelled. Somebody had pulled it out from under the sink.

I ate in silence, thinking about going down to Willy's house before Mom thought of something for me to do. I held my spoon suspended when I heard voices in the next room.

I quickly finished my cereal and eased my bowl into the mess in the sink, then hurried towards the door on my toes so I wouldn't make any noise.

"Joey?" Mom called. "That you in the kitchen?"

I frowned. "Yeah."

"Come here, will you?"

At the dining room table just around the corner, Stella and Mom were separating bills. There were two stacks of envelopes, one about three inches high, and the other half that. The two of them looked like sisters, Mom wearing cutoff shorts just like Stella's, with her hair all long and shimmery clean.

"I'm going to Willy's house," I said.

"How long has it been since you looked at these bills?" Stella asked Mom.

"I don't know if I have enough in my checking account to pay them," Mom said. She worked in a tourist gift shop on the other side of the island. Not a bad job, but she was always scraping coins out of the bottom of her purse. My dad, who now lived in Las Vegas with his new wife, Marissa, wasn't all that good about sending us money like he was supposed to.

"Look," Stella said, shaking her head. "It's not as bad as it seems. See these phone bills. You have three of them, so automatically you can throw the two earlier ones away, just pay the latest one."

"Am I that far behind? Joey, listen, I want you to mow the lawn today, okay?"

"You can probably cut this whole mess of bills in half," Stella said.

"I'm going to Willy's," I said again, then started to leave.

"Take the trash out to the garbage can, all right? Then take the garbage can out to the street," Mom said. "And what about cutting the grass?"

Stella snorted.

"What?" I said.

She shook her head, but said nothing.

I went back into the kitchen, jamming my hand down into the cereal box for a handful of Kix before heading out through the garage. I munched them one by one as I strolled down the street to Willy's. It felt good to be out of the house. Freedom. Fresh air. Sun warm on my head.

I was about to put another Kix in my mouth when I remembered I'd forgotten to take out the trash. Dang. Then I shrugged and continued on down to Willy's. Stella could do it.

Later, when I came back home, I saw Mom wrestling our big metal garbage can out to the street. She was dragging it, making a horrible scraping noise. I hid behind a hibiscus hedge a few houses away and waited until she went back into the house.

I sat in the shade and let some time pass, feeling a little bad that Mom had to drag the garbage out. But she should have told Stella to do it. That's what Stella was there for. To do stuff.

ABOUT SEVEN O'CLOCK THAT EVENING, LEDWARD CAME OVER. The sky was pinky-blue, with a good hour of light left in it. Mom told Ledward she needed to talk, so they went out through the backyard gate and headed down to the beach for some privacy.

When they came back about a half hour later, Mom

was clinging to Ledward like a lizard on an ironwood tree. He towered above her, his wavy black hair greased back and catching reflected glimpses of the last light of day.

They stood out in the ankle-high grass with their arms around each other.

I was hiding in my room, spying on them from the edge of the window. Once, they turned and peered my way.

Finally, Ledward kissed Mom on her forehead and, as he headed toward his Jeep, said, "I'll call you."

Mom stood smiling after him with her hands in the back pockets of her shorts.

I stepped back into the shadows of my room.

"Howzit," Ledward said as he passed by my window. I thought he was talking to someone else out there who I couldn't see. But he stopped and peered through the screen. "I seen you there from when we first got back," he said, then chuckled.

"Uh . . ."

"Come outside, boy. We go walk, you and me."

"Huh?"

"Come outside. I like talk to you."

I went out. The sky, now, was the color of pearls, the air warm and silky. Next to Ledward I felt about a foot tall, since he was the same height as a telephone pole.

Mom went into the lighted house and stood at the big front window, watching us.

Something was up.

I followed Ledward down the sloping grass to the edge of the swampy canal that crawled past our yard. We stopped and stood, looking out over the rusty water. It smelled like sulfur. Flecks of bug life swarmed inches above the surface. A bufo near my left foot hopped out of the grass and headed into the marsh.

Ledward pointed his chin toward the toad. "You know how come got bufos in the grass?"

"No."

"'Cuz you no cut um. They like um long, bufos. They come inside, dig down. Make a home. They like that long grass."

So? I thought. Who cares if toads live in the grass? Except for when you mow it and accidentally chop one of them up. "I cut the grass," I said.

"Yeah, but no more nuff, ah? When the grass stay short, they no come inside. That's the key."

I stared at the spot where the toad had vanished.

"So tomorrow afta school you cut um, ah? For your mama."

"You're . . . you're not my boss."

Ledward grinned. "Ha! You funny, boy."

I scowled.

"Well, how's about you cut um now, den? Go get that lawn mowah, go. I wait. I help you start um up."

"I'll do it later. And . . . and anyway you can't tell me what to do, you know."

"You think so?"

"Yeah."

"Who going cut it, then? Your mama? The girl?"

I shrugged.

"You like I do um for you?"

"You can do what you want."

"Hokay. No problem . . . but, boy . . ."

He paused and studied me.

"What?"

"Afta I do um this one time you going do um ev'ry Sataday now on, ah? Keep um short so the bufos no come inside."

I watched a half-submerged branch drift down the river, part of it sticking up like a claw. Who did he think he was, anyway?

"You're not my boss," I mumbled.

"Huh . . . I guess nex Sataday we going fine out. Hokay?"

"Find out what?"

"If I your boss."

"What does *that* mean?"

"Sataday come, and you no more cut um, den you going fine out what I mean."

"I'm telling Mom you threatened me."

"You call that one t'ret?"

"Yeah . . ."

Ledward looked off toward the mountains. "Huh," he

said, then looked back. "Anyways, we going see Sataday, ah?"

Then he cut the grass. In the dark.

A COUPLE OF DAYS LATER, DARCI AND I WERE IN THE KITCHEN poking around for something to eat. We'd just gotten home from school. Stella wasn't there yet, because now that Clarence was driving her she got back later than ever. Mom would spit bullets if she knew Stella wasn't there to meet Darci when she got home.

But I wasn't about to rat on her.

I didn't want Stella getting into trouble, and then telling Clarence it was my fault. I could just see him creeping along behind me as I walked home from school, his rat-trap car rumbling along at one mile an hour. My whole body shivered just thinking about it.

Darci reached into a box of Kix and grabbed a handful of oats for Harry, then headed out to the backyard. "Let's take Little Richard out of his cage," she said. "We can hold him."

I had to laugh. Darci with those rascally eyes . . . and a great idea.

"Stella will *kill* us, Darce."

Then I figured, how's she gonna know? And anyway, Willy told me they clipped parakeets' wings so they couldn't fly away.

We crept out to the patio where Stella liked to keep

the birdcage during the day. She said since poor Little Richard was in jail, the least she could do was put him outside so he could talk to the mynah birds. I didn't tell her the mynah birds would probably have Little Richard for lunch if he ever got out.

Darci fed Harry first, cupping her hand under his mouth — then eating the Kix herself. But she saved some of them, and dragged one of our corroding old metal-and-vinyl patio chairs over and stood on it. Biting her lower lip, she opened the cage door and reached in. She crushed the leftover Kix and opened her hand, revealing the crumbs.

Little Richard bobbed his head, his shiny black eyes darting between me, Darci, and the feast in Darci's hand.

He plopped down on her wrist.

Hopped towards the crumbs.

Darci let him peck and nibble, then dropped the rest of the crumbs onto the newspaper that covered the bottom of the cage. When Little Richard fluttered down after them, Darci grabbed him.

Little Richard screeched and shrieked and nipped at Darci's thumb, mad as a wasp. Darci winced, but wouldn't let go.

She eased him out of the cage.

"Don't squeeze him so hard, Darce."

Darci cooed and stroked Little Richard's head with

her finger. When he calmed down, she opened her hand.

And Little Richard flapped up into the sky like a freed balloon.

"*Ahh!*" I said. "Why'd you do *that*?"

Darci jumped off the chair and ran after him, calling, "Here, birdybirdybirdy," like he was a cat, or something. "Here, birdybirdy!"

What a joke.

I was going to wring Willy's neck next time I saw him, because that bird was *gone*.

WHEN STELLA CAME HOME, YOU'D HAVE THOUGHT THAT Darci and I had just come home from church, and that we each wore our own little gold cross around our necks. But our fine acting was lost on Stella, who was in an excellent mood.

She gave Darci a pat on the head, and said, "Don't you look sweet today," then she headed into the kitchen to get the bag of birdseed for Little Richard's feeder. She hummed to herself, reaching for the bag, which was on top of the refrigerator. "Aren't you going to feed Harry?" she said, looking over her shoulder at Darci.

Darci gulped, then got the box of Kix and grabbed a handful of oats.

Stella smiled and went out to the patio, humming.

Darci glanced at me, then at the Kix in her hand.

Stella filled the feeder.

Humming, humming.

We cowered like startled puppies as she started to pull out the water bowl.

Stella went silent.

A fat fly buzzed past my ear. A car horn tooted out on the road beyond our backyard fence.

Stella dropped the water bowl and put her hand on her throat, staring into the empty cage. I stopped breathing.

"You *kids!*" Stella screamed. *"Where's Little Richard?"*

Darci and I stood still as concrete birdbaths.

Where was Mom when you needed her?

Stella stormed over and breathed down on us. "Where *is* he?"

Darci shrugged.

Stella turned to me. "You little pissant. *You* did something to him, didn't you?" She grabbed my arms and squeezed.

"Ow, that hurts," I said, jerking away.

Her cheeks turned pink. Her eyes bulged, then squinted down to razors. I could see the white outline of her jawbone popping through the skin.

I backed away, rubbing the finger marks on my arms.

"I just wanted to hold him . . ." Darci whispered.

Stella's eyes shifted away from me.

". . . I didn't mean to let him go."

"*You* did it?"

"He . . . he flew out of my hand."

Stella's face flushed sunburn pink. She seemed to be stuttering in her mind, thinking of what to say, what to do. Finally, she blurted, "Maybe I should take something of *yours* and lose it, huh? How would you like *that*?"

Darci inched behind me.

Stella spun around and slammed down the hall to her bedroom. Soon after, she blasted back out and bolted from the house.

A couple of hours later Stella sulked back, looking as if she'd lost her last friend in the world. I could hardly even glance at her puffy, red eyes. She looked lower than one of the dried-out run-over toads that littered our street. Stella didn't have a mom and dad somewhere who she could go to when things got tough. She had to live with us just to survive.

For the first time, I wondered where she'd actually come from. I'd never even thought about that before.

TWO DAYS AFTER LITTLE RICHARD ESCAPED, MOM NOTICED that the cage was empty. She studied it a moment, then raised her eyebrows and went into her bedroom and turned on the TV. She never asked about Little Richard. Ever.

ON FRIDAY NIGHT, LEDWARD'S JEEP PULLED INTO THE DRIVEway. He and Mom had been out on another date. Those two argued almost every time they got together, and on the phone, too, but they couldn't stand to be away from each other. I didn't get it.

Anyway, I'd stayed up late flipping channels on Mom's TV, and had just come out to my room and fallen into bed.

The Jeep coughed and jerked to a stop. The engine died as Mom jumped out. Ledward got out, too, faster than I'd ever thought a guy that big could. He caught Mom by her arm in three giant strides.

"Angela, wait," he pleaded. "You don't understand."

"Oh, I understand all right," she spat, struggling to free herself from his grip.

But Ledward wouldn't let go. "Lissen," he said, "please . . . I don't know nothing about kids . . . maybe I could figure it out . . . but —"

"Let me go!" Mom said. "You have no right to say that about him, no right!"

Ledward let go and Mom backed away, glaring and rubbing her arm. Then she spun around and hurried through the garage and into the house, slamming the door and sending what sounded like a frying pan whanging around the kitchen floor.

Ledward swore under his breath. He paced, once, twice. He kicked the left front tire on his Jeep. Then he got back in and started it, and sat with the engine idling for a good five minutes before backing out and driving away.

Who was the *him* Mom was talking about?

Who Broke Harry's Head?

I'd almost fallen asleep when my eyes popped open at another loud thump. I sat up and listened.

But that was the end of it.

THE NEXT DAY I GOT UP EARLY AND PEEKED INTO THE kitchen. No one was up. I quietly got a bowl and a box of cereal and ate at the far end of the counter near the door to the garage.

Mom came in a few minutes later to brew her morning coffee before getting dressed for work. Her eyes were puffy, as if she'd just that moment dragged herself out of bed. I tried to blend into the wall paint. I did a pretty good job, too, because she didn't say one word to me.

I finished my cereal quickly and went outside.

I glanced at the grass and remembered what Ledward had said about cutting it. Forget it, I thought. Who cared what he said? Who was he to tell me what to do?

And anyway, the grass wasn't important, because that was the day Darci discovered the murder.

I went back into the house after Mom drove off to work. I found Darci in the kitchen with a box of Froot Loops that Mom had bought in a moment of weakness. "Where's Stella?" I asked. "She ever come home last night?"

"Sleeping," Darci said.

I grunted, and stuck my hand in the Froot Loops box.

Darci finished quickly, antsy to treat Harry to a handful of colorful oats.

She grabbed some and went outside to round him up.

And screamed.

"Somebody killed Harry! Joey, Joey, somebody killed Harry!"

I ran out to see Harry's white head hanging by a few splinters off the rest of his body. Along the jagged break, raw wood gaped out like torn muscle and tendons. It was creepy. I mean, rocking horse heads don't just fall off on their own.

I pulled Darci close to me and glanced around the backyard for anything else that wasn't as it should be. But all I saw was dirt and sand and splotchy grass.

"Holy cow, Darce."

Darci sobbed and sobbed. Fat tears gushed down her cheeks. Harry's oats were scattered all over the concrete patio. I didn't know what to do, so I patted her back and said, "Somebody'll fix it. So stop crying, okay? Come on, Darce."

"Somebody . . . broke . . . Harry's . . . head," she said, hiccuping.

"Maybe he just got old and fell apart. Things don't last forever, you know."

That was so lame it only made her sob louder. She ran back into the house, banged down to her room, and slammed the door.

I stood with my hands on my hips, studying Harry's dangling head.

Who Broke Harry's Head?

I noticed a slash of white paint on the brick just behind him. The same color as Harry. Like maybe his head came off because somebody kicked him into the wall. Not only that, one of the patio chairs was sprawled nearby, upended. On the ground next to it I saw a cigarette butt, which was even creepier than Harry's busted head, because nobody in our house, and nobody I knew, smoked.

Unless you counted Clarence.

My scalp felt as if a small herd of spiders were crawling all over it.

But that wasn't all. When I bent down to study the cigarette butt, I saw the faint stain of lipstick on the filter.

I frowned.

No one who smoked ever came over to our house. Mom used to smoke, but not now. Stella was always yakking about what a dirty habit it was. And Darci certainly didn't smoke.

I rubbed my chin.

Maybe Stella did it. Because of Little Richard.

But murdering rocking horses wasn't her style.

Maybe the cigarette butt and Harry's head weren't related. That could be.

So who broke Harry's head?

THE SIGHT OF HARRY ALL BROKEN UP LIKE THAT FILLED DARCI with such misery that her heart burst every time she peeked out into the backyard. "I want Harry back," she cried.

"Oh, stop that nonsense," Mom said that night when she got home from work. "You're too big for a rocking horse, anyway."

But Darci moped around, producing giant tears whenever she thought the occasion called for them.

Mom still wasn't moved.

But Stella was, because the following week she came home with a brand-new Harry. I mean, a completely new horse, not a fixed one.

"Where'd that come from?" I asked.

"Clarence made it in shop," Stella said.

"No kidding?" It was pretty good. "Why?" I asked.

"Why what?" Stella said.

"Why'd he make it?"

"Because I asked him to."

"Why?"

"What are you, the FBI?"

"But Darci let your bird go."

Stella frowned. "Some brother *you* are."

"What do you mean?"

Stella shook her head. "I feel sorry for you, you know?"

"What'd I do?"

"Beat it. You're driving me crazy."

"Why?"

Stella rolled her eyes and walked away.

But Darci fed and groomed and rode New Harry like he was a real, true-life horse. Rode him and rode him and rode him. All day long, she rocked on that horse.

She kept him penned up alongside old Harry, whose head Stella had duct-taped back into place, though it sagged off to one side.

But now I was really confused. I wanted to know who broke Harry's head. And why.

My brain was overworked.

This crime was getting to me.

All through the next week Stella acted secretive. She'd come home and hide out in her room. Whenever the phone rang she'd burst out and dive for it before anyone else could answer it.

"What's going on?" I finally asked her.

"What do you mean?"

"I mean you stay in your room or just sit around staring out the window. And where's Clarence, anyway? I haven't heard his horn in more than a week."

Stella waved me off.

"Come on," I said. "Tell me. You can trust me."

Stella laughed.

"Well, you can," I said. "Really."

She must have been anxious to talk, because she believed me.

She pinched my T-shirt and pulled me into her bedroom. "Okay. Don't you tell anyone. Can I really trust you?"

"Sure."

"I met this guy," she whispered. "He's a Marine. His name is Buddy. He . . . he asked me to marry him."

"*What?*"

"Shhh."

"But you . . . you're just . . . you . . ."

I must have looked like a bug-eyed bufo, because she gave me this kind of sad, I-pity-you face that told me I was a bigger fool than she'd thought. But still, she couldn't have known this Buddy guy for more than a week.

Stella grinned, watching me calculate the days.

"Well, what did you say?"

Stella crossed her arms. "I said I'd think about it."

"But . . . but what will we do if you leave?"

Stella scowled. "I haven't said I'd marry him, all right? And maybe I won't. But if I did, your mom would definitely need help around this place. She can't handle it by herself."

Stella looked into my eyes. Whatever she saw there softened her. A little.

"Listen, your mom's okay, you know? But . . . she needs help. She doesn't have what it takes to deal with you two twerps alone. She's got . . . her own problems. I know this is a laugh, but I guess it would be up to you to help her, huh? You or that he-man she drools over, though I doubt he'll ever find the guts to pop the question. But God help you if you get stuck with him."

"What do you mean she doesn't have what it takes?"

"You're so blind. If you were my kid do you think I'd let you get away with all the rot you get away with? You come and go whenever you please. You take and you take and you push your mom all over the place. You don't help out. Somebody has to scream at you just to get you to take out the garbage or cut the grass. Noooo, I wouldn't put up with that. I'd beat you to a pulp. But your mom won't because she's too weak. Haven't you noticed she's never home? That's because it's too much for her. And you just take advantage of that. You run all over her."

"I do not."

Stella smirked, then pinched my cheek. "Yes, you do, little sweetie."

I batted her hand away.

"You just don't have a clue about what it means to give, do you?" she said. "I hate to tell you this, big boy, but try pulling that kind of stuff outside of this little protected world of yours and you'll find out real fast what I'm talking about."

Stella glanced out the window into the backyard. Darci had the two horses sitting side by side, and was standing on them, balancing with one foot on each saddle, like a trick-rider in a circus.

"Do you smoke?" I said.

Stella turned back. "What?"

"I found a cigarette butt on the patio. It had lipstick on it. Right by where Harry was murdered."

"Murdered?" Stella laughed.

"But do you?"

When Stella didn't answer, I said, "Did you break Harry's head?"

Stella eyed me, smirking. "You are so much dumber than you look, you know that?"

"At first I thought maybe you told Clarence to do it. Because of Little Richard."

"*Pfft* . . . Clarence wouldn't do that."

"He looks like he would."

"He's a teddy bear. And are you forgetting that he made Darci a new horse?"

"If he's so nice, then how come you're dumping him?"

She shrugged. "Buddy has a future."

"Why did you say God help me if I got stuck with Ledward?"

Stella snorted, an ugly sound. "I mean your stupid little life will change. Oh, boy, will it."

"Why?"

"Because you're so selfish, dummy. You think he-man's gonna put up with that? Oh, no, Joe-Babes. He'll show you the *real* world, and you're not going to like it."

"What do *you* know about the real world?"

Stella paused, gazed down at the floor. She took a deep breath and looked me straight in the eye. "A little more than you do, unfortunately."

We were silent a moment.

Her eyes jumped back and forth across my face. Then she looked away. I knew Stella couldn't have killed Harry. She loved Darci. She was the only one who ever spent time with her. And she'd never even chewed Darci out for letting Little Richard go.

I must have looked confused, or lost, because Stella cupped my face in her hands. She smiled, and her eyes started to water. They looked warm and kind. She pulled me close, and kissed me square on the lips.

"Ahh!" I said, jerking away. "What'd you do *that* for?"

"There got to be a reason for everything?"

I ran my tongue over Stella's lingering kiss as if it were still there, then touched it again with the back of my hand. Stella's lips were softer than anything I'd ever felt in my life.

Stella laughed and walked out of the room, leaving me with the taste of her lipstick on my tongue and my heart leaping in my chest. For as long as I lived I would never understand what made people like Stella tick. Who knew what went on in her mind? Or anyone's mind.

I turned toward the screened window when I heard fat drops of rain start to plop onto the cracked concrete of our patio. Fresh earth smells wafted in and filled my lungs with sweetness. Darci was still out there, oblivious of the rain, the horses rocking madly under her feet.

ON FRIDAY NIGHT MOM HAD ANOTHER SHOUTING TELEPHONE conversation with Ledward. She slammed the receiver down and locked herself in her room.

Stella was supposed to go out with Clarence, or maybe Buddy, I didn't know which, but she stayed home instead, because she was worried about Mom. So was I. Every time I knocked on the bedroom door Mom said, "Go away."

My fingers started to tremble. "Stella," I whispered. "Something's wrong with Mom."

"Listen," Stella said, taking me aside. "You have to talk to her. Make her come out. Darci's taking this all in and that's not good. Your mom doesn't know what she's doing to her."

"But what's wrong with her?"

"I don't know. Maybe she's depressed. It happens. But you've got to talk her into coming out."

"What do I say?"

"I don't know, just think of something."

I knocked. "Mom?"

"Go away."

I stood with my ear to the door, hearing nothing but

the hum of my own body. I tried the doorknob. It was locked.

"Mom, come out. You're scaring us."

She said nothing.

I could open the door with a butter knife, I thought. Just stick it in the slot and turn. I told Stella.

"Okay, do that. We need to know what's going on in there, you understand, Joey? We *need* to know. Now go open the door."

I got a butter knife from the silverware drawer and took it down the hall. I stuck it in the slot.

Pop!

I inched the door open, afraid of what I might see.

Mom was sitting on her bed with her legs crossed, her back against the wall. She was staring straight ahead with eyes as glazed as a cow's.

"Mom?"

"I'm such a failure, Joey."

I eased down on the edge of the bed. Not too close. I'd never seen her like that before. "No, Mom, no. You're not a failure, really, you're not."

She turned her glassy eyes towards me. I saw a small glimpse of light in them. "Thank you, Joey."

I looked down.

We sat still and silent.

Finally, I said, "You hungry, Mom?"

"No."

I waited.

"I can . . . I can make us some soup. I think we have some chicken noodle. And I can make cinnamon toast. How's that?"

She turned towards me again, and stared for the longest time, letting her eyes explore my face. "You can do that?"

"Well . . . I think so."

Mom's eyes flooded with tears. "Yes," she said. "Yes, Joey, make us some soup. Make soup for all of us."

I stood. "Okay, Mom. You just . . . you just rest here. I'm going to keep the door open, okay?"

She nodded and closed her eyes.

I went into the kitchen and found a can of soup and a pot to cook it in. I read the directions, then dug through the drawer I thought the can opener might be in.

And that's when I found the cigarettes.

Way in the back, behind all the junk.

Kools.

I stared at them. Kools — Mom's old brand.

"What are you doing?" Stella said, suddenly there.

I grabbed the can opener and slammed the drawer shut.

And made soup for the first time in my life.

Stella watched the whole time, at first smirking, then nodding.

"What?" I said.

"Wonders never cease."

THE NEXT DAY, SATURDAY, WAS ONE OF THE FEW MOM got off.

I woke up early, about ten o'clock. Darci was already out in the backyard with her horses. I frowned, still unable to figure out how or why Harry got his head knocked off.

After a bowl of cereal I went out to the garage and dragged out the smelly old rotary lawn mower. I hated that thing. It was nearly impossible to start and it wasn't self-propelled.

While I was struggling with the pull-rope, Ledward drove up in his Jeep. He stepped out and flashed me a white-toothed grin. He reached back into the Jeep and came out with a bouquet of wild yellow ginger.

I frowned and gave the pull-rope another rip. The lawn mower coughed and spat and went back to sleep.

Ledward loomed over me. "You like me for pull um?"

I stood back. "Sure, why not?"

He handed me the bouquet, then squatted down and rewound the pull-rope. He looked up and winked. Then yanked the cord, smooth and clean.

The lawn mower started right up.

He adjusted the throttle and stood.

I handed him the ginger. "Thank you."

"No," he said. "T'ank *you*."

He tapped me on the back and went into the house through the garage.

Thank me?

Why?

I stood with the lawn mower idling high while the fuzzy-edged pieces and events of the past couple of weeks slowly started to sharpen in my mind. Most of it came into focus later, but I got the important part right away — Harry's busted head; the cigarette butt with lipstick on it; what Stella was trying to tell me, and Ledward, in his strange way; the pack of Kools hidden in the silverware drawer; and the image of Mom dragging the garbage can out to the street.

And now Ledward, thanking me for hauling out the lawn mower.

It was all about me.

And how I was making everything too hard for Mom.

I frowned as that small light flickered on in my brain. I had pushed her and pushed her until she couldn't take it anymore. She might have done the kicking, but I was the one who broke Harry's head.

Me.

I looked up when a small yellow bird flew past. It landed in a tree across the street. I blinked, and it was gone.

Who Broke Harry's Head?

Author's Note

In Kailua, my sister had a rocking horse named Harry. Somebody knocked his head off. We never knew who did it. It was a mystery then, and is a mystery now. We also lived, for a while, with a teenage live-in nanny who taunted us mercilessly. I loved going head-to-head with her. It was a challenge. She was crafty. But so was I. And, to be honest, I had too much freedom for my own good, all the way up until seventh grade, when my mom finally got wise and sent me away to boarding school on the Big Island. So even though "Who Broke Harry's Head?" is fiction, I exist in the story in a large way. Only I didn't know what I was writing about when I first started this story — what it all meant. Now I do. Hoo boy.

GRAHAM SALISBURY is the author of several books for young readers. Most notable are *Under the Blood-Red Sun*, winner of the Scott O'Dell Award for Historical Fiction, the California Young Reader Medal, and Hawaii's Nene Award; *Blue Skin of the Sea*, winner of the Judy Lopez Award, and Parents' Choice Award; *Lord of the Deep*, the 2002 *Boston Globe/Horn* Book Award winner and *School Library Journal* Best Book of the Year; and his recently published collection of short stories, *Island Boyz*. His latest book is *Eyes of the Emperor*, a companion novel to *Under the Blood-Red Sun*. Though he returns to Hawaii several times a year, he now lives with his family in Portland, Oregon.

The Troddler

Bruce Coville

ANDERS HATED THE STONE TROLL THAT STOOD AT THE COR-
ner near his house. Every time he walked past it, it reminded him that his father had been lost to the trolls:
"Troll-taken," as the neighbors put it.

"Serves you right," he would say to the statue each
afternoon as he came home from school. "If you'd stayed
underground where you belong, you wouldn't have
been turned into stone."

Yet some days he couldn't help staring at it, fascinated
by the tragic look on the troll's face. Even so, on the
afternoon that everything changed, Anders passed the
statue with no more than his usual insult and continued
straight to his house, where he burst through the front
door with his daily cry of, "I'm home!"

He paused, waiting for his mother's standard response
of, "And I'm in the kitchen!"

He was greeted by nothing but silence. With a shrug,
Anders ambled into the kitchen, expecting to find a
plate of his mother's baking with a note tucked under-
neath to explain where she was.

The table was bare.

It was then that Anders noticed something else, something that sent a tremor of fear rippling through him.

Faint, but unmistakable, he caught the cold, stony scent of troll.

His hand crept to the sprig of trollbane he wore around his neck. He didn't know if the plant really kept trolls away; some of his friends claimed the idea was mere fogwump, and his father had never told him either way. Even so, it made him feel better to know it was there.

Setting his schoolbooks on the table, Anders moved his other hand to the dagger at his waist. Then he shook his head. What foolishness! No troll could be here now, not during the day. Wasn't the statue at the corner — not to mention the other three statues he passed on the way to school — proof enough of that? After all, each had once been a living troll who had been caught by the trollwatch and dragged into the light to be petrified.

Yet even if no troll were here now, Anders' nose insisted one had been recently.

"Mother?" he called nervously. "Mother, where are you?"

No answer.

He dashed through the house, checking the living room and the dining room, then up the stairs to look through all four bedrooms. He found no sign of her — but neither did he find any sign of a struggle, any hint that she might have been taken against her will.

Anders forced himself to stay calm. It was possible she had simply gone to the market, or across the way to visit old Gerda, who had been sick recently. But without leaving a note? That was not like her. His mother always left a note if she was going to be away when he got home, even if she was only going across the street.

Anders sat on the edge of his bed to think. Trolls could not go out in the daylight. So when could a troll have come into his home?

It had been dark when he left for school, of course, as it would be every morning until winterdim finally ended, some four months from now. So there had been an hour after he left for school that trolls might have been out and around — though it was hard to imagine how one could have gotten past the trollwatch.

All right, what about his mother? It was unlikely she would have gone out before the weak winter light had straggled into the sky. Wait — had she been here when the troll came? Anders felt a new surge of panic. He tried to fight it down by telling himself that since there was no sign of a struggle she could not be troll-taken. He repeated it out loud — "My mother has not been troll-taken!" — and his panic began to subside. But it still left the question: If not troll-taken, where was she?

And why the smell?

He was about to head for Gerda's cottage, to see if his mother might be visiting the old woman after all, when he heard a noise from across the hall.

"Who's there?" he cried.

Silence.

Slipping his dagger from his belt, Anders tiptoed to the door. He paused, holding his breath, listening intently.

Silence . . . silence . . . then, from his mother's room, a whimper.

Anders bolted across the hall. The room — dark from the drawn curtains — was still empty. He turned to the closet. He had not looked inside it on his previous inspection of the room; it had never occurred to him that his mother might be in there. But that whimper had to have come from somewhere.

"Mother?"

No answer.

Gripping his dagger more tightly, Anders yanked the door open — then cried out in astonishment and disgust. Crouched in the corner, gnawing on one of his mother's shoes, was a baby troll. The creature looked up at Anders with wide eyes, then took the shoe out of its mouth and began to scream, a terrible, high-pitched keening. At the same time, Anders saw a blaze of light in his own hand — his dagger, flashing a troll alert, just as it had been created to do. No wonder the little monster was screaming. Small as it was, it must have sensed that the dagger had been made to cut troll flesh.

Anders hesitated. Much as he hated trolls, he couldn't bring himself to simply stab a baby one. But the thing's screeching was piercing his ears. He hesitated, then thrust the dagger into its sheath.

Instantly the little troll stopped squalling. Anders pulled the dagger partway from the sheath. The troll's voice rose again. Anders pushed the dagger back. The shrieking subsided.

Clutching the haft of the dagger, ready to draw it again if needed, Anders crouched to look at the creature more closely. *Thor's belt but it was ugly!* Anders wasn't sure which was worse: the huge, pointed ears; the squashed nose with its gaping nostrils; the blunt fingers and toes; or the cracked, stone-gray skin.

What was he supposed to do now? His mother had taught him all sorts of manners and rules, but she had provided no advice for a situation like this. And her all-purpose rule — "When in doubt, simply be kind and honest" — surely couldn't apply to trolls.

Could it?

How did one go about being kind to a troll anyway?

Anders sat on the corner of his mother's bed, trying to think. A troll had been in the house. His mother was missing. Now he had found a baby troll in the closet.

He felt a sudden surge of panic. Could the thing's parents be here as well?

No, he told himself. *That's not possible. There's no place a full-grown troll could be hiding.*

But what did it all mean? And what should he do now?

Well, the last question was easy. He *should* just drag the little monster outside and let the lingering sun turn it to stone. But when he looked at the creature, he remembered the agonized expression on the statue at the corner, and found he didn't have the heart to petrify it.

The other choice was to take it to the constable. Of course, if he didn't want to turn it to stone, he couldn't do that until after darkfall, which was still an hour away — far longer than he wanted to wait with this creature.

Maybe he should just go for the constable by himself.

No. He couldn't leave a troll — even a baby one — alone in the house. It might be hiding in the closet now, but who knew what havoc it might wreak by the time he got back?

His stomach reminded him that he had been starving when he came home. He decided to get something to eat while he worked out the problem. "Stay there!" he ordered the baby, shutting the closet door.

Not that he expected the thing to understand him.

Closing his ears to the little troll's pathetic whimper, Anders headed for the kitchen, where he sliced himself some cheese and meat. He put them on a plate, then drew a mug of cider from one of the big taps in the wall. He had meant to eat downstairs, but he kept worrying about what the baby troll might be doing and finally decided to go back upstairs with the meal.

After putting the plate on the corner of the bed, Anders opened the closet door. The little troll stared up at him with huge eyes, then farted. Anders cried out in disgust and backed up against the bed. He waited for the rotten-cabbage odor to fade before he picked up his plate again.

The little troll watched solemnly as Anders began to eat. After a moment it lurched to its feet. So it was a troddler, a troll just learning to walk. Moving carefully, setting one blunt foot ahead of the other, the troddler wobbled towards him. Then it leaned against his leg and stared at the plate, its wide nostrils twitching. After a moment it made a sound that pretty clearly indicated hunger.

"Go away!" said Anders sharply.

The troddler reached up and made the same noise.

Anders sighed. Being kind to a troll, even one that was only a troddler, seemed like the height of stupidity. But "be kind" was the advice his mother had given him for situations like this. So he broke off a piece of cheese and handed it to the little creature.

A wide grin split the creature's face, revealing seven or eight gray teeth that looked like small stones set in its jaw. The grin revealed something else, too: a piece of paper stuck to one of the creature's teeth — paper with writing on it.

The troddler was about to pop the cheese into its mouth when Anders grabbed its hand. The baby began to squawk. That was all right with Anders; squawking forced the thing to keep its mouth open. Fighting an urge to vomit, Anders darted his fingers over the thick, gray tongue and into the gaping mini-cavern of the trod-dler's mouth. With a cry of triumph, he snatched out the scrap of paper.

When he let go of its arm, the baby instantly jammed the cheese into its mouth and began to chew, smacking noisily.

Ignoring the creature and its sounds, Anders hurried to the bathroom, where he placed the moist paper on the shelf, then carefully washed his hands to get rid of the thick, sticky trolldrool. Once he had dried them again, he picked up the paper. It was sticky, too. He considered trying to wash it off, but was afraid the ink would run more than it already had. Working carefully, he unfolded it and smoothed it against the mirror. He was able to make out some of the words, which were indeed in his mother's handwriting, but between the smears and the chew marks, it was frustratingly incom-plete:

Dear And

been called away   rgent mission.
not sure   I will   to return.
*   much not told you.*
*   meant to, soon.   need to find out for*
yourself   dare not write it all
*   become dangerous   try to*
follow   snowflakes lead you to the red
stone. The red stone is the key. You need only

father's name for troll
you will be frigh
much you think you know is fal
Do not go for help, or all will be lost!
ve,
Moth

Anders shook his head in mystification. What could it possibly mean?

He took a deep breath. Well, the first thing it meant was that his mother had not gone against her will. That was good. But what were the things she had not told him — things she did not even dare write down? Why couldn't he go for help? And how in the world were snowflakes supposed to lead him to a red stone?

Hearing a sound, he turned towards the door. The troddler stood there, gazing at him with wide eyes. A string of orange spittle ran from one corner of its mouth and it was clutching the rest of the cheese in its stubby hand.

Anders was about to shout at the little creature for chewing up the note when it held the cheese out to him. The gesture was touching, and not at all what he would have expected from a troll. But even though it calmed his anger, the idea of eating something that had just been in a troll's hands was too much for him, and he pushed the cheese back.

"Gurk!" said the troddler happily. Then it popped the cheese into its own mouth.

Still clutching the soggy note, Anders returned to the bedroom. The troddler trailed behind him and stared with wide, eager eyes as Anders picked up his mug. Anders took a deep swallow of cider. Then, against his better judgment, he passed the mug to the troddler. It gulped down the remainder of the amber liquid, then belched happily.

Anders stared at the piece of paper again, trying desperately to make sense of his mother's fragmented words. They indicated trouble, and urgency, but not panic. He was more mystified than ever.

"How did *you* get here?" he asked, glowering at the troddler. "And where's my mother?"

"Glurp?" it asked, not very helpfully.

Anders sighed and pushed himself to his feet to start another search — not for his mother, this time, but for more clues to where she might have gone.

He started by examining her room. He felt hesitant and shy, as if he were spying on her, and didn't go so far as to open the drawers in her dresser, telling himself he would do that later, if he absolutely had to. Finding nothing, he stepped into the hallway. The troddler came tottering after him. Anders started to shoo the creature back into the room, then decided it was better to keep it nearby.

He had finished with the upstairs and was searching the kitchen when he found his first clue: a small, white flower lying beside the doorway. Anders stared at it for a moment, then felt his heart leap. The common name for the flower was "winterkiss," but he and his mother had always called the blossoms by his baby name for them: "snowflakes."

. . . snowflakes lead you to the red stone . . .

The troddler reached for the blossom, but Anders held it back, which caused the thing to squall again. Fortunately it stopped when he tucked the blossom into the pouch he wore at his side. He straightened his shoulders, feeling a surge of confidence now that he had figured out the first clue. Then he realized he had lost sight of the troddler.

"Now where have you gone?" he muttered.

It took only a moment to find the baby; it was sniffing around the door to the cellar. Beside the door, tight against the frame, was another white blossom.

Anders felt a clench of fear. He had not checked the cellar on his first tour of the house. The scary stories his father had told about it when Anders was little had left him with a permanent reluctance to enter. His mother, he knew, felt the same way. It would never have occurred to him to think she had gone down there.

Now he had to think about it.

He pulled the door open.

Cool, dank air rolled out.

The stony scent of troll was stronger here, terrifyingly strong. He might have turned away — except he saw a small white blossom lying on the third step down.

Anders swallowed nervously. Everyone knew if a troll was going to enter your house, it would come through the cellar.

But his mother's note . . .

He shook himself and muttered ferociously, "If that's where she's gone, that's where I follow."

He went to the cupboard to fetch one of the torch-sticks old Gerda made in return for the soup his mother so often took over. Returning to the cellarway, he whispered, *"Ignis."* At once the upper end of the stick began to glow. The troddler gasped in fear and pulled back, landing on its rump.

"It's all right," said Anders soothingly. But the trod-dler just looked at him with wide eyes and whimpered. Anders sighed and took the little creature's hand. Its skin was thick and bumpy, but pleasantly cool. The creature burped happily as Anders pulled it to its feet.

They started down the stairway, Anders leading the way, the troddler scooting along behind, sliding from step to step on its bottom. The torchstick glowed more brightly, automatically adjusting to the increased darkness.

Suddenly Anders stopped, cursing himself for six

kinds of a fool. The troddler bumped into him from behind, but he scarcely noticed. The stairs were coated with dust. He should be looking for footprints!

Holding the torchstick ahead of him, he bent to study the next step. It was clear enough that something had disturbed the dust — disturbed it so much that he could not see a clear footprint. How many feet had passed over this stairway?

Extending the torchstick farther, he could see a small footprint two steps down. That had to be his mother's! The surge of relief he felt was quickly replaced by terror. One step below it, near the edge of the stair, was another print, wide and blunt, too big for the narrow plank to hold completely.

The mark of a troll foot.

Anders shuddered. Part of him wanted to bolt back up the stairs and flee the house. Another part insisted he had to go on. His mother had told him to follow the snowflakes, and he could see another blossom lying right at the base of the stairs. He took a deep breath. Onward it was.

"All right," he said to the troddler. "Let's go."

When they were all the way down, Anders found a new problem: Dust did not show on the moist, earthen surface of the cellar floor the way it had on the stairs. And he did not see another snowflake.

It was the troddler who provided the solution. It began sniffing, its wide nostrils growing even wider, then lunged forward as if it had caught a scent it wanted to follow.

For lack of a better idea, Anders let the little creature lead the way.

At the far side of the cellar an old carpet hung over a hole in the wall. The bottom of the hole was about a foot and a half above floor level. Oval-shaped and four feet high, the hole led to a root cellar where the family could store vegetables for the winter. Except they never did, since that would have meant coming down here to fetch them. Better to get them at market!

Anders drew the carpet away from the ledge you had to step over to enter the root cellar. There he discovered another white blossom.

He picked up the snowflake and climbed in.

The troddler scrambled after him.

The torchstick grew brighter in response to the deeper gloom. Anders, easily able to see the whole of the small room, felt a surge of relief at finding nothing awful, and at the same time a sharp stab of disappointment, as he realized he had come to a dead end. Raising the torch-stick, he turned in a slow circle, looking for anything that might indicate his mother — or anyone else — had been here. Nothing. But as he turned to leave, the trod-dler began making urgent noises. Then it scrambled for-ward to point at the back wall.

"Come on," said Anders, reaching for its hand. "We have to go."

The baby still resisted. Anders stepped closer to pull it away, then gasped. Caught between two stones was a piece of fabric — troll fabric, easily identified by the dull color and coarse weave. He stared at it in astonishment. How could a piece of cloth have gotten stuck between the stones?

He looked more carefully, then caught his breath. One of the stones had a distinct reddish tinge.

He took out the remains of his mother's note and examined it in the light of the torchstick:

. . . snowflakes lead you to the red stone . . .

The red stone is the key. You need only . . .

The rest of the sentence had been chewed up by the troddler. Nearly ready to scream with frustration, Anders pushed the stone.

Nothing happened.

He tried to twist it.

Nothing.

Feeling foolish, he blew on it, whispered to it, hit it, kicked it, struck it with the torchstick.

Nothing, nothing, nothing, nothing, and nothing.

Then the troddler waddled up to the wall. Anders was about to pull the little creature back when it smacked the stone with the flat of its palm. A sudden grinding sound made Anders back away in surprise. His surprise was even greater when the wall pulled apart to reveal a low, wide tunnel. Even without stepping forward, he could see the small white blossom that lay just on the other side.

Anders put his hand on the troddler's head. "I don't know how you did that," he said. "But if I had some more cheese I'd give it to you right now."

"Gurk!" said the troddler. It was clearly eager to enter the tunnel. But Anders hesitated. His mind was racing with questions: What did it mean that there was a tunnel under his home? Was this how the trolls had come for his father? If that was so, why had they waited so long to return? Most important, what was he going to do if he actually came upon a troll?

Well, he still had his dagger. And he had the troddler. Maybe he could use it as a hostage.

He wondered if that would make any difference to a troll, if it would even care about a baby.

Finally unable to resist the mystery of the tunnel, and the sense that it might lead to his mother, Anders hoisted the torchstick and started forward.

After a few steps he murmured, *"Diminis,"* and the torchstick went to half-light.

No sense making his presence too obvious.

The tunnel continued for some distance without change: cold, dank walls; low ceiling; occasional puddles of slimy water. A few times he heard the squeaking of a rodent. At least, he hoped that's all it was. . . .

The troddler stuck close to him, clutching the leg of

his trousers. He found himself oddly glad to have it so near.

Finally the tunnel began to widen, then quickly grew so wide that Anders could no longer see the walls on either side. He hesitated, then murmured, *"Ignis."*

When the torchstick came to full light he saw that he had entered a large cavern — so large he could not see the opposite side. He heard a rumbling noise behind him and turned just in time to see the mouth of the tunnel sliding shut. With a cry of horror he rushed back. He was too late; the opening had become a solid rock wall. Frantic, he began searching for some way to open it again. But the stone was seamless, without even a hint of what might be the edge of a door. After several minutes of desperate searching he laid his head against the stone in despair, trying not to weep. He didn't even pull away when the troddler reached up to hold his hand.

A moment later he heard a deep chuckle. Icy fear clutching his heart, Anders turned . . . and found himself staring straight into the belly of an adult troll! He fought back a scream even as the troddler screeched with delight and wrapped its arms around the big troll's leg.

Anders put his hand to the haft of his dagger, which somehow helped him find his voice.

"Where is my mother?"

He didn't expect an answer — didn't really expect anything other than a skull-crushing blow to the head

— so he was astonished when the troll spoke. In a voice like stones rubbing together it said slowly, "I will take you to her."

"Is she all right?"

"Of course," rumbled the troll. Then it stooped to pick up the troddler. "I am glad you brought back little Kratz-Kah. We were very worried about her. Follow me."

Ignoring Anders' volley of questions, the troll turned and walked away. The boy waited a moment, then scurried along behind. After a while he realized they were actually following a downhill path, marked on each side by a row of reddish rocks. Eventually they crossed a stone bridge that spanned a dark chasm. He could hear water running beneath it — far beneath it.

On the far side of the bridge the path leveled out, and Anders saw the first of the troll dwellings, crude cottages made of stone. They didn't seem to have roofs, which struck him as odd until he realized there wouldn't be much need for a roof underground. It wasn't as if the trolls needed to keep out the rain!

The dwellings became more numerous. Soon Anders realized he had entered a village. His nervousness increased. Was his mother a prisoner here? How could he possibly help her? What was going to happen to them?

Trolls peered from their windows. Troll babies sat in the front yards, sucking on rocks. Older troll children chased one another around the cottages with a slow, clumping gait, but stopped to stare as he went by. Two old troll women, gossiping across a stone fence, turned and smiled toothlessly at him.

Anders tried to question his guide, but the troll did not speak again. Yet even as his fear was growing, another part of his mind registered surprise that the village appeared so . . . normal.

At last they came to what was clearly the town square. It was dimly lit by hanging cages filled with large, glowing slugs. In the center of the square was a table. Seated at the table were six trolls — and Anders' mother. When she saw Anders approaching, she leaped to her feet, smiling in relief.

"Anders!" she cried, spreading her arms to welcome him. "I'm so glad you're here!"

He ran to her embrace. "What's happening?" he gasped. "Are you all right? Are we prisoners? I don't understand!"

She held him close. "No, we're not prisoners, darling. It may be some time before we can leave here, but that won't be because of the trolls. It's because we're not safe at home. Listen, Anders, I'm sorry I had to leave so quickly. Thank goodness you were able to follow the clues in my note. I'm sorry I couldn't be more clear, but the danger was too great."

Anders laughed. "That note was less clear than you expected. There was a troddler in the house, and she ate most of it."

He took the remains of her message from his pocket and handed it to her.

His mother examined the tattered paper with dismay. "But how did you manage to find your way here?"

"I worked out the clues from what was left."

"But the tunnel —" She looked at the note again, then at him. "How could you possibly open the tunnel without knowing you had to put your hand on the stone and say your father's name?"

Anders blinked at the idea. "Is that what you're supposed to do? I tried everything I could think of. Finally the troddler —" He paused, then corrected himself. "Finally Kratz-Kah put her hand on it, and it just . . . opened."

Understanding dawned on his mother's face. "Of course! The tunnel will always open to a troll's touch. Thank goodness you kept Kratz-Kah with you. You would never have found your way here if you hadn't. You might even be in prison now."

Anders looked at her in shock.

"This morning we learned that the trollwatch has found out about your father and me. That's why I couldn't come back today, or come to school to get you. They might have been waiting for me."

"I don't understand," said Anders plaintively. "What do you have to do with the trolls?"

"Your mother has been helping us for years," said one

of the trolls at the table. "Now it's time for us to help her."

"Actually, both your parents were helping, until your father was taken," said a male troll at the other end of the table. He had a pair of stones in his hands, and was rubbing them idly together.

"But it was trolls who took him!" said Anders angrily.

His mother shook her head. "That was the story we put out, to discourage suspicion." She closed her eyes for a moment, and it was clear the next words were hard for her to speak. "Anders, your father was killed by the trollwatch."

"What? Why?"

"For daring to help the trolls. They caught him one night, as he was coming back from a meeting." Tears welled up in her eyes, and the sorrow in her voice brought back Anders' own sense of loss. "We were lucky they couldn't identify him after the dogs were done with him," she whispered. "If they had figured out who he was, they would have come for us, too."

Anders felt his knees grow weak. "Why didn't you tell me all this before?" He gazed around at the trolls, creatures he had been taught to hate and fear. "You lied to me all these years."

"Your father and I didn't know what else to do. We didn't dare tell you the truth about the trolls when you were little. One slip at school, even one suspicious sentence, and the trollwatch could have taken your father and me away, and put you in an orphanage. It was safer not to let you know. The time was coming to tell you everything, but I didn't know when or how I was going to do it." She shook her head and smiled ruefully. "I did hope to do it more gently than this!"

"I still don't understand what you have to do with trolls!" he said, part baffled, part angry.

"Your mother is a great healer," said the troll sitting next to her. "Though we do not fall ill very often, and it is hard to injure us, our stony flesh is also slow to heal. Your mother knows how to help us, as did her mother, and her mother's mother before her. As, we hope, will you."

"That's why we have a troll tunnel leading to our cellar," said his mother gently. "Ever since the new government banned trolls and humans from mixing —"

"Because that way it was easier to make us work as slaves in their mines," growled one of the trolls.

His mother nodded. "Ever since the government decided to do that, I have been forced to do my healing in secret. Otherwise, I could be sent to prison." Her indignation flared. "Sent to prison for healing! Can you imagine?"

Anders looked around at the troll village. "How often do you come here?"

His mother shrugged. "Only when a troll needs me. Probably not more than once a month. Usually I came at night, while you were sleeping. But just after you left for school this morning I learned that the trollwatch was after me and I had to flee at once. If I had not, you would still have come home to an empty house, because I would have been in prison." She took a breath, then added bitterly, "Or, more likely, dead from an 'accident' arranged by the officials."

"It was I who brought the warning to your mother," said the troll next to her. She was bouncing the troddler on her knee. "I did not know Kratz-Kah here had followed me. We have been looking all over for her. Thank you for bringing her back." She wiped a tear from her eye. "I was terrified for her."

Kratz-Kah made a gravelly chuckling sound. The troll woman wiped a string of drool from the corner of the troddler's mouth. Kratz-Kah squirmed and held her stubby, stony arms out to Anders.

He hesitated, then reached out to take her.

She was even heavier than he expected.

"So," he said to his mother, as Kratz-Kah wrapped her arms about his neck. "How long will we need to live down here?"

"Until the trolls are free again."

Anders looked around at the faces of the creatures he had been taught to fear for so long. The creatures his father had died fighting for.

They began to smile at him. The smiles were ugly and lopsided, filled with misshapen teeth. But they were also warm and genuine.

"All right," he said, holding the troddler closer. "What do we do now?"

UNEXPECTED

Author's Note

Students are often asked to answer essay questions about what an author intended in a given story. The truth (at least for me) is that often I have no idea what I'm writing about until long after the writing has been finished.

"The Troddler" is a good example. Though it was the first story I wrote after my mother's death, it wasn't until several days after I started working on it that I looked back at the opening pages and realized they were all about a boy who comes home to discover that his mother is missing. And it wasn't until well after I had finished it that I fully realized the implications of Anders going underground to search for her. It may be obvious in retrospect what was going on in my head, but while I was writing it, I had no idea. I was just writing.

I find that fact a little scary, and also kind of fun — which is exactly the feeling I was trying to evoke when I wrote "The Troddler."

BRUCE COVILLE has published more than ninety books for children and young adults, including the international bestseller *My Teacher Is An Alien*, and the wildly popular Unicorn Chronicles series. He has more than sixteen million books in print, in over a dozen languages. He is also the founder of Full Cast Audio, an audiobook publishing company devoted to producing full-cast, unabridged recordings of material for family listening. Bruce lives in Syracuse, New York, with his wife, illustrator Katherine Coville.

Infinity Jinx

〰️

Margaret Peterson Haddix

THEY ALWAYS PUT HIM TO BED EARLY, WHILE IT WAS STILL light out. He was never sleepy then. He'd lie in bed, wide awake, watching the curtains blow in and out the open window. If he squinted, he could almost believe the window was alive, and breathing.

That thought would have scared him when he was younger. But he was five now. He'd been five for a very long time. His turning-five birthday seemed so long ago that he could barely remember it. But if he squeezed his eyes shut, he could remember leaning down toward a ring of fire — five blazing candles on a chocolate-iced cake — and Mommy behind him saying, "Blow out the candles, Timmy. Blow hard and make a wish!"

Sometimes, if he concentrated really, really hard and squeezed his eyes together as tightly as possible, he thought he could remember another birthday, even longer ago. That birthday's cake had white icing and it was Daddy behind him saying, "Blow out the candles! Blow hard and make a wish!" But that cake had had five candles on it, too.

He had to be remembering wrong. Maybe he'd even counted wrong. Probably he'd just been turning four on the white-icing birthday, and he hadn't known the difference between four candles and five.

Because how could someone turn the same age twice?

IT WAS DAYTIME NOW, AND MOMMY AND DADDY WERE AWAY at work. The robo-nanny was in the kitchen cleaning up the dishes from lunch. Timmy was supposed to be watching TV. He was always supposed to be watching TV, but today he didn't want to. Today the TV seemed too small, and the room seemed too small, and even the whole apartment seemed too small. He wasn't sure he could stand sitting still a minute longer, let alone the rest of the day. He wanted to go to the park, but the robo-nanny never took him there. Just Mommy and Daddy did, after work or on Saturdays, and it was hours and hours until they'd come home from work, and days and days until Saturday.

Somebody knocked at the door.

Timmy wasn't supposed to answer the door. Even the robo-nanny wasn't supposed to. But every other time someone had knocked — Timmy could remember it happening only once or twice — the robo-nanny had gone whirring over to the door to lift her eyestalk to the peephole. And then she'd stood there, guarding the door until whoever it was had given up and gone away.

This time the knock was very soft. Probably the robo-nanny hadn't heard it over the TV noise from all the way in the kitchen. Timmy looked quickly over his shoulder, then tiptoed over to the door. He had to stand on the arm of the couch — something else he wasn't supposed to do — so he could be high enough to lean over and look out the peephole.

Another boy was standing out in the hallway.

The boy had his thumbs stuck at either side of his mouth, pulling the corners back into a monster face. He'd fanned his fingers out beside his head, like antlers. He was looking up toward the peephole, and he must have been able to see Timmy's eye, because suddenly he jerked his hands down from his face.

"Oh, sorry," he said. "Didn't know anybody was there."

At least, that's what Timmy thought the boy said. His words were muffled by the door between them.

Without thinking, Timmy slid off the couch and opened the door. Just a crack.

Alarms began sounding as lights flashed all around the door frame. Timmy jerked back. His hand was still on the doorknob, so he accidentally yanked the door all the way open. The floor itself started glowing red and blaring out siren sounds. The robo-nanny zipped out of the kitchen, faster than Timmy had ever seen her roll. Two of her arms were reaching for him, and a third was stretching towards the door. Timmy knew that in seconds, he'd be scooped up and the door would slam shut, and he'd never see the funny-faced boy again.

But Timmy was wrong. The other boy dived into the room. He seemed to be trying to dive *under* the robo-nanny's wheels. And then, a second later, the robo-nanny froze, with her arms still suspended in the air.

Timmy stood frozen, too, for a little while, unable to believe that she wasn't going to finish grabbing him. He watched the other boy get up and feel along the wall beside the door. Seconds later, the lights stopped flashing and the sirens stopped, mid-roar. The boy grinned over his shoulder at Timmy.

Timmy looked down and saw that there were only inches between the robo-nanny's hands and his waist. Very carefully, he stepped back, so she now reached out for empty air.

"H-how'd you do that?" he croaked to the other boy.

The boy shrugged.

"It's easy if you know what you're doing," he said. "Control panels are in the same place in every apartment in this building, I bet. So I just —"

Timmy was too astonished to wait for any explanation.

"But — *her*," he said, pointing at the robo-nanny. "How'd you make her stop? I've never seen her stop." He waved his hand in front of her partially extended eyestalks. For the first time ever, her eyebeads didn't track his every move. A terrible thought struck him. "Is she — is she *dead*?"

"Oh, geez," the other boy said, rolling his eyes. "Robots can't die. They're not alive to begin with. I just disabled her. What do you think your parents do with her every night when they're recharging her energy cells?"

Timmy had never thought about that. He'd always figured that the robo-nanny prowled the apartment all night long, watching over him and his parents, keeping them safe. He wasn't sure he wanted to believe what this strange boy was telling him.

"I'm Jack, by the way," the other boy said. "Who are you?"

"Timmy."

"How old are you?"

"Six," Timmy said. He didn't know why he lied. He didn't even think about it — the wrong word just flew right out of his mouth on its own.

Or maybe he did think about it. Jack looked even older than six. Timmy didn't want Jack thinking he was just some little baby, too young to even talk to. He had never met an older kid before. He didn't want this one to run away.

"Oh, it's okay, then," Jack said, his shoulders relaxing. Timmy was glad he'd said six instead of five. "For a minute there I thought — oh, never mind. I'm nine. Why aren't you at school?"

"School?" Timmy said.

"You know — books? Robo-teachers? Tests? Torture? I got out of going today because I faked being sick. But they left the robo-nanny to watch me, so I couldn't do anything — boring! I waited until noon to disable her, because I know my mom always checks in by remote about eleven-thirty. And now I'm looking for some fun. I thought the whole building was empty — boy, am I glad I found you. What do you think we should do?"

Jack said all that in such a rush that Timmy felt dizzy. He was so glad that Jack didn't keep asking questions about school — whatever that was. And the "we" at the end — "What do you think *we* should do?" — made Timmy feel like jumping for joy.

"Maybe we could play —" Timmy started saying, at the same time that Jack burst out with, "Hey! Let's play —"

Timmy stopped talking, so he could hear what Jack had to say. Jack stopped for just a second and then screamed out, "Jinx!"

"Huh?" Timmy said.

"Don't you know anything?" Jack asked.

Timmy was afraid Jack was upset now, and he'd stomp away, and never come back. And Timmy would be stuck with a disabled robo-nanny.

But then Jack grinned, showing teeth as big as a grown-up's, only crooked. "It's a game. If we both say the same word at the same time, the first person to say 'jinx' puts a, well, a jinx on the other person, and so now you're not allowed to say anything until I say your name three times."

"Oh," Timmy started to say, but then he caught himself, his mouth stuck in a silent circle. He looked desperately up at Jack. How could this be a game? Games were supposed to be fun.

"All right," Jack said, grinning again. "This is more fun when you want someone to shut up. Timmy, Timmy, Timmy. See, now you're un-jinxed. You can talk now."

"Thanks," Timmy said, feeling as relieved as if Jack had ended a real jinx, some sort of true-life fairy-tale spell keeping him silent.

"Hey, cool," Jack said, looking beyond Timmy into the rest of the apartment. "You've got smooth floors. We've got carpet *everywhere*. I bet my remote-control cars would run great in here. Want to try?"

He pulled two miniature cars out of his pocket, and a tiny control panel. And, miracle of miracles, he handed the remote control straight to Timmy.

"The green button's go, red's stop, and the arrows are for turning. What are you waiting for?" Jack asked.

JACK CAME OVER TO PLAY WITH TIMMY ALMOST EVERY DAY after that. It was almost always late in the afternoon.

"I can't play sick every day, or my parents will catch on," Jack said early on. "But I'll come after school whenever I can. I promise. You know we're the only kids in this whole stupid building? I can't believe I never met you before. Did you just move in or something?"

Timmy was glad that Jack didn't wait for an answer to that question. Timmy had lived in the same apartment for as long as he could remember, for his whole life. Timmy wondered why his parents hadn't taken him around the building, looking for other kids. Didn't they want him to have friends? At the park on Saturdays, they always nudged him towards the other kids in the sandbox, "Go on. Go and play with your buddies." They'd just laughed when a little girl at the park, Molly, had put her arm around Timmy's shoulder and said, "When we grow up, Timmy and me are going to get married." Timmy had tried to run away, but Dad had pushed him back towards the other kids, and muttered, "Don't worry, Timmy. Believe me, you don't have to be afraid of Molly proposing any time soon."

But Molly was just a little kid, like Timmy. None of the kids Timmy played with at the park were as old as Jack. Come to think of it, none of them were any older than Timmy.

Timmy had never thought much about it before, but wasn't that strange?

He wanted to ask his parents or the robo-nanny — or maybe even Jack — why he'd never been allowed to play with any kid older than five, but he was afraid. He was afraid that question would lead to him not being allowed to play with Jack.

So Jack was his secret, the first secret he'd ever had in his entire life.

Jack taught Timmy how to disable the robo-nanny and the alarm panel. They had their little routine. Every weekday afternoon, Jack would tap lightly on the door. Timmy would spring up from watching TV, disable the robo-nanny, disable the alarm, then open the door for Jack. Jack even showed Timmy how to erase part of the robo-nanny's memory banks, so she couldn't tell Timmy's parents she'd been disabled. It was perfect.

Except Jack always had ideas for making any plan better.

"It's dangerous, me knocking," Jack said one day, a week or so after Timmy had first met him. "There might be some extra sensors we don't know about. I always get home from school at the same time. Why don't you just look at the clock and disable everything at three-thirty every day, right before I get here?"

"Clock?" Timmy asked hesitantly. "What's a clock?"

"Oh, geez. You know, like —" Jack looked around at the walls. He seemed puzzled. He darted into the kitchen, then the bedrooms in turn. Each time he returned to the living room, his nose was more wrinkled up, his eyebrows were more furrowed, and his eyes held even more bafflement. "Don't your parents have a clock anywhere?"

"I don't know," Timmy said.

"Well, that's weird," Jack said, shaking his head.

"Here. I've got a portable clock. You can have it. We've got dozens at my place."

He pulled something from his pants pocket that looked like a small coin. He held it out to Timmy and Timmy saw glowing symbols on the face of it — strange combinations of squiggles and lines and dots.

"What are those?" Timmy asked, pointing.

"You're joking, right?" Jack asked. "Don't tell me you don't know your numbers yet."

"Sure," Timmy said defensively. But Jack was looking at him so doubtfully, he felt he had to prove himself. "One, two, three, four, five, six, seven, eight, nine — what's the last one? Oh, yeah. Ten."

"Silly," Jack said, laughing. "Ten's not the last number. Numbers go on forever. To infinity."

Timmy was not about to ask what infinity was, not with Jack already laughing at him.

Jack stopped laughing. His puzzled look came back.

"But you've never seen numbers written down, have you?"

Timmy shook his head, too ashamed to look Jack in the eye.

"Hey, it's okay. I just thought, with your parents and the robo-nanny home-schooling you and all . . ."

"They're not home-schooling me," Timmy muttered. "I don't think."

"Really? Are you sure?" Jack said.

Timmy shrugged.

"Okay, okay. Whatever," Jack said, as though he knew Timmy was embarrassed. "Here. I'll teach you numbers, so you know when to let me in every day. Got any paper?"

Timmy did have that. For the rest of the afternoon, Jack scrawled numbers and taught and quizzed Timmy. He wasn't satisfied until Timmy himself could make shaky versions of all the numerals.

"Well, you learned fast," Jack said at the end, while the two of them sat there admiring Timmy's best efforts. "I don't know why your parents haven't taught you this yet." He was silent for a minute, then said, "Maybe —"

But Timmy said, "Maybe —" at the same time. "Jinx!" he yelled out, feeling triumphant to have beaten Jack at the game.

Jack made an elaborate charade of pretending to zip his lips, turn a pretend key, and throw the pretend key over his shoulder.

Timmy laughed delightedly. "Jack, Jack, Jack," he chanted.

Then Jack had to pretend to search all over the room for the pretend key. He finally "found" it in the disabled nanny's ear. By the time he'd gone through another melodramatic act to unlock his lips, he seemed to have forgotten whatever "maybe" he'd started to suggest.

"Oops, look at the time," he said, glancing down at the portable clock. "I've got to go. Take the clock, so you know when to disable everything tomorrow. And

— hey — show your parents your numbers. They'll be so proud."

Timmy watched Jack leave. But he hid the clock and the sheets of numbers before he turned the robo-nanny back on.

Because the "maybe" he'd been about to say was, "Maybe they don't want me to know."

THAT NIGHT, TIMMY WATCHED HIS PARENTS CAREFULLY. THEY returned as usual in their business suits and shiny shoes, and ruffled his hair and hugged him.

"His hands are clean, aren't they, nanny?" Mommy asked, like always. "I don't want dirty handprints all over my clothes."

They asked him questions about his day, but didn't seem to listen to his answers. They announced that it wasn't a good night to take Timmy to the park. And they both let out tired-sounding sighs as they sat down to the dinner nanny had fixed.

"Is work hard?" Timmy asked, tilting his head in a way that often made Mommy laugh and say, "Isn't he cute?"

But Daddy was the one who laughed over this question.

"Silly boy," he said. "Of course work is hard. Be glad you're a kid."

Then Daddy took another bite of roast beef.

What would happen if Timmy said, "Guess what I

learned today? I can write numbers now. Want to see?" Or, "Why don't we have a clock anywhere in our apartment?" Or, "How come you never let me play with older kids?"

Timmy thought he knew what would happen. His parents would find out about Jack. And then they'd never let him play with Jack again.

The questions weren't worth the risk.

"Bedtime, Timmy," Mommy said, smiling.

Timmy got up and brushed his teeth and changed his clothes. After Mommy tucked him in, he pulled the coin-sized clock Jack had given him out of his pajama pocket and stared at the blinking numbers. 7:01. 7:02. 7:03. All those minutes gone.

It was funny. Before he'd had a clock, he'd never known that time changed at all.

THE NEXT DAY, TIMMY DISABLED THE ROBO-NANNY AND THE alarm system at 3:25 P.M., and was waiting in the doorway when Jack came down the hall at 3:30 P.M.

"Perfect," Jack said. "You remembered!"

"What do you want to play today?" Timmy said, letting Jack in. "Remote-control cars? Soda-bottle bowling? Bumper ball?"

"Oh, I don't know," Jack said. "Wait — yes, I do. Let's tell scary stories. I'll go first."

Jack wouldn't quite look Timmy in the eye. Timmy

didn't know why, but that made his stomach feel funny. It was like Timmy's gut had figured out something before Timmy's mind.

They sat down on the couch where Timmy always watched TV.

"Once upon a time, a long, long time ago," Jack began, "a bunch of grown-ups got together to complain about their kids. 'We love our children, but they change so fast,' they said. 'One minute they're babies, the next minute they're taller than we are. It isn't fair. It all ends in the blink of an eye.'

"Most of the people were just whining and moaning over nothing, like grown-ups do. They didn't mean anything by it. But one of the men in the group was a scientist. And he said, 'A-ha! This is a problem I can fix!' So he went to his laboratory and mixed up vials and vials of different chemicals. And he came out with a syringe full of red liquid. And he called all the other parents back together, and he held the syringe up in the air in front of them and he said, 'I can make your kids stop growing!'

"Well, none of them believed him. So he took his own son, a three-year-old boy, and he stuck the needle of that syringe right in his little boy's arm. 'Come back next year,' he told those other parents. 'You'll see.'

"So they did. A whole year later, they all met again in the exact same place. And that little boy was there, and he looked exactly, 100 percent the same. He was no taller and no heavier and he could still wear the same clothes. Even his hair hadn't grown at all.

"And some of those other parents had children who had been younger than that three-year-old boy, but they looked and acted older now. Some of the parents said, 'Wow, can you do that to my kid, too?' And some of the other parents said, 'This is wrong! You're an evil man! You should be thrown in jail!' So then they all had a big argument and — Timmy? Timmy, are you listening?"

Timmy was listening as best he could, but his ears didn't seem to be working right anymore. And it wasn't just his ears — or his stomach. His whole body felt jangly and weird.

"Timmy, your face is as white as paper. You're not going to faint, are you?" Jack asked.

It seemed to take all of Timmy's energy to shake his head. Then he managed to whisper, "I think — I think I had that shot."

Jack didn't look surprised.

"I thought so!" he exclaimed. "I just didn't know if you knew."

Slowly, Timmy shook his head. No. He hadn't known anything.

They were both quiet for a minute, like even Jack didn't know what to say then. Finally, Jack bit his lip and burst out, "But Timmy, there are rules, see? About how people can use the shot on their kids. That's what came out of those arguments the grown-ups had. Nobody's supposed to use it on anyone who's older than five. Because — well, it gets too complicated. Kids who are six or older already know too much. So your parents are breaking the law. They — they're going to have to go to jail."

"I lied," Timmy whispered. "I'm only five. I — I didn't want you to think I was a baby."

"Oh," Jack said. He got a funny look on his face. "Then I'm the one breaking the law. Paused kids — that's what they call people like you, 'paused' — paused kids aren't supposed to have anything to do with regular kids. They have separate playgrounds, and everything. Paused kids aren't even supposed to know that regular kids exist. So it's always the regular kids' fault if they get caught together."

Now Timmy really did feel like he was going to faint. This was going to lead to him never seeing Jack again. He knew it.

"But you didn't know," he protested desperately. "And nobody else knows that I know you. My robo-nanny doesn't, and your robo-nanny doesn't, and our parents don't. . . . So it doesn't matter, does it?"

Jack didn't get up and leave. But he had doubt written all over his face.

"This is serious stuff," he said. "It's kind of like,

well, maybe I'm contaminating you. Maybe I already have, giving you the clock, and teaching you to write numbers . . ."

Timmy liked having the clock. He'd liked learning numbers. And more than anything else, he liked playing with Jack.

"I don't want to be paused," he burst out bitterly. "I want to be a regular kid like you!"

"Do you?" Jack asked.

Timmy nodded stubbornly. He stuck his lower lip out, putting on what his parents always called his sulking face.

"I don't know," Jack said quietly. "Sometimes I think it might have been fun to have stayed a little kid forever. You don't have to go to school, and you don't have anyone telling you, 'Do your homework! Do your chores!' And nobody expects you to learn fractions — do you know how hard it is to multiply fractions? Maybe you're lucky to be paused. You won't ever have to grow up."

"I think my parents think it's good," Timmy said, suddenly understanding a little more. He remembered what Daddy had said the night before. *Of course work is hard. Be glad you're a kid.*

He was glad his parents hadn't paused him just to be mean.

But he still didn't like it.

"I should probably go," Jack said.

"No!" Timmy shouted. Without Jack, life would be the same as before — the same old TV shows and the same old lunches with the robo-nanny and the same old Saturdays playing with the same old kids in the same old park for years and years and years. He didn't think he could bear that anymore. "Jack, you've got to help me. Being — what'd you call it? — paused? It's like — like a jinx."

"An infinity jinx," Jack muttered. "Because there's no end to it."

"Isn't there any way to stop it? Any way to un-pause me?" Timmy asked.

"Yeah, there's another shot that reverses the pausing. You could always just tell your parents you want to grow up," Jack said. Then he frowned. "But they can always tell you no."

And they would, Timmy thought, his heart sinking. He thought of the way his parents hugged him when they came home from work. He thought of the way his mother kissed him when she tucked him into bed. They liked him being a little kid. Would they still like him if he grew up?

"Nobody tells regular kids much about paused kids," Jack admitted. "I used to think it was all just a story, like fairy tales. And it's something people joke about. When I do something bad, my parents say, 'Don't you wish we'd paused him back when he was too young to get into so much mischief?' But in the stories, there is one way for paused kids to force the adults to let them grow up."

"What's that?" Timmy asked, so eager he almost fell off the couch.

"By learning how to read," Jack said.

THAT NIGHT IN BED, TIMMY FORCED HIMSELF TO STAY AWAKE for a long, long time. Darkness was creeping in around the edges of his blowing curtains, and the numbers on his glowing clock flickered all the way from 7:01 to 8:01, and still he resolutely kept his eyes open. When the numbers blinked over to 8:02, he slipped out of bed and tiptoed quietly to his door. He pulled it open without making a single noise, and peeked out.

His parents were sitting on the couch. But they weren't talking or staring at the TV as they mostly did when they knew he was awake. Instead, they were both peering down at rectangular objects held open in their laps.

Books. Jack was right. Grown-ups did do this thing called reading.

Timmy tiptoed back to bed, but now too much was tumbling around in his brain for him to even think about sleeping.

"See, reading's like, you've got these things called letters," Jack had said that afternoon, "and they all make different sounds, and you've got to remember which sound goes with which letter so you can put the sounds together. And the sounds make words. Every word there is, you can spell with letters."

"What's that got to do with growing up?" Timmy had asked.

"I don't know," Jack said. "I guess, once you know how to read, nobody can control you as much, because you can find things out for yourself, and you can think for yourself. So once you can read you can't stay paused anymore, 'cause you're always learning new things."

Now Timmy thought about his parents bent over their books. They must have always kept their books hidden from him in the daytime. They must have kept all sorts of secrets from him.

Maybe they were just trying to protect him; keeping him safe and innocent.

What if reading was dangerous?

But how could it be worse than never having a sixth birthday?

Timmy thought about the last thing Jack had said to him before he'd left that afternoon.

"If you want, I can teach you to read," he'd offered.

"Yes," Timmy whispered into the darkness now. "That's what I want."

JACK ARRIVED THE NEXT AFTERNOON WITH SCHOOLBOOKS under his arm and sheaves of paper in his hands.

"This is *A*," he said, writing three connecting lines on the paper. "You've got to start with *A*."

" 'A'," Timmy repeated agreeably.

Reading, it turned out, was harder than learning numbers, but easier than disabling the robo-nanny. Within a matter of days, Timmy knew the whole alphabet, and the sounds all the letters made. In weeks, he'd mastered short words and small books. After a few months, Jack pushed back the books one afternoon and said to him, "You know, you can read now. When are you going to tell your parents?"

"I don't know," Timmy said miserably. "Shouldn't I know how to read really, really well first?"

Jack didn't say anything, and just handed him another book.

The TV shows the robo-nanny wanted him to watch all the time seemed dumber than ever now. Sometimes in the mornings, even when it'd be hours before Jack would get home from school, Timmy would disable the robo-nanny just so he could pull out one of Jack's books and practice reading. The pictures in the books didn't jump around the way the TV characters did, but Timmy decided he liked that. He could study them better this way, see how they changed from page to page.

He started shutting off the robo-nanny earlier and earlier in the day, and leaving her off longer and longer.

One morning, he turned her off the minute his parents walked out the door. Then he pulled out some of Jack's books and curled up on the couch to read.

Suddenly, the door flew back open.

Daddy burst into the living room calling out, "Don't panic, robo-nanny, I just forgot my briefcase." And Mommy was right behind him, saying, "Robo-nanny? Why aren't you picking up my remote feed?"

Timmy had time to hide the books. Lies flocked in his mind — convincing ones, too. He could say the robo-nanny broke. He could say he couldn't figure out how to turn on the TV without her.

But he stood up and held out the book in his hand.

"Mommy? Daddy?" he said. "I know how to read." And he looked down and began, "'Once upon a time, in a village far, far away . . .'" He read the entire page. Then he read another page, and another, all the way to the story's end. Finally he looked up.

Tears were streaming down Mommy's face. Daddy's face was frozen, his mouth hanging open in surprise and dismay.

"I'm sorry," Timmy whispered.

Mommy folded him into her arms. Timmy wasn't sure if it was a hug or a stranglehold.

"He's so smart," she muttered. "We ought to be proud. I *am* proud. But —" She sniffled. "Do you know what this means?"

She was talking over the top of Timmy's head. She was asking Daddy, not Timmy. But Timmy answered.

"You have to let me grow up now," Timmy said, pushing away from Mommy so he could see his parents' faces. He wished he didn't have to look up so high to see them. For the first time in his life, he wanted to be able to look his parents straight in the eye.

"Maybe he can forget," Daddy was saying to Mommy in a choked voice. "Maybe we can pretend this never happened."

Mommy looked down at Timmy. "Oh, honey. If you grow up, you won't want to snuggle anymore. You won't be excited when we get home in the evenings. You won't want us to kiss you good-night. And someday — someday you'll leave."

Timmy's neck was starting to hurt from looking up.

"Is that why you paused me?" he asked. "I'll stay. I promise. Of course I want to stay with you forever."

Mommy laughed, but it was a sad, strangled laugh. She crouched down so she was finally face-to-face with him.

"That's what you say now," she said. "But you'll change your mind. People change when they grow."

Daddy sank into the couch so he was on Timmy's level now, too.

"We had so many reasons for pausing you," he said. "Growing up — it's hard. And being an adult . . . Given a choice, why would anyone want to have to worry about mortgage payments and insurance premiums and commuting and bosses —"

"Instead of finger painting, and lying on your back

watching a cloud for an entire afternoon, and thinking an ice-cream cone is the most thrilling treat in the world?" Mommy said. "Your life is so much better like that. And, Timmy, you're so wonderful the way you are right now. So innocent and trusting. It's so much fun being a five-year-old!"

Timmy felt like his chance was melting away. Maybe he would forget how to read. With his parents gazing at him so beseechingly, the book already felt strange in his hand. Desperately, he hugged it to his chest.

"But you don't have fun with me," he accused. "You come home and you just pat my head and you don't even look at me. You don't have to, because I always look the same. And at the park, you just tell me to run off and play. And you put me to bed early so you can do grown-up things. . . . You're — you're bored with me."

Mommy gasped, and all the color drained from her cheeks.

"But I was bored with me, too," Timmy said. "I wasn't having fun. I didn't have any new thoughts about clouds or finger painting or ice cream, so those things weren't fun anymore, either."

Timmy felt like he'd flung down a challenge. Mommy was shaking her head — *no, no, no* — like someone trying to fend off a nightmare.

"Is that true?" Daddy asked, sounding stunned. "Is that why you taught yourself to read?"

Timmy was glad they seemed to think he'd figured it all out on their own, so he didn't have to get Jack in trouble.

"I like reading," he said. "I know my numbers, too. And how to tell time. And I know what infinity is — and what it isn't."

Even without any antidote shot, Timmy realized, he'd grown and changed and become an entirely different person from the little boy who'd looked out a peephole and opened a door all those months ago.

"We can't stop him now," Daddy said to Mommy.

Mommy looked back at Timmy and nodded, her face happy and sad all at once.

"So what do we do now?" she asked.

"You un-pause me," Timmy said firmly. "And then — can I have a birthday party soon? I *really* want to see six candles on a cake!"

Daddy and Mommy laughed. Then Daddy said, "But we can't invite any of your friends from the park. They're all paused."

"I'll make new friends," Timmy said, thinking of Jack. Still, he felt a stab of fear. Growing up would mean lots of things would be new. Some of the new things would be good, like Jack and reading. But some of the new things might be bad.

"Maybe we —" Daddy said.

"Should we —" Mommy said.

"If we —" Timmy said.

They all said the "we" at once.

"Jinx!" Timmy cried out. Mommy and Daddy stopped talking and just looked at him. He didn't know if they understood about jinxing, or if they just didn't know what to say.

"Mommy, Mommy, Mommy," he chanted. "Daddy, Daddy, Daddy." And it was like he was breaking a real spell, a spell of all their fears and worries about him growing up.

Timmy wasn't scared or worried anymore, either. He would grow up. And as he grew, every jinx would have an end.

Author's Note

For many years, my husband and I had kids and no pets; several of our friends had pets and no kids. In the early stages of parenthood, I was amazed at how often the two were compared. ("Your baby cried all night? Oh, so did our puppy when we first brought him home. . . .") Even as my kids got older, I was surprised that many parents I met seemed to regard their children as, essentially, glorified pets.

Later, I wrote a book, *Turnabout*, about scientists being able to toy with the aging process — turning 100-year-olds into teenagers again. My biggest problem writing the book was that I kept thinking of alternate ways to play around with age.

Then my kids hit a phase when they were fascinated with 1) the concept of infinity; and 2) jinxing each other. So I began imagining what an infinity jinx would be. . . .

MARGARET PETERSON HADDIX has written numerous books for kids, including *Running Out of Time*, *Double Identity*, and the Among the Hidden series. Her books have won readers' choice awards in several states. She and her family live in Columbus, Ohio.

Marked for Death

Will Weaver

Eyes on the ground, clutching my hunting rifle, I hurry along the forest trail. I tell myself this is not happening. This is not real. But the glistening red dabs along the trail grow to spatters and splashes, and there — at the base of a tree — is a large spray of color, as if a paint ball has exploded. Ahead I hear a groaning. It is not the sound of a deer. It is human. One part of my brain understands that. Another part knows that my life has changed forever. . . .

Three months earlier . . .

When I walked into Gun Safety class, the boys laughed. Their thirteen-year-old voices croaked like toads.

"Hey," a pimply-faced kid whispered, "aren't you in the wrong room?"

I pretended to check my registration sheet, then looked at him. "No, I'm good. But Dermatology is just down the hall."

A few boys chuckled. Pizza Face, a.k.a. "Tanner" (we had to wear stick-on name tags), looked at me dumbly. "Forget it," I said. I glanced around, then took a front desk; since I was the only girl, I might as well be a cliché.

UNEXPECTED

The instructor, Mr. Johnson, soon came into the room. "Good morning, class!" he said. He was a school industrial arts teacher, but today he wore a camo cap and a Dorks-Unlimited shooting vest, and carried two long guns plus a bunch of handouts.

"Don't be afraid, they're only guns," Tanner said.

I glanced at them. "Looks like a .22 rifle and a twenty-gauge shotgun," I replied. "Though I prefer a sixteen-gauge myself. The dram load is a little light for ducks and geese, but it's perfect for partridge hunting — wouldn't you agree?"

Several boys snickered — at Tanner this time.

"Huh?" he said to me. He was still staring at the guns. I suddenly realized he might have been talking to himself about not being afraid, and I felt stupid. I usually wasn't this cruel, not even to geeky boys.

"Well, well, well!" Mr. Johnson said, his eyes lighting up as he saw me.

Spare me, puleeeeze, I thought.

"If it's not Miss Samantha Anderson."

"Sam," I said.

"Samantha's father happens to be one of the top marksmen in the Midwest," the instructor said loudly, "and a professional hunting guide as well. If she shoots anything like her father, you boys don't stand a chance."

There were a few uncertain laughs.

"Maybe you could, like, turn a big spotlight on me?" I said to Mr. Johnson.

This got a big laugh from the boys; Mr. Johnson drew back. He cleared his throat, looked back to his list, and moved to a different spot in the room.

I checked my watch. I had to pass this class in order to get my gun safety permit, which meant I could go deer hunting — real hunting, as in carrying my own gun — for the first time, which, for Midwestern kids, is kind of a big deal. The even bigger deal was this: I'd be hunting with my father — just me and him. He wasn't around much — right now he was guiding in Alaska — but we had been planning this for years. "When you turn thirteen, just me and you, honey," he always said. My brothers, Jake, Ben, and Andrew, had their turn; now it was mine.

First, however, I had to get through this day. Stuck inside a classroom on a hot August Saturday — the last one before school started — was bad enough, but most of my friends were off to the Mall of America in Minneapolis on one last shopping trip for school clothes. Growing up with three brothers, I constantly worried about being perceived as a helpless princess — that's why I was so harsh to Tanner.

"Today's class will cover the basic principles of firearms operation and hunting safety," Mr. Johnson droned as he distributed handouts. I sighed again.

My family lives in Wisconsin, in the countryside north of La Crosse, and we target shoot right in our backyard. I've shot nearly every kind of gun, including deer rifles; my father got me started with a BB gun when I was about five. These days he's gone almost all the time. What can I say about that? Nothing. I think my parents are kind of married, kind of not. I don't ask. I only know that my mother has made a big deal of me knowing how to do all the stuff my brothers can do, such as ride a horse, clean fish, use cables to jump-start a vehicle with a dead battery, etc. She's a real outdoorsy woman herself, though she doesn't like to hunt. Anyway, I can do lots of things that many girls can't. But I don't make a big deal about it, especially around my friends from La Crosse. It's a tomboy thing.

"There will be a test at the end of the day," Mr. Johnson said, "so pay attention — unless you think you know it all."

He glanced sideways at me; I pretended to study the handouts, which were at least easier on the eyes than a room full of thirteen-year-old geeks. After the teacher moved on, I snuck another look around. The boys were painful to look at: It was as if they had all been dropped as babies.

Meanwhile, Tanner had drawn something rude on his desk, and was trying to get the next kid to look at it. He was so lame I sort of felt sorry for him.

"We'll start with the fundamental, number one issue

of gun safety: muzzle safety," the instructor said. He held up the small rifle. "If the bore, or 'business end,' of a gun is never pointed at a person, no one can ever be shot accidentally."

He took ten minutes saying the same thing ten different ways. I checked my watch again, just to make sure the battery wasn't dead. . . .

After muzzle safety, it was on to more bonehead facts and information, including a filmstrip (I thought they went out with the last century) on moving safely through the field while carrying a gun. "Always be sure of your target, and never, *ever*, run with a gun."

Okay. Got it.

"The next part of our class contains graphic images," the instructor said as he set up his slide projector.

"All right!" Tanner whispered to anyone who would listen.

"These photographs were taken at the scene of actual hunting accidents."

"Cool!" Tanner said.

Everybody ignored him. If Tanner were a character in a Hollywood movie, he would be marked for death — you know, the swimmer who paddles away from the others in a shark flick, or the camper who wanders into the woods at night in a slasher film.

"Fair warning: Some of these slides are explicit, or, as you youngsters might say, 'gross,'" the instructor said.

No one seemed to mind.

"Their purpose is to shock you," the instructor continued, taking his time, making us wait. (Clearly this was his best stuff.) "I want you to see the effect of an accidental misfire."

I got ready by squinting my eyes. The first slide was of a hunter facedown in brown leaves with a big black splotch on the back of his orange jacket; compared to the computer games Jake, Ben, and Andrew played, it wasn't *so* awful.

"That's what he looked like in the field," the instructor said. The next slide flashed onto the screen — I looked away but not in time — and there was a sucking in of breath around the room. "This is what he looked like in the coroner's office."

A stainless-steel table. A naked man on it. And a big gunshot wound in his side. I stared. My breakfast Cheerios moved in my stomach.

The slides continued. I watched the next one from the very corner of my eye: I could just make out enough to know that it was no computer game.

"This hunter died fast," the instructor announced.

Two dead hunters were enough. I ended up watching Tanner watch the slides; his jaw dropped farther and farther with each flash of light on his bumpy face.

"Okay, that's enough," the instructor finally said. He shut down the projector and turned on the lights. There were exhalations and murmurs and thumping desks.

After another short filmstrip on target shooting and safety, it was lunchtime at last.

Even better, we got to go outside.

On the elementary school playground we took our bag lunches towards some grass. Tanner carried only a twenty-ounce Mountain Dew. "Hey, everybody, did you see that dead guy's butt?" he said. Everybody ignored him. We sat down. Tanner kept looking for a group to join, but nobody would let him in. I was just about to give in and make room for him, when he raced across to the swing set. He took a swing and began to pump himself higher and higher. Gradually we turned to watch him. Soon, at high arc, the chains began to slack and he free-fell with harder and harder jerks. "Hey, everybody, higher?" he called.

"Yeah — way higher!" several boys called, and snickered.

Tanner stood up in the swing and pumped. I held my breath.

"Anybody, want to see me jump?"

"Yeah — for sure!" several guys called. They stood up so they could get a good look at Tanner breaking his neck. I'd had enough; I went over to the swing set. "Tanner, cut it out! You're gonna get hurt!"

His head jerked sideways and he stared down at me. Then he looked at all the boys. I realized I'd just made things worse for him. Luckily for all of us, Mr. Johnson stepped through the door. "The bus is here," he called. In an instant, the boys all rushed away.

"Hey, everybody, wait up!" Tanner shouted.

I waited as he braked himself in a cloud of dust, and then jumped. He did a running flip, and landed on his back with a thud. His mouth fished for air, and then he sat up gasping.

"See, what did I tell you?" I said. "Those guys just wanted to see you get hurt."

He looked at me, and for a second his eyes were not crazy and jumpy. It was like there was a normal kid buried somewhere inside his head. But really deep inside.

"Race you to the bus!" he said.

THE YELLOW SCHOOL BUS TOOK US TO THE LOCAL TARGET range for actual shooting — in other words, the exciting part of the day.

"I've never shot a shotgun before," Tanner said to me.

The boys all looked at one another, then rolled their eyes.

"Does it kick?" he asked me.

"Some," I said, "but just keep the butt of the stock tight against your shoulder. That and your cheek tight on the wood."

"Okay," Tanner said easily. I was amazed. Tanner was possibly the only thirteen-year-old boy in the world who didn't mind taking directions from a thirteen-year-old girl. The other boys rolled their eyes again; however, as the shooting range approached, they all began to stare out the bus windows. I got the feeling that *most* of the class had not shot a shotgun.

First, everyone shot the little .22 caliber rifle. Three shots in the three main positions: prone, sitting, and standing (off-hand). The first boy couldn't figure out the sitting position — that is, which elbow to place on which knee. We all giggled. When my turn came, I put all three shots in the center of the bull's-eye. Eventually we moved to the shotgun, and by the end of the day I had twenty new friends — Tanner in particular — not to mention my Hunting and Gun Safety certificate and badge.

For the boys, the big question was where to sew on their badge: cap or hunting jacket? They even included Tanner in that debate. Me, I slipped mine in my pocket and got out of there.

"How'd it go?" my mother asked. She was waiting for me in the parking lot beside our Jeep. Tanned and lean, she wore her usual Saturday outfit: jeans, dusty cowboy boots, and the leathery, soapy smell of Penny, our horse.

"She can shoot like heck!" Tanner called across to my mother. "She's totally cool!"

I shrugged. "Tanner, my new very best friend."

My mother smiled. "Thatta girl." She put her arm around me right there in the open.

"Please, Mother," I said instantly.

"Sorry," she said.

I watched the boys head off with their fathers. All except for Tanner, who got on a battered bicycle with a wobbly back tire. My mother started the car and we drove away. I kept looking back.

"What?" she asked. When I didn't say anything, she said, "You miss your Dad?"

I was silent. Then I said, "Well, don't you?"

She paused a moment too long. "He'll be home soon."

"Whatever," I answered. We didn't talk much about him; there was lots of unsaid stuff about him being gone. I think she thought I blamed her, and maybe in some ways I did.

When I got home I left my father a voice-mail message about passing the Gun Safety class; he hardly ever answered his cell phone, but then again, if you're a hunting guide, the last thing you need is your phone to start beeping.

Sometimes I called his number just to hear his voice message, and today I listened to it twice before I hung up.

THE FIRST DAY OF SCHOOL WAS A DISASTER. EVERYBODY HAD grown a foot except me, and the bad news didn't stop there. I was standing with Tara and Melanie, the cool kids, in the eighth-grade hallway, when a loud voice called, "Sam — hey, Sam!"

I looked over my shoulder. I froze.

Tanner came rushing up. His pimples were better some, and he had on a clean shirt, but he was wearing old, busted-out tennis shoes and ratty jeans. His hair needed a major washing. The girls around me drew back.

"It's me, Tanner! Remember? From Gun Safety class?"

"Oh, yeah," I said. I checked my watch.

"Hey, Sam, I was thinking — maybe we can go hunting someday!"

I felt my ears began to burn, which meant they were probably turning red. "We'll see. Actually, I gotta go to class, Tanner," I said.

"Okay, see you around, Sam," Tanner said cheerfully, and turned away.

"Who was *that*?" the girls said in unison.

"Just this . . . kid," I said, and felt my entire face turn really red.

As school continued that first week, Tanner ricocheted from group to group. Nobody wanted anything to do with him, so I ended up talking to him a couple of times. The only conversation he could really stay with was about going hunting, or someday even owning a hunting gun of his own. I tried to be nice to him but he was like a stray dog: Feed him and he only comes back more often; chase him away and you feel like dirt. Since I had a soft spot for lost pets (and kids whose fathers weren't around), I ended up being his only friend.

One day I asked him about his parents.

"My foster parents or my dead ones?" he said.

I swallowed. "Whichever."

"My foster parents are okay. But my real parents died a long time ago."

"I'm sorry."

"My father, that is," he added. "My mother's in California in this drug treatment place."

I tried to think of something to say.

"Actually, it's a prison," he added. "She's in prison." He looked straight at me. "I usually lie about her."

"Well, I'm glad you didn't," was all I could think to say. But with Tanner that was enough. He smiled like he was the happiest kid in the world.

After that, Tanner attached himself to me like a wood tick. I swear he was sucking my blood, and he certainly didn't help my hall life. The more I talked to Tanner, the less the Tara-and-Melanie crowd talked to me. If I were honest, those girls were kind of Mary Kate and Ashley-ish anyway; however, the tomboy thing always worried me — that and explaining why my father was never around.

As October rolled around, and with it the opening of small-game season, Tanner pestered me daily about going hunting. "Mr. Johnson said he's going to find someone to take me grouse hunting," he said. "When we go, want to come with?"

"We'll see," I said.

"You could show me how to wing shoot and stuff like that." He smiled hopefully.

"We'll see," I muttered. It was the only answer that worked with Tanner, the only response that made him go away. Not yes, not no. "We'll see."

Then the leaves turned yellow and red, geese honked high overhead as they flew south for the winter — and my father came home. Suddenly one day there he was in his dusty black Ford Explorer, waiting for me after school right there in front of the buses and everybody.

"Daddy," I shrieked. I raced into his arms. I didn't care if anybody saw me. In fact, I hoped they did.

"Sam, honey!" he said, lifting me off the ground and swinging me around. He smelled like cigar and leaves and wood; his trimmed beard had flecks of snow in it, a speckled whiteness that I never noticed before. There were also new, fine wrinkles around his eyes, which were tired, and a little sad, as if he'd been working too hard or had lost something important. I began to cry.

"Honey, honey, what's the matter?" he said, flashing me his old smile.

"Nothing," I said, rubbing away my tears.

"Well, I sure hope not," he said.

I managed a grin.

"Hey, is that your dad?" a loud voice said.

Tanner. He lurched up beside us.

"Hello there, young man," my father began.

"Go away!" I said suddenly to Tanner.

Tanner flinched as if I had kicked him. My father looked at me with disappointment — which only made the moment worse. I rushed into the Ford and slammed the door. My father came around and settled into the driver's seat.

"What was that all about?" he asked.

"Just . . . this . . . boy," I blubbered.

My father smiled and started the engine. "Oh, that," he said.

"No — you don't understand," I said, even more annoyed. I looked out the window; Tanner was still standing there, staring after us with his mouth-open-deer-in-the-headlights look. More than ever, I wished I'd never met him.

For the rest of that week, the one before deer season, my father picked me up every day after school. And every day, Tanner found some excuse to be there. "What's the deal with this Tanner?" my father said.

I shrugged. "I met him in Gun Safety class this summer. He just sort of attached himself to me."

"He's new in school?"

I nodded.

"Does he have any friends?"

"I'm it," I said sarcastically.

My father looked in his rearview mirror at Tanner, then across to me. "I'm proud of you, honey."

On Wednesday afternoon, when I came to meet my dad, I saw the Gun Safety instructor, Mr. Johnson, talking with my father.

"There she is," Mr. Johnson said immediately when he saw me; it was like they had been talking about something important but not for my ears.

"Hey, Sam, guess what? Guess what!" Tanner shouted as he raced up behind me.

"What," I said flatly.

"Mr. Johnson says I might get to go deer hunting with you and your father!"

ON THE WAY HOME, I SAT AS FAR AS I COULD FROM MY father and stared out my window. Tears burned in my eyes; I wouldn't let him see my face.

"It's not like that, Sam," my father said again. "And anyway, what could I do? Bob Johnson tells me this kid's story — how he's bounced around foster homes all his life, how he came to the Gun Safety class all on his own. The one thing the kid wants to do is go deer hunting. What could I say?"

"Like, 'No'?"

My father nodded. "I considered that. But sometimes we have to . . . share what we have. The luck. The gifts. Think about it: This kid has no one. For starters, you've got two parents."

"Sort of," I said instantly.

My father fell silent.

I glanced over at him. His eyes had a hurt look, and they stared straight down the road.

"I'm sorry," I said. I felt my own eyes burning again.

"It's okay, baby," he murmured, and touched my hair.

"It's just that . . ." I began, but my voice broke.

"I know, I know: 'just you and me.' That's what we always said. But it will still be almost like that. I've got it figured out. I'm going to make a deer blind for Tanner that's way away from us. You and I will take the tree stand, and I'll check on him once in a while. It will all work out, okay?"

I bit my lip. I didn't say anything.

On Thursday night after school, my father took Tanner and me to the shooting range. "I just want to make sure he knows what he's doing," my father said. I made my statement by staying in the truck. And anyway, my gun, a twenty-gauge shotgun set up for deer hunting, was long since targeted in. Tanner was using one of my brother Andrew's old guns, a single-shot "starter" twenty-gauge. The range was busy with last-minute shooters; guns boomed and crashed. Tanner's first screwup was to wave the muzzle sideways across the line of bench shooters — including my father. I sucked in a breath. A couple of hunters drew back and glared, and my father snatched the muzzle downward. I flashed back to the slides in Mr. Johnson's class. But the gun was not loaded, and I saw my father mouthing stern words to Tanner, who hung his head. Then my father got Tanner situated at the bench, and the gun pointed in the right direction. At first Tanner flinched and jerked each time he fired. Dust kicked up yards below the target. But gradually he began to lean more tightly into the stock, and keep his cheek on the wood when he squeezed the trigger. My father nodded approvingly. When the round of firing stopped, and hunters walked forward to check their targets, Tanner raced wildly downrange and came rushing back against traffic as he waved the target.

"Look, Sam! I hit it three times!" Tanner shouted.

"Great," I said without expression. He had shot at it ten times.

"Not that bad for your first time with a new gun," my father said, as they returned to the truck.

Still holding the shotgun, its muzzle waving, Tanner hopped up and down with excitement. My father quickly took the gun from Tanner. "What did I tell you? Never jump or run with the gun!"

"Sorry," Tanner said with that instant kicked-dog look in his eyes. My father glanced at me.

"But you did all right today," my father added. "Saturday morning, if you promise to be safe and remember what you learned, we'll go hunting."

"I promise, I promise! Oh man, I can't wait!" Tanner said.

My father smiled, but something in my stomach clenched; I had a terrible feeling about this, and it had something to do with my father. But he was a pro, and he had worked with hunters of all kinds. He had to know what he was doing.

We dropped Tanner off at his foster parents' place, a double-wide trailer with several battered plastic tricycles lying about.

"What time will you pick me up Saturday morning?" Tanner asked.

"Let's say five A.M."

"I could be ready earlier," Tanner said.

My father patted Tanner on the back and shooed him out of the pickup. "Five A.M. I'll be here."

Tanner raced up to the double-wide. At the door he braked and brought up his hand as if to knock. Then he changed his mind and rushed inside, slamming the door so hard the wall quivered.

My father stared after him. Then he looked at me. I looked away, out my window.

"Hey, you want to get a Dairy Queen or something?" my father asked. "Just you and me?"

ON OPENING MORNING WE DROVE INTO TOWN TO GET Tanner. It was chilly and pitch-black outside, and the streetlights were bright as we entered La Crosse. In the trailer park with its curving streets, Tanner was the only moving thing. He stood outside, stamping his feet up and down against the cold and puffing frosty breaths.

"Wow, am I glad to see you!" he said, leaping into the truck. He shuddered from the cold, and there was frost on his eyelashes.

"How long you been waiting?" my father said, turning up the heater fan.

"Not that long," Tanner shrugged. In the dark cab of the truck, my father's teeth shone white as he smiled.

North of town, at the dark edge of the woods, which we owned, my father let the truck coast to a stop. "It's very important to enter the woods quietly," my father said to Tanner. "I'll take you to your stand."

Tanner nodded continuously. He could not stop grinning. "I can't believe this," he said to me.

"Remember, you'll stay there until I come for you," my father said to him. "It takes a lot of patience to wait for a deer."

"Why can't I, like, track them and sneak up on them?"

"That comes later, with more experience," my father said patiently. "Most hunters start out on the stand, or a blind."

Tanner nodded with some disappointment.

"Sam and I will take the tree stand. Whistle if you need help of any kind, all right?"

Tanner nodded, and then the two of them headed off

into the darkness. My father's little flashlight bobbed along the trail like a firefly. It became a little speck, then went dark. I sucked in another breath.

After ten minutes or more, my father's bobbing light reappeared, and I began to relax. We went to our stand. It was a platform about six feet off the ground, sort of like a tree house with two chairs. It had a tiny little heater if we needed it, and a railing on which to rest our guns. We settled in, and after we were quiet, the forest gradually came alive: Invisible ducks whistled overhead; an owl went "who-who"; there was a sharp skittering sound in the leaves below.

I tensed and gripped my rifle.

"Squirrel," my father whispered. And he was right.

Gradually the light came. First to appear were the silhouettes of spruce trees; then a broad duskiness spread downward from their points. The grayness softened and slipped groundward, and soon we could see the deer trail that ran parallel to our stand. My father checked his watch. "It's legal shooting time," he whispered. And almost on cue, I heard soft steps coming down the trail.

"Get ready," my father said.

I clicked off the safety.

The shape of a deer appeared; at walking speed, it was coming right toward us.

"Let's see what it is first," my father whispered.

The deer was not large, but clearly a buck; there was a pale flash of horn.

"Spike buck," my father said. "Let him pass."

As we watched, the buck stopped to paw for some acorns, and found a mouthful; he chewed audibly as he looked around. Then he moved on and disappeared down the trail.

"A very good sign," my father murmured, and we settled back to wait for a bigger and better deer.

By ten A.M. we had seen nothing but chickadees, a pileated woodpecker that chipped giant-sized chunks of wood from a dead pine tree, and at least a dozen gray squirrels. But it was fun just sitting there talking with my father.

He told me all about his job as a fishing and hunting guide, how some people were great but others were total slobs and jerks.

"Same with school," I said. I was about to tell him about my friends — at least I thought they were my friends — when *Boom!* went Tanner's gun.

My father and I looked at each other; then we heard Tanner's whistle.

"I'd better go check," my father said quickly.

"Be careful!" I said suddenly.

"Don't worry, honey. I'll be right back."

I waited alone in the stand. I could hardly catch my breath. I kept having this terrible feeling. But soon enough my father returned, shaking his head and smiling.

"He says he saw a deer of some kind, and had a good

shot. But we looked all over and couldn't find blood. I'm sure he missed him cleanly."

"Good," I said.

"Now, now," my father said, smiling again, and we settled back into our chairs. The sun was out now, though still low (it was November), and by two P.M. the woods slowly grew dusky again. My father dozed for a little while; it was nice waiting there, holding my gun while he napped — like I was keeping guard for him.

When he woke up, we continued talking, about my friends this time, about boys I liked. I was surprised to be telling him stuff.

He nodded. "When I was a junior in high school, I was dating this really pretty senior girl," he said. "She sort of picked me, you could say. Anyway, we went to her senior prom, and afterwards she wanted to get more serious. But I wasn't ready, so we didn't." He glanced sideways at me.

"So, Dad, is that my lecture on boys?" I teased.

He smiled and said nothing. We turned to stare out at the forest in comfortable silence; it was one of the happiest moments of my life.

Suddenly there was a scattered, crunching sound on the trail. The sky was grayer now, and the air colder — as if the woods were coming alive again.

"Get ready!" my father whispered.

Two does came bounding along with their brown-and-white tails erect.

"There must be a buck close behind," my father whispered.

And sure enough, hot on their tracks came a buck with tall antlers, at least eight points. He was moving too fast for a good shot, and in a couple of seconds he was out of sight. I let out a disappointed breath and lowered my muzzle.

"That's okay, honey. You didn't have a clean shot. Don't worry, you'll get another chance."

But not at that buck.

Boom! went Tanner's gun for the second time.

My father looked at me. Then we heard Tanner's voice calling for us. "I hit him, I hit him," he shouted faintly.

"Wait here," my father said. "I'll go check."

"Be really careful, Daddy!" I said again.

He looked at me oddly. "Always, honey," he said. And left.

I watched him disappear down the trail.

Several minutes passed; it was as if the woods held its breath.

"There he is," Tanner suddenly shouted. His voice was to the right now, as if he had left his stand and were running through the woods. "I think I see him!"

Then *Boom!* again.

And a hoarse scream — a wailing.

No, no, please. "Daddy!" I shouted. Dropping my gun, I leaped to the ground. I raced through the loud leaves underfoot, past the slapping, stinging branches. "Daddy!" I kept crying.

"Over here, Sam!" my father called. His voice sounded terrible — as if he couldn't breathe.

I rushed into a clearing. Beside a fallen, mossy log, my father was slumped over — slumped over Tanner, who lay on his back in the brown leaves.

"Look, Sam! I got him!" Tanner said to me as he pointed. Twenty yards away a large buck lay brown on the brown leaves; an antler curved up darkly.

Tanner held his other hand over his stomach. His face was bone-pale and his eyes white and sort of popped-out. My father said, "Sam — we have a shoot-ing accident here. I want you to run back to the stand — my cell phone is in my backpack. Call 911."

"I'm sorry!" Tanner said to us. He started to cry. "I re-loaded, then was running, I must have tripped. . . ."

"Go, Sam!" my father said.

I ran as fast as I ever have — made the call — then rushed back up the trail toward Tanner, following the blood on the leaves — the deer's blood or his blood, I couldn't tell. But there was so much blood.

My father met me before I could see Tanner again. He tried to block my view. "Sam, I want you to go back to the truck," he said slowly. "Wait for the ambulance, then show them the way here. I'll wait with . . ." Then his voice broke, and he drew me fiercely into his arms and held tight.

*   *   *

AT TANNER'S FUNERAL, WE PUT THE DEER'S ANTLERS ON HIS coffin. Melanie and Tara and some of their friends from school attended; at first I was pleased, and we all hugged, but later I saw Tara whisper something, then giggle under her breath at the others, who cried continuously, as if Tanner were their best friend. For a second I hated them for coming, but then let go of it. At least they were here.

The preacher was bald and had a voice like Mrs. Krabappel, the teacher on *The Simpsons* (and twice he called Tanner "Tyler"); the eulogy was mainly clichés about "the less fortunate among us" and life as a "flickering candle." Tanner's foster parents were there, but their baby began to wail, then throw up, and they had to leave. Quickly the service was over. Tanner's body was to be shipped somewhere — Minneapolis, I think — so there was no trip to the cemetery, no burial. After the church service there was punch, coffee, and cake in the chilly church basement. The lunch was hosted by a flock of blue-haired old ladies who chattered cheerfully among themselves in the kitchen. There were more of these church ladies than people who actually came for Tanner.

I stayed close to my father, as did my mother. I hadn't seen them together, dressed up, in forever. Mr. Johnson, the Gun Safety teacher, came up to us. "Well, Tanner got his deer," he said.

I realized one thing about funerals: People say incredibly stupid things.

"He wasn't ready to hunt," my father said, staring across the room. "I should have known that."

"It's all he wanted to do — go hunting just one time," Mr. Johnson said.

"Excuse me," my father said. I could see the pain in his eyes.

"Let's go, Daddy," I said.

He nodded and let me take him by the arm and out the door. My mother followed. It was bright now, the sun breaking through patchy clouds, and the three of us drove home in silence.

At home we all ate dinner, still in silence. Even my brothers used their best manners.

"I've been thinking," my father said. "I have an offer to manage a sporting goods store here in La Crosse."

My mother looked up quickly.

He swallowed. "I'm thinking of taking it."

We all stared at him.

"The owner wants to sell eventually, and I've got some ideas on new sports lines, new gear."

My oldest brother, Ben, perked up. "Hey, you could hire us!"

"And go broke immediately," my father replied. There was laughter all around.

"Seriously, what do you think?" my father said. He looked at my mother.

"Could you stand being inside a store all day?" she asked.

"I'd do some Midwestern guiding on the side — if I could find good help for the store."

Andrew, Ben, and Jake took their cue and began to poke and laugh at one another.

"I think I'll take the offer," my father said suddenly. He looked at me. "Life's too short."

I looked down; my eyes felt hot and then they spilled over.

"Hey, what's a matter with her?" Andrew called.

"Nothing," my father said quickly.

And he was right. After our family dinner, I went to my room and lay back on my bed. I stared at the ceiling and thought about life. I had to admit that the preacher was right: Life is like a lit candle, and the wind is blowing. But the part he left out was how other people can touch our lives. And change them forever.

On Monday, back in school, I didn't try to hang out with the cool crowd. I didn't care. Instead, I said hello to kids I'd never met before, kids who looked interesting. They smiled back shyly, and it was a great feeling. I felt, for the first time since grade school, like I was totally myself.

Author's Note

Up in Minnesota, where I live, lots of women and girls hunt deer. Their fathers taught them, and now hunting is part of their lives. That's why "Marked for Death" is a bit of a role reversal, then, in terms of what we expect. In my story it's the girl who is the crack shot, the good hunter. The annoying boy who attaches himself to her at school is "marked" for sadness, and nothing she does — especially teaching him how to hunt — can change that.

WILL WEAVER is the author of five novels and many short stories for young adults. His recent titles include *Claws*, *Memory Boy*, and, of course, the Billy Baggs series: *Striking Out*, *Farm Team*, and *Hard Ball*. His new young-adult novel, *Full Service*, was released in 2005. An avid outdoorsman, he lives near the headwaters of the Mississippi in northern Minnesota.

The Telltale Croak

∽∾∽

Laura E. Williams

CHAD STARED DOWN AT THE DEAD BODY.

His stomach churned as he staggered sideways, falling against the warm hood of his father's 1979 Trans Am. Rebuilt engine, five cylinder, four on the floor, candy-apple red — Dad's pride and joy. Now, front fender dented.

He was dead.

No, *he* wasn't dead — not yet at least — but Marky was.

Marcus Hornik, known around the neighborhood as Marky. Only five years old. How could the Hornik family allow him to play outside at this hour? He should be home in bed, safe and sound.

Chad had tried not to hit him. He had wrenched the wheel to the right and then swerved to the left, but the sickening thud had come a split second later.

His eyes burned, but he blinked back his tears, too frightened to cry — too frightened to move or to think. All he could do was stare at Marky's lifeless form lying in the glare of the Trans Am's headlights.

The road was quiet except for the accusing growl of the car's engine. It was a back road, rutted and bumpy, in need of new paving. No street lights, just the moon

227

and the stars to give direction. But Chad didn't pay attention to the wide-open sky — Orion and his hunting dogs sprawled out above him, the flickering shadows all around, the warm, comfy, night air. All he could do was stare at the body.

No blood pooled under Marky's head. No blood trickled down from any visible cut or scrape. No blood, no proof, no evidence.

No evidence?

The plan flooded Chad's brain. If he buried the body, there'd be no way anyone would know what had happened. Marky would simply be missing. A search party would never find him. No one would know that fourteen-year-old Chad had taken his father's car out for an illegal joyride while his parents and little brother were at dinner and a movie. No one would know what he had done.

He had to hurry before anyone drove by — before his family came home. He could see his house off to the west and across the fields, the lights from the windows blazing like watchful, disapproving eyes.

He jumped into the car, and with hands he knew would shake for as long as he lived, he steered the Trans Am over to the shoulder and pulled onto a dirt road hidden from the main road by tall grass and drooping trees. He shut off the engine. The silence that greeted him rang in his ears. His heart thumped like a dog's wagging tail hitting the floor.

Then the little sounds came to him through the open window. The crackle of a night creature scurrying through the underbrush. The nearby katydids chirping. The surrounding fields rustling in the wind with hushed voices as if they told a secret they didn't want Chad to know. The bullfrogs croaking down by the pond, one especially loud. *Ribbet . . . Ribbet . . .*

Only, the croak twisted grotesquely in Chad's head until all he could hear was: *Murder . . . Murder . . .*

He shuddered, jumped out of the car, and ran back to the road. Without the headlights spotlighting the body, Marky looked like just another lump of roadkill. Only, it wasn't a deer or a possum or a skunk. It was Marky. Innocent Marky, who had just started waiting for the school bus last year. Marky, who loved to play catch. Marky, who ate peanut butter cookies like they were going out of style. Marky, who was dressed up like a ghost last Halloween. Now he *was* a ghost.

Trying to clear his mind before he freaked himself out, Chad slowly stepped forward, afraid that the body would suddenly rise and come for him on stiff, Frankenstein legs, eager to rip out Chad's heart.

Now he was right up close to Marky, but Marky, fortunately, stayed dead. No, that was *unfortunately*, but *fortunately* he wasn't like Frankenstein, but *unfortunately* he was dead, but — Chad shook his head frantically. Too confusing. Too jumbled. Stop thinking. Just do something.

He bent over. No gag-inducing whiff of death. It was too soon for the decay and the bugs and the stink. Gingerly, he scooped one arm under Marky's shoulders, the other arm over the hips and then under his butt. Chad grunted. Marky was surprisingly heavy and awkward to carry with all four limbs sprawled out, head flopping with each step.

Carefully but quickly, he carried Marky to the side of the street, down the dirt road, past the parked car, and onward as the land dipped to the hidden pond, which was actually called Hidden Pond. Hidden, but everyone knew it was there. Yet no one came down here much, now that the pond was more marshy than pond-like. Only his little brother seemed to like the place for frogging. Otherwise, it was pretty much deserted. The perfect place to hide a murder.

The bullfrogs croaked louder, like they knew he was there and they were trying to tell him something. Chad wished they'd all jump off their lily pads and drown. He couldn't concentrate with all that noise. He laid the body on a clump of grass and searched by moonlight for a good burying place.

Suddenly he heard the distant sound of tires over loose gravel. He held his breath. Even the bullfrogs seemed to hold their breaths as the car rolled by on the street above. Chad caught only the occasional flicker of the headlights as the light flashed through the trees and underbrush lining the side of the road. Would the car stop? No, there was no blood on the road, no evidence. It kept going. Only when the sound of tires on pavement had faded like a snake hissing away did he breathe again. And the bullfrogs started croaking in unison: *Murder . . . Murder . . . Murder . . .*

Just like a dog, Chad clawed at the damp earth, digging a grave for Marky. Even though it was late summer, the earth chilled his knees as he knelt. Cold dirt caked his fingers like gloves.

The sweat beaded on his upper lip. Digging was hard work. He stopped and looked at the grave. Too shallow. He looked at the glowing hands of his watch. His family would be home any minute.

A shallow grave was better than no grave, he decided quickly. He grabbed Marky's legs and dragged him into the ditch so he was lying on his right side. Then Chad dumped the displaced dirt over the body. When he was done, a pale ear stuck up like a flag of surrender. Chad pushed a clump of earth over it. There.

He sat back on his heels and surveyed his work. The grave looked like a mound. Like a dead body lay under it. A murdered body.

Still on his knees, he leaned forward and tried to smooth out the obvious angles. The shape of the head, the sideways shoulder, and the hip jutting up. No more time. No time for making gravestones. No time for prayers. Well, maybe a quick one. He clasped his dirty hands together and bowed his head, squeezing his eyes shut so that God would know he really meant this.

Murder . . . Murder . . .

Chad's eyes sprang open. His head jerked up. He gasped and stared right into the bulbous eyes of a giant bullfrog sitting on the mound, right above where Marky's unbeating heart lay in the dirt.

Murder . . . Murder. . . it croaked.

Chad leaped to his feet and sprang away. He ran for the car. Before he got in, he hastily rubbed the dirt from his knees and hands, then he jumped in, turned the key, and ground the gears into reverse, the tires kicking up dirt as they screeched into motion. Once on the road, he pushed the gas pedal to the floor. But still, even over the roar of the engine, over the *whoosh* of the wind blowing in through the open windows, he heard the deep, accusing croak of the bullfrog.

Murder . . . Murder . . .

It took only two minutes to get home. Recklessly, he careened into the driveway and pulled the car into the garage. He ran inside. He took a shower, washing away all traces of his crime. He put on his pajamas, and went to bed.

When his family came home a few minutes later, they stopped in his doorway.

"Asleep already?" his father asked.

"Isn't he sweet?" his mother whispered.

"He's a good kid," his father agreed. "We couldn't have asked for two better sons."

"Only I'm the betterer one," Joey, his little brother said, not bothering to keep his voice down.

His father hushed the seven-year-old with a soft laugh. His mother sighed with happiness as they tiptoed away.

Chad couldn't move. It was as if he were buried himself, his sheets wrapped like shrouds around his body, his dark room an airless tomb.

Breathe. Keep breathing, he told himself, gasping for air. His heart thudded.

What if his father saw the dent in the fender of his pride and joy?

What if someone found Marky's body?

What if he'd left a clue at the scene of the crime? He'd watched too many cop shows not to know that even the slightest bit of tissue or carpet fiber or strand of hair could mean a guilty verdict, ten to life, no parole. He was too young to go to jail. He was too young to drive!

Murder . . . Murder . . .

Chad froze.

Murder . . . Murder . . .

It wasn't possible! The pond was at least a mile away. No way could the bullfrog have followed him home. But . . . but maybe it wasn't a frog. Maybe it was Marky's spirit. . . .

Murder . . . Murder . . .

233

Chad pulled the covers over his head.

Murder . . . Murder . . .

He buried his head under his pillow.

Murder . . . Murder . . .

He stuffed his fingers into his ears.

And waited.

The croaking finally stopped.

WHEN CHAD WOKE UP THE NEXT MORNING, HIS FINGERS were still in his ears, which had turned bloodred, and his hands were cramped, as though he had been using them to dig.

Memories of the previous night exploded in his brain. Or was it just a nightmare?

Of course. He loosened his tense muscles. That's all it was. A nightmare.

He stretched his fingers. Traces of dirt, like slivers of a muddy moon, were visible under his nails. Nightmares didn't leave dirt behind. His muscles tensed right back up. He ran to the bathroom and scrubbed his nails clean until his fingertips felt raw.

He dressed quickly, then he sat on the edge of his bed — nowhere to go. It was Saturday. Mom and Dad were probably downstairs eating waffles. Joey was either in the basement or outside already, digging for worms.

He looked out the window. Heavy, gray clouds dumped rain. Lightning licked the sky with forked tongues, and thunder applauded. So Joey was in the basement then, concocting awful-smelling potions, using up Mom's best shampoo and nail polish and Dad's aftershave and car wax till the stink sent one of them down there to investigate and punish. It was like this every Saturday.

But this wasn't every Saturday.

This one was different.

This Saturday he was a murderer.

The doorbell bonged. It sounded like church bells — funeral bells.

"Chad," his mother called up to him. "Lisa's here, dear. Come on down."

Lisa. Lisa Hornik.

His legs trembled. Could he suddenly get the flu like he used to when he hadn't studied for a spelling test?

He heard a weird choking sound. Then his mother said, "Oh, Lisa, I'm so sorry, sweetheart." Then more choking.

He sidled to the top of the stairs. It wasn't choking, it was sobbing. His mother pulled Lisa into her arms and hugged the shaking girl.

Lisa looked up and saw him. Slowly he came down the stairs.

"Oh," he said.

"Marky's missing," Lisa said before he had to ask. As if he didn't know.

"Oh," he said.

"Since last night," his mother added while Lisa sobbed. "He wandered out when no one was looking." She patted Lisa's back. "I'm sure he'll wander back, or the police will find him."

"I — I think he was snatched," Lisa got out between gasps of air.

Chad's mother gave her a squeeze, then let go. "I'll leave you two alone." She disappeared into the kitchen.

Lisa looked at Chad with red, swollen eyes. Puffy eyes. Bulging eyes. Frog eyes.

Chad blinked. No, no, no.

"I can't believe it," Lisa moaned, sinking into the couch, burying her face in her hands. Blond strands, wet and curly from the rain, fell across her cheeks like writhing worms.

"I —" Chad said. Then stopped. *I what? I killed Marky? I hit him with Dad's pride and joy? I buried him out by Hidden Pond? Yeah, right.*

"I know, I know," Lisa said, wiping her sleeve across her eyes and standing up. "I know you're sorry."

I'm sooo sorry.

"It's not your fault."

But it was.

"I just wanted to let you know, in case . . . in case you see him or something."

Something like buried him?

She reached out and hugged Chad, as though he were

the one who needed comforting. "I gotta go. Mom's freaking out. There's going to be a search party if you want to join."

"Uh," Chad said.

Lisa smiled through her tears. "Thanks." Then she was out the door into the storm.

Murder . . .

Chad whirled around, his heart in his throat. Joey grinned at him. But the bullfrog — where was the bullfrog?

Joey opened his mouth and burped again. It sounded just like the croak of a bullfrog.

Murder . . .

Chad stared, then he melted with relief. He laughed uneasily. "You're a disgusting little kid," he said to his brother.

Joey flashed a gap-toothed smile and tried to burp again, but he couldn't.

Chad ran upstairs and turned on his bedroom light to fight off the gloom. Maybe he should help Lisa's family hunt for Marky after all. He could lead them away from the grave and away from the scene of the crime.

He pulled on some heavy socks, and he was just about to pull on his rubber boots, when his father knocked on the open bedroom door.

Chad looked up, his heart catching, skipping a beat, then starting again, faster than before. "Hi, Dad."

His dad frowned. "Son, do you know anything about a dent in the Trans Am?"

Chad tried to swallow the sudden frog in his throat. He couldn't speak, so he shook his head instead.

His father frowned harder. "Very odd," he said. "Are you sure?"

Chad nodded.

His father walked off down the hall, calling to Chad's mom.

Chad collapsed onto his bed.

Murder . . . Murder . . .

He looked around. Joey? It had to be Joey burping again.

Murder . . . Murder . . .

He twisted on his bed, looking around for his little brother, who must have slipped into the room.

Murder . . . Murder . . .

Chad froze. Lightning flashed. The bullfrog sitting on his desk flicked out its tongue. *Murder*, it croaked, staring at Chad, unblinking. *Murder . . .*

Chad rolled off his bed and fell to the floor on all fours, like a dog. "It was an accident!" he shouted at the frog.

Murder . . .

"I didn't mean to kill Marky."

His voice was drowned out by the thunder. The storm had stalled right above the house.

The lights flickered, then went out. Rain beat against the windows. Lightning flashed. Thunder bashed.

The lights flicked back on. The bullfrog was gone.

Chad collapsed on the floor and sobbed into a pile of dirty socks. Pretty soon the stink got too much for him and he sat up. In the kitchen, he heard the phone ring. Maybe it was the police. Maybe they'd found Marky's body with a single strand of Chad's hair. They'd DNA-tested it, and it was a perfect match. They were calling to let his parents know that they were on their way to take him to prison for the rest of his life.

But it was only an accident, he wailed silently.

"You shouldn't have taken the car out," said the imaginary judge, who looked way too much like his father.

I didn't mean to kill Marky.

"What a disappointment," said one of the jurors, who looked like his mother.

I'm sorry.

"Murder," croaked another juror, who looked like Joey. "Murder!"

He couldn't bear it. He pulled himself to his feet and stumbled downstairs, knees weak, palms sweaty. His parents were in the kitchen.

"Mom, Dad," he said. "About the Trans Am —"

"That was the police who just called," his father interrupted.

"Ohhhh," Chad groaned, sagging onto one of the chairs.

"Are you all right?" his mother asked, pressing a cool palm against his forehead.

Chad shook his head.

His father cleared his throat. "They told me that a man called to admit that he had accidentally backed into my car at the drug store yesterday. I guess his guilt got to him."

"What?"

"So that explains the dent," his father finished.

"But —" Chad said. *But what? But I took your pride and joy out for a spin so I could brag to my friends? But I accidentally killed Marky, and that's why there's a dent? But don't worry, I buried the body?* "Oh," he said.

His mother smiled. "What was it you wanted to tell us, dear?"

The doorbell rang for the second time that morning. *Bong, bong, bong.*

"I'll get it," Joey shouted, his feet pounding over to the door.

"It's about Marky," Chad said to his parents. He took a deep breath. Telling the truth wasn't easy. Especially when it was about mur —

Two wet paws suddenly pressed against his arm and a slobbering tongue licked his cheek.

Chad turned. "Ahhh!" he shouted, terror freezing his limbs. "Ahhh!"

Lisa Hornik hurried forward. "Down, boy," she commanded. The dog dropped to all fours.

Chad stared at the beast in horror. Back from the grave. Risen from the dead. He expected to see worms and maggots crawling through the animal's flesh, but instead, the dog sat on his haunches, his nose black and wet, his tongue red and drooling. He looked absolutely healthy and completely alive.

Lisa chirped on happily as though she didn't notice Chad's pale face and his open mouth. "Marky came home!" She bent down and gave the dog a hug. "He was all muddy and he has a bump on his head and a little bit of a limp, but other than that he's doing fine."

Just then Joey bounced into the kitchen.

"Did you find Freddy?" his mother asked.

Joey grinned. "Yup." He held up his hands.

"Ahhhhhhh!" Chad screamed again, nearly tipping over backwards in his chair.

Bulging eyes stared out from in between Joey's clasped fingers. Then the bullfrog puffed up its throat like a yellow balloon.

Stupid, it croaked.

UNEXPECTED

Author's Note

I love *The Twilight Zone* shows where there was usually a great twist at the end of the story. I also love those old gothic mysteries where everything is doom and gloom and there's usually a storm raging. When I decided to write this story, I remembered the famous tale by Edgar Allan Poe called "The Telltale Heart," and I wanted to put a modern spin on it. After adding a bunch of frogs, a storm, and a twist at the end, *voilà* — I ended up with "The Telltale Croak." Remember, now, before you do something wrong: Those guilty consciences never leave you alone. *Ribbet!*

LAURA E. WILLIAMS has written or contributed to over thirty published books. She loves writing everything from picture books to middle-grade and young-adult novels. Her bestselling children's novel, *Behind the Bedroom Wall*, won the Jane Addams Honor Book Award, and her picture book, *The Long Silk Strand*, was highlighted on *Reading Rainbow*. She currently lives in Connecticut, where unexpected things happen to her all the time.

Dear, Dear Kitty

∞∞∞

Marion Dane Bauer

JEREMY NOTICED THE GHOST THE FIRST DAY HE AND HIS FAMily moved into the new house. Well, that's what he called it, anyway — the forbidding cold that seemed to hover at the turn in the stairs halfway up to the second floor — a ghost. But, of course, Jeremy was a rational, twenty-first-century kid. He didn't believe in ghosts, really. He told himself, in fact, that what he felt was an odd pocket of stagnant air due to faulty circulation. Even in a brand-new house such as this one, plopped down on the Minnesota prairie as part of an instant village where there was never anything before, there were going to be mistakes. Especially about air circulation. Air circulation, his father said, was a science that seemed to be a mystery to most builders. The thought of a ghost appealed to Jeremy, though. He even tried to scare his little sister with the idea.

Only she didn't scare. She was four years old, probably too little to get the concept. Or if she did get it, she thought of friendly Casper in the cartoons, not of a real ghost.

In fact, when he told her — "Did you know, Lilly, there's a ghost on our stairs? It hangs around in the corner of the landing" — she only nodded absently and said, "Yeah, I know. She cries all the time."

"She?" Jeremy held back a smile. He often had to work at holding back smiles with Lilly. She was that kind of kid. Very serious about herself. Insulted if you thought she was being funny when she didn't mean to be.

"Yeah," Lilly said. "It's a girl. Dressed kind of funny. She's wearing a long dress and a . . . what do you call it? Like a blanket thing around her shoulders."

"A shawl?" he suggested.

"Uh-huh," she said. "And she's crying. All the time she cries."

Jeremy decided to let the matter drop.

THEY WERE HUNGRY, SO HUNGRY. SARAH HAD TAKEN APART the keg that had once held flour and sat in the meager warmth of the iron stove, licking and sucking the last traces of flour from the wood. Mr. Lincoln, her black-and-white tom, almost as gaunt as his namesake had been, lay curled in her lap.

A pot of snow melted on the stove. Papa had put it there, though Sarah couldn't imagine what he was going to find to put into it. The potatoes were gone, the carrots and turnips, too. And there wasn't a grain of wheat left to grind into flour in the coffee mill. They had eaten even the precious seed Papa had been holding back for springtime planting.

"It won't do any good to save this for planting if we don't live to see the spring," Papa had said.

The idea had made sense at the time, though now spring — if it ever came — loomed before them, appearing even emptier than winter had been. Nothing to eat. Nothing, even, to plant.

The pot was beginning to boil.

"Sarah," Papa said. And she looked up to see that he was standing in front of her holding a knife, the one he had used long ago to slaughter Gert, their only hog. That was when they had been so rich as to have a hog.

At first she didn't comprehend. Couldn't comprehend. What could Papa possibly want with a knife? And what did he expect to put into the boiling pot, anyway?

Then she saw where his gaze had fallen, onto the black-and-white cat curled in her lap, and she knew.

"No!" she screamed. She sat straight up in bed, jerked awake by her own fierce cry. She clutched the bedclothes to her breast as if they were the cat she must save from Papa's knife, though Mr. Lincoln, she knew immediately by the pressure against her feet, slept unmolested at the foot of her bed.

"What is it, child?" It was her father's voice, reaching her from the other side of the dark soddy. "Is something wrong?"

"Nothing, Papa," she said, her voice trembling. "It was a dream. Only a bad dream."

And she knew she was right. It had been a dream.

Papa and the knife and the boiling pot and her cat could come together so terribly only in a dream. Even so, before she lay down again, Sarah lifted Mr. Lincoln and tucked him away with great care beneath the covers and out of sight.

"WHAT ARE WE GOING TO DO, PAPA?" SARAH STOOD STARING out of the south window of the soddy, the only one that wasn't barricaded with snow. She had been standing there for a long time, though there was little to see beyond the small window set deep in the sod wall. This was late March, and winter should be losing its grip. The ice had even gone out of the Buffalo River, which ran nearby. Nonetheless, for the past three days a blizzard had howled, driving snow across the plains with unrelenting winds. Now, though the winds had quieted and the sun blazed in a vivid blue sky, nothing was visible except an endless expanse of glittering white.

She turned from the window, picked up the cat that had been twining around her ankles, and said it again. "What are we going to do? We have no more flour. No more anything."

Papa smiled, though his smile did nothing to erase the worry lines that had settled in the past two years — the Minnesota years — around his eyes and mouth. "Don't worry, daughter," he said. "We will soon find something to eat."

Something! As though it were only a matter of looking hard enough and food would fall into their laps!

Sarah ached to say it: *Don't you think it's time, Papa? Time to give up and go back to Illinois?*

Time to go back to a two-story clapboard house on a shady street instead of this dirt hovel squatting beneath an endless bowl of sky. Back to stores that sold ready-made dresses and bright-colored ribbons and bread and meat and apples and penny candies and every other thing a person could dream of. Back to school and her friends. To Mama's grave. Mama's and the baby's.

Sarah studied Papa's face, but he looked so sad, she couldn't say any of it. He looked almost as sad as he had when Mama and the baby had died. They had traveled here to Minnesota to escape that sadness, but it had caught up with him — caught up with them both — even here.

She looked down at Mr. Lincoln, draped in her arms, and stroked him until he began to purr — a rough motor that started in small bursts, then stopped, then started again. Even he was a reminder of sadness. Perhaps Mama would have chosen a different name for the scrap of a black-and-white kitten that had appeared at their door if she had known the president would be killed. She had named him for the black fur that covered his chin and edged his white face, making him look as though he wore a beard and dark hair. Perhaps she had named him for the look in his amber eyes as well, a look that seemed both melancholy and wise.

"I can sell Nelly and the wagon," Sarah's father was saying, his voice too cheerful, too loud. "That will get us more food . . . and seed for planting, too. This is the best wheat country in the world, daughter. All we need is one good harvest, and we'll be set."

"How will you plant without a mule?" she asked, squeezing Mr. Lincoln until he chirped a protesting mew and leapt down from her arms. What she really wanted to ask was, *How will we go back to Illinois without Nelly and the wagon?*

But Papa was already pulling his coat down from the peg by the door. He answered neither the spoken question nor the one she dared not give voice. "The Christophersons will be glad for another mule. I know they will," he said. "And they probably have seed to spare. Potatoes and cornmeal, too, I'll warrant. Maybe even some dried apples. We have come too far to give up now."

But Sarah had never thought of going home as giving up. She had always thought of it as more of a reward, like the medals the teacher used to give out at the end of the year for lessons done well. From the day she and her father had crossed the Mississippi and headed north and west, rumbling along in that creaking wagon behind Nelly, she had regarded this journey as temporary. First they would go, then they would come back.

Mr. Lincoln twined between her father's ankles, mewing insistently, the tip of his tail curved into a question mark.

"What does *he* want?" Papa pushed the cat away with a booted foot.

"Same as us, I suppose. He wants food."

Unrelenting, Mr. Lincoln returned to rub once more against Papa's legs, and he pushed the cat away again, a bit more roughly this time. "How foolish it is," he grumbled, "to feed a cat when we can barely feed ourselves!"

Sarah hurried to scoop her pet up and away. "He's kept us free of mice all this time," she said, burying her face in the soft fur. "Truth be told, he's been such a good mouser, they have quit coming in to be caught!"

"Truth be told," her father grumbled, but then he said no more. He pulled on his wool hat, wrapped a scarf around his neck.

"I'm going to ride Nelly to the Christophersons'," Papa said. "I won't be long."

"Yes, Papa," Sarah answered, her voice muffled by the bundle of black-and-white fur. But then she lifted her face to speak more clearly. "Papa?"

"Yes." He paused, one hand on the door latch.

"The Christophersons have a large family. They may need all the provisions they have. What if they care not to trade either food or seed for a mule?"

For a long moment her father stared at her as though he had forgotten who she might be and what matter they were discussing. At last his gaze fell from her face to Mr. Lincoln, encircled by her arms. "If they care not to sell," he replied, speaking as though to the cat, "then we must have faith. God will provide."

What will He provide? Sarah wanted to ask, her dream of the past night suddenly flooding through her veins. But she only clutched her cat harder.

Her father opened the door to a rush of wind that brought sharp cold and a sudden swirl of snow into the room. "Have a pot boiling," he said. "I must walk back, but I'll be home by evening." And he left.

Have a pot boiling! Sarah shivered and squeezed Mr. Lincoln until he began, once more, to protest.

The day dragged by, and the always-dim light in the soddy grew even dimmer. Sarah busied herself with the quilt she was making, assembled except for the final quilting. Although she sat as close as possible to the stove, her fingers soon grew cold and stiff and her stitches began to be crooked and too large.

It was Mama's fault, really. She should have stayed around longer to teach her daughter how to quilt properly, to teach her all the womanly arts. The first time Sarah had tried to make bread here in the soddy — the first several times, really — had been a waste of good flour. Who would believe that a person had to knead the dough steadily for an hour or more for it to rise properly?

Mr. Lincoln didn't help with the progress of the quilt,

either. He kept jumping into her lap, bumping the hand that held the needle.

Sarah looked over at the pot of snow-melted water simmering on top of the stove. What would Papa bring home to fill the pot? And the more urgent question: If the Christophersons had no use for another mule or had no spare seed and food to trade for one, would God, indeed, provide?

At once Sarah rose from her stool and sought out the butcher knife in the cupboard. After searching the small, open house for a place to hide it away, she finally dropped the cruel instrument unceremoniously between the cupboard and the sod wall.

"There," she told Mr. Lincoln. "He will never look there." The cat's sad amber eyes gazed into hers, and he mewed as though to tell her she had done the right thing.

But the pot still steamed on the stove.

There had been a great pile of buffalo chips by the stove when Papa had left, but they burned hotly and quickly. Sarah had to put on her shawl and go out several times along the side of the soddy to bring in more chips. The snow, even where it hadn't drifted, reached to her knees.

Each time she went out, she stopped at the corner of the house and put up a hand to shade her eyes so she could study the vast, white prairie that stretched towards the Christophersons' homestead. It didn't matter how long she stood there looking, though; no dark figure made its way back toward her, carrying food. The wind, which had grown still during the night, had started up new again, and soon she could no longer make out Nelly's prints, leading away from the soddy. Papa hadn't taken the wagon. He would have to wait until snowmelt for that, probably for the spring mud to dry up, too.

And then, at last, on her fourth trip out for chips — or was it her fifth? — she saw him. At first she hesitated to admit that the dark spot moving towards her could be her returning father, because the figure she could make out — just barely because the wind had now grown more fierce, flinging about so much snow that she could hardly see anything at all — was clearly riding.

Papa was returning on Nelly, the trade refused!

Sarah stumbled back inside the soddy without bothering to pick up chips, pulled the door closed, and leaned against it. Papa was coming back without food! Now they would have no choice but to make do with what God provided!

Her gaze fell on the simmering pot, then on Mr. Lincoln stretched out on the floor, half under the stove.

"No," she said to the dusky room.

She ran to the startled cat, who stiffened his legs at being snatched up so abruptly and pressed sharp claws into her arm. She ignored the claws, looking wildly around the small soddy. But a cat was much more difficult to hide than a knife — especially in a small, open room.

So Sarah turned to the only place possible, the only place she could think of where there was space to hide anything at all.

"Dear Mr. Lincoln," she said, and pushed out the door again, her cat held tightly against her body, beneath her shawl.

"Dear, dear kitty," she said again, and, stumbling through the growing drifts, pushing against the ever-increasing wind, she headed onto the open prairie.

MARTIN BENT INTO THE WIND, WHICH HAD BEEN GROWING more fierce all afternoon. The temperature had been growing colder, too. But the worst was the wind. It picked up the new-fallen snow and drove it ferociously, throwing it at him like millions of icy knives. One kind of blizzard followed by another. This one called a ground blizzard.

How kind Christopherson was to give the food without taking the mule, to tell him to keep Nelly and, knowing that a man had his pride, that he could work off the food — even the wheat, enough for bread and for seed, too — by helping clear sod for more acreage on the Christopherson homestead come spring. And spring wasn't far away. This blizzard might be fierce, but it would, most likely, be the last they saw of snow until another winter.

He readjusted the bulky bag slung behind him over the beast's rump and gave Nelly her head. She was a good mule. She would find her own way home.

If only there were a bit of meat, too. Not that he would have asked for meat — certainly not. But Sarah had grown pale in the time they had been in Minnesota. Her face used to be so pretty and round, and now it was thin, even drawn. He would have liked to have been able to offer her the extra strength only meat could give.

He hoped she hadn't exerted herself too much while he was gone, that she had stayed inside beside the stove, that the chips he had piled there had been enough to last through the day so she had no need to venture out for more. At least the extra supply was in a lean-to, right up against the wall. If she did have to leave the warmth of the soddy for chips, there was no danger of her moving away from the wall and getting lost in this whiteout.

No danger at all.

IT WAS THREE DAYS BEFORE MARTIN FINALLY FOUND HIS daughter. Three days of hopeless misery. He had arrived home to a cooling stove, a pot of lukewarm water, and no sign of Sarah. No sign, even, of the cat.

When he and Nelly came across her at last, curled into a ball in a slight depression in the land, the snow had finally melted enough to reveal her small shape. He sat for a long time, his arms and legs hanging limp, gazing at the frozen figure. She lay on her side, her shawl covering her head and shoulders, clutching that blasted cat.

What could have prompted her to leave the soddy? And why, in heaven's name, had she taken the cat with her?

Finally, he got off the mule and lifted Sarah awkwardly — how could a girl near thirteen years old be so light? — and carried her back to the soddy. When he got there, he wrapped her in the quilt she had been working on and laid her on her bed. Then he pried the frozen cat out of her equally frozen grasp.

The last thing he was going to do was bury her with the cat in her arms the way her mother had been buried with her newborn son.

He carried the stiff bundle of black-and-white fur to the door, then hesitated there, at the door that opened into sunshine and the first signs of warmth. It might have been a rabbit he held in his hands, though the sad-looking creature hadn't much meat left on him. Martin couldn't help but note, though, that what was there had been perfectly preserved by the cold. He turned the carcass over and then over again, considering. A man was grateful enough for potatoes and wheat, but a bit of meat was always a blessing. After all, how much different would this creature be from rabbit in the eating?

But then something — some prick of conscience, perhaps — drew him to glance back at the quilt-bundled figure on the bed, and he turned again to the door. This time he stepped through it and carried Mr. Lincoln across the distance to the riverbank. The ground was still frozen, and he wasn't going to leave the remains where he might stumble upon them later and be reminded, once more, of his daughter.

Despite the recent spate of cold, the river was open, the water roiling and muddy. He dropped the thing in. Instantly the muddy water reached up to clutch the frozen carcass, pulling it down and out of sight. Then the black-and-white corpse emerged again, popping to the surface like a floating log, and the current carried it away.

Let the river take the thing where it will — first to the Red River, then farther north into Canada. That was entirely enough ceremony for a cat.

Martin turned away. There was little left for him to do now but to bury his only daughter.

As much as Jeremy tried to put the idea of a ghost out of his head, he couldn't help but notice the way their cat, Abe, reacted strangely to the corner of the landing, too.

Abe was a silly name for a cat, he knew. It was their

mother who had named the critter, before Jeremy had even been born. She had always loved American history, and she said that when the tiny kitten with sad amber eyes showed up on their doorstep, somehow she could see the long-ago President's face in his. Maybe it was the way his black fur seemed to form hair and a beard at the edges of his white face.

Abe was old and crotchety now. About the only one he got along with these days was Lilly, and no one knew why he put up with her. She hauled him around like a sack of potatoes, even putting doll clothes on him sometimes. He'd lay his ears back and scowl ferociously when she dressed him, but he wouldn't do anything to stop her, just crouch there, waiting for her to take the stuff off again. Jeremy had agreed to help dress Abe once. He'd only been trying to button the polka-dotted playsuit Lilly already had put on the cat, and Abe had left red tracks the length of Jeremy's arm. Go figure!

Anyway, ever since they'd moved to the new house, the cat had been acting strangely. He would pace at the bottom of the stairs — or at the top, depending on which side of the stairs he was caught away from Lilly — and wail. He wouldn't set one paw on the steps to go up or down, and when Lilly carried him with her in either direction, he spat and hissed at the corner of the landing as they passed.

"Hush, Abe," Lilly would say, smoothing down his bristling fur. "She's just sad. She won't hurt you."

Jeremy considered mentioning the strange behavior — both Abe's and Lilly's — to his parents, but then he thought better of it. This hadn't been a particularly happy move.

Dad had promised Mom that they would stay in Minneapolis. "Forever," he had said. "We'll never have to move again." And Mom had been foolish enough to believe him. But when his company decided that they needed him, just for two or three years, to manage this plant they'd built out in the sticks — heck, there weren't even sticks in this place, just flat-as-a-cracker prairie — what could he say? Mom, however, had said plenty and was saying it still.

So Jeremy didn't tell his parents about "her," as he had come to think of the sudden pocket of cold air in the corner of the landing. He only watched and waited. But while he was watching and waiting, he found himself walking on the banister side of the stairs, as far from the cold corner as he could get. Curiously enough, he noticed that his parents did the same. He wondered if they had any idea what they were avoiding, treading on the narrowest part of the stairs. Only Lilly walked right up the middle, and when she did, she often stopped, cocked her head to one side as though she were listening, then spoke a few quiet words before continuing on her way.

"She wants Abe," she told Jeremy once, with her usual serious air. "I told her she can't have him."

"Why can't she?" Jeremy asked, hoping to discover more by continuing the conversation, however meaninglessly.

"Because he's afraid of her. He won't go with her, 'cause he's scared."

The idea of fierce, old Abe being scared of anything was enough to bring on an undisguised smile. Still curious, Jeremy said, "Would you let her have him if he got over being scared?"

Lilly thought about that. "If he wanted to go, I'd let her have him. She needs him real bad. And Abe is getting kind of tired."

"Tired of what?" Jeremy asked.

But Lilly only shrugged. "Just tired," she said.

Once Jeremy asked Lilly why the ghost always stayed in that one place, halfway up the stairs.

"It's where she was buried," Lilly said, in her flat, matter-of-fact way.

"There?" Jeremy asked, envisioning a corpse floating in the air. But then he remembered how they had flattened this land to make room for the houses, as though the natural undulating ripple of the prairie was a defect to be bulldozed away. It was possible, he reminded himself, that a grave could have been dug in ground that had been somewhat higher than where their house now stood.

Not, of course, that he believed in Lilly's ghost.

Jeremy had read about little kids like Lilly having

imaginary playmates, but something about her "ghost" made him uneasy. He told Mom she ought to get Lilly into some kind of preschool program right away so she could bum around with some kids her own age.

After a time, Jeremy mostly forgot about the pocket of cold air in the corner of the landing. Lilly never talked about *her* unless he asked, and as soon as he started at the new school, he was much too busy to think about such silliness. He'd gone out for football, and some of the guys on the team were pretty darned good. He had to work hard if he was going to make the first string. Besides, what seventh grader wants to get caught believing in ghosts?

And it was no trouble, really, staying to the outside of the stairs.

THE FIRST TIME JEREMY SAW ABE STRETCHED OUT IN THE corner of the landing, a small, self-satisfied smile curling beneath his whiskers, Jeremy stopped in astonishment.

"Well, fella," he said. He reached to rub the old cat's head, but his hand encountered — well, *seemed* to encounter; there was certainly nothing to be seen — a wall of sudden cold, and he jerked it back and rubbed it on his jeans instead.

"They're friends now," Lilly said solemnly from the top of the stairs. "She's not crying anymore."

"Who?" Jeremy asked, almost impatient. "Who's not crying?"

"Sarah," Lilly answered, as though the name *Sarah* would tell him anything. "Her name is Sarah. She wants him to go with her, but she can't pick him up. He's too heavy."

"Oh," Jeremy said, rather stupidly, he noted to himself, and he hurried up the stairs to his room. Basketball was under way now, and he had almost forgotten his uniform.

JEREMY WAS STOMPING UP THE WALK THROUGH THE FRESH snow — everyone said it always snowed during the high school basketball tournaments in Minnesota — when he discovered the footprints. Small. Precise. They marched across the porch, down the steps, and across the front yard at a distinct but determined angle.

Abe! What was he doing outside? It was entirely unlike the old cat to be out in the snow by his own choice. He might mew at the door, but the moment he discovered the bad weather on the other side, he accordion-pleated himself inside his skin and turned back to the warmth of the house. Or to that place on the stairs — as cold as the air always seemed to be there — where he spent more and more of his time these days.

Who could have lured him out into the storm?

There wasn't a single footprint to be seen except those of the cat.

And it was entirely too cold out here for a cat, especially one accustomed to warm registers and blankets and every comfort of a house. Besides, Lilly would be plenty upset if anything happened to the old bag of bones. Jeremy figured he'd better find him.

He followed the small indentations in the snow that led in an unwavering line away from the house.

Jeremy hadn't gone far before he came upon the cat — Abe, curled up right there in the snow, one paw and his black-and-white tail curved over his nose as though that alone would be sufficient to keep him warm.

"There you are, cat!" he said. "Aren't you cold?"

The temperature had been below zero for hours, not to mention the fierce winds, the kind that robbed heat from living flesh. Jeremy bent quickly to scoop Abe up, but the instant he touched the black-and-white fur, he knew. Abe was more than cold. He was dead.

"DEAR KITTY," LILLY SAID, RUNNING HER HAND ONCE MORE over the plush fur to brush away the last of the snow. "Dear, dear kitty."

Clearly she didn't understand. "Lilly," Jeremy said, speaking slowly and carefully, "I'm real sorry, but Abe is . . ." He couldn't say the word. Not to a just-barely five-year-old. "He's . . . gone. Can't you see?"

"I know," Lilly replied, lifting her small pointed chin

to gaze solemnly into Jeremy's face. "Abe is dead." And then, apparently, wanting to console her big brother, she added, "But it's okay. Really. Sarah needed him a whole lot more than we do."

"Who is Sarah?" Jeremy demanded, filled with sudden frustration. It was time — far past time — to put an end to this.

"She's the girl who was crying," Lilly replied, speaking in the same slow, careful way Jeremy had used with her, as though he might not be quite bright. "Only she's not crying now." Then she picked up Abe, just lifted him casually and cradled him in her arms as though she were accustomed to toting around dead cats, and added, "I'll tell Mommy we need to have a funeral . . . like we did when I found the dead bird. Do you want to come, too?"

"No." Jeremy said it quickly, almost before he had a chance to decide whether he wanted to attend Abe's "funeral" or not. Even as he spoke, though, he was heading for the stairs.

He had reached the top before he paused and looked back down, staring at the landing. Had it really happened? Had he walked right through the middle of the landing without feeling even a trace of that heavy cold?

He shrugged and turned away. He was, after all, a rational twenty-first-century kid.

He certainly didn't believe in ghosts.

UNEXPECTED

Author's Note

When I was doing research for my Dear America novel, *Land of the Buffalo Bones*, I found myself fascinated by the hardships endured by those people who settled — or tried to settle — the Great Plains in the mid-1800s: blizzards, hailstorms, tornadoes, drought, prairie fires, plagues of grasshoppers. And hunger. True hunger.

What would it be like, I kept wondering, to wake up in the morning knowing that there was no food to be had anywhere? The thought wouldn't leave me. You might even say it haunted me. I put it to rest — finally, I hope — in this story.

MARION DANE BAUER is the author of over forty books for young people, ranging from picture books and early readers to nonfiction books on writing and novels. Her work has received many awards, including an American Library Association Newbery Honor for her novel, *On My Honor*. She was the first Faculty Chair and continues on the faculty of the Master of Fine Arts in Writing for Children and Young Adults program at Vermont College. She lives in Eden Prairie, Minnesota.

Sleuth 2500

◌◌◌◌

Dian Curtis Regan

"Heads up, son! Mattress coming."

I stop opening boxes to watch two men finagle a mattress through the doorway and plop it onto the box springs. Moving aside, I lean against a built-in desk beneath the window to admire my new room — pleased I don't have to share it with my brother, Troy, who stayed behind in Denver to start college.

Leaning over the desk, I peer out the window. It's a three-story drop to the patio of the walk-out basement. The house was built in the '70s, so we've taken to calling it our "new, old home."

The men leave. I continue unpacking, eager to finish so I can explore my neighborhood here in Wichita during the final week of summer vacation.

I unearth old CDs. Grabbing a chair, I climb up to put them on the top shelf of the closet. *Hey, someone's left papers up here*, I notice. Hopping off the chair, I smooth them out on the desk. Looks like homework: *Phillip Hutte, grade 6*.

"We're the same age," I mumble, then spot the date: *March 12, 1975*. "Whoa, we're not the same age at all. Today, he'd be . . . thirty years older — plus twelve. Forty-two. Same as Dad."

"What about me?"

My father, wearing his faded Colorado tee and a tool belt, is wandering the house, looking for things to repair — much to my mother's dismay.

"Hey, Dad, look what I found."

He chuckles over the date. "Ah, 1975. Sixth grade with Mrs. Conover. I'll bet she never forgot *me*." Dad hands the paper back with a cryptic wink. "Come downstairs. I need help tightening the banister."

After the deed is done (and has passed Mom's worried scrutiny), I head back to my room. Sitting on top of the desk, gazing out the window is . . . a *girl*?

"Who are you?" I ask.

Startled, she hops off the desk and acts confused. "Hi. I'm, um, Blasey."

She's dressed weirdly — in a celery-colored, gauzy one-piece thing that flutters around her ankles. Lots of beads. I'm guessing we're about the same age — only she's taller. I hate it when girls are taller.

"Blasey?" I repeat. *Odd name*. "I'm Kit Gallagher. How'd you get in?"

She shrugs. "Back door?"

"We don't have a back door." Then I realize she could mean the patio door. "What are you doing in my room?"

"The house was *supposed* to be empty," she explains, glancing at something in her hand. I can't tell if it's a cell phone or a video game.

"Is that a — ?"

"No!" She shoves it into a pocket. "It's just my, um, Palm planner."

"Oh." I'm still confused. "So what do you want?"

"I was checking out the scene of the crime."

Chills flitter across my shoulders. "A crime was committed in my room?"

"I should probably leave," she says, sidestepping around me and heading towards the door.

"Wait. Tell me. What happened?"

Pausing, she glances at her watch, then cocks her head as if listening to something I can't hear. "I'll do what I want," she snaps — obviously not to me.

Glancing my way, she says, "A boy fell to his death from your window. Years ago. They say it was an accident, but *I* think he was pushed."

"Wow. How do you know?"

"It was in the . . . um, newspapers. He was only twelve," Blasey adds. "And his name was Phillip Hutte."

IT'S MIDNIGHT BEFORE I UNPACK THE REST OF THE BOXES and help Mom put sheets on the bed. We can't find my comforter, but it's not necessary on this hot August night.

Mom met Blasey when I walked her outside; however, I spared Mom the worry of a possible murder in our new, old home on Parkwood Lane.

Moonlight spills across my bed from the window —

that window. I cannot stop thinking about Phillip and whoever pushed him thirty years ago. And . . . why?

I cannot stop thinking about Blasey, either. How'd she get up to my room without anyone seeing her? And why would she care about a crime that happened thirty years ago?

She kept tapping keys and speaking into a tiny microphone on her Palm planner. She wouldn't let me see it up close. Very weird.

Finally, I sleep. My dreams are filled with falling — *me* falling, then waking in a panic before I hit the ground.

Poor Phillip Hutte. For him, it wasn't a dream.

THE NEXT MORNING, I SPEND A LOT OF TIME LOOKING OUT my window and thinking about what happened. Something in the yard catches my eye. It's Blasey, leaning against the trunk of a cottonwood, talking into her planner.

I hurry outside. It's a million degrees — even in the shade of the cottonwood. Denver is hot in August, too, but not boiling like this. "You, again," I say.

"You weren't supposed to see me."

How can I miss? Her outfit is as flowery as the neighbor's garden. Frilly blouse and skirt. Headband grazing her eyebrows. "Still investigating the crime?" I ask.

"Yeah, well, it's sort of a . . . game."

"Game? Somebody falls to his death and you call it a

game? Gee, can I play?" I'm being sarcastic, of course, but she gives me an interested look.

"You want to? I mean, we're not supposed to . . ." Pausing, she drops her voice to a whisper. "I don't see why you can't help. Especially since you live at the scene of the crime."

I peel some loose bark off the tree trunk while considering my options. "I'll help under one condition."

She raises an eyebrow, causing the headband to slip.

"You explain *why* you're so interested in this crime, and who is listening to our conversation."

"Oh!" She acts surprised that I've figured it out. "My sister can hear, but only when I have the speaker on. She feeds me clues through the earpiece." Cocking her head, she yanks back her hair, but I don't see an earpiece. It must be tiny.

"Where is your sister?" I motion at the surrounding houses.

Blasey laughs. I was not trying to be funny. "My sister's in our room."

"Ah, you have to share a room? Too bad," I tease. "Is she older or younger?"

She ignores my teasing, giving me a bored grimace. "Everyone has to share. And we're the same age."

"Twins?" I ask, wondering what she means by "everyone has to share."

"Of course we're not twins." Frowning, she flaps her arm as if it's not important. "If you want to play the game, we have to locate the murderer and get him — or her — to confess."

"So, you're out to *solve* the crime? What then? Go to the police?"

"No! Once we figure it out, the game is over. We go home and pick another unsolved crime to play. It's fun."

"I don't get it. You don't tell anyone? You let the murderer go free?"

"That's how the game works."

"*What* game? How come I've never heard of it?"

Blasey hesitates, then takes the object from her pocket. "This isn't really a Palm planner; it's an ESD, or Electronic Sleuth Device."

I peer at it. SLEUTH 2500, I read. UNSOLVED CRIMES OF THE 20TH AND 21ST CENTURIES. The words glow, then fade as soon as I've read them.

"Very cool, but we're not far enough into the twenty-first century to have an overabundance of unsolved crimes."

"Oh, there are *lots* to choose from," she says. "We just figured out this really bizarre disappearance that happened in Nevada in 2085."

"Excuse me?"

She slaps a hand over her mouth. "I shouldn't have told you that."

"Very funny," I say, letting her know that *I* know she's

goofing on me. "Okay, I'll play your sleuth game. What do we do next?"

She yanks me around the tree, out of sight of the kitchen window. My mom is working on the cabinets. She's a shelf-paper maniac. Every surface must be covered with colored vinyl before we can unpack dishes.

Blasey keeps a firm grasp on my arm while punching lighted keys on the ESD.

"What are you doing?" I ask, trying to pull my arm away.

She freezes mid-punch. "Oh, wait, I'd better not do it this way." Squinting up into the cottonwood branches, she contemplates her next move. "Do you have bikes?"

"Sure. Mine and my brother's old one. Are we going somewhere?"

Grinning, she drops the ESD into her pocket. "Just follow me."

I STEER THE BIKES OUT OF THE GARAGE AND GIVE HER MINE. I ride Troy's.

Blasey blasts off to the corner, then heads down Woodlawn. I cannot imagine what she's doing, but then, I haven't been able to figure out anything she's done since I discovered her in my house.

Turning on 21st Street, she leads me down several long blocks, then stops in front of a police station, which surprises me. I hit the brakes and slide sideways, coming to a full stop. "I thought you said we wouldn't go to the police."

"We won't *tell* the police. Big difference."

"Then why are we here?"

"Because, according to my sister, who is reading game facts to me, this *may* be where we find the guy who pushed Phillip out the window."

WE PARK OUR BIKES AND GO INSIDE. I WATCH WHILE BLASEY inquires about Officer Rooney. When asked if we have an appointment, she mumbles something about a school assignment.

One minute later, we are sitting alone in a tiny office, messier than my brother's side of our former room. Blasey whispers into the ESD: "Papers scattered on the desk. Scent of cinnamon coming from a gadget plugged into an outlet. Pillow on the chair."

"Collecting clues?" I ask, wondering what all this has to do with Phillip. I answer my own question: "I know — rules of the game."

"My sleuth assistant is making fun of me," she pretends to complain into the microphone. (I know she's pretending because she doesn't want her sister to know about me. Rules.)

Officer Rooney arrives. He's a towering bear in a blue uniform. "Hello, kids. What's up?"

He looks about the same age as my father, which would be the same age as Phillip — had he lived.

"We'd like to interview you for our school paper," Blasey chirps, acting like Miss Efficiency with a notebook and a pen in her lap.

"Has school started?" he asks. "My kids haven't gone back yet."

"No, we're, um, just getting a jump on the first issue. Stories have to be in before school starts in order to print an issue the first week."

Oh, she's good, I think. *I'd* still be saying, "Uh, uh, uh . . ."

"So," Blasey begins. "You have kids?"

"Yes. Amy and Phillip."

Whoa. Blasey and I exchange quick glances.

"Were they named after, um, anyone special?"

"Oh, sure," he says. "Amy is named after her Grandmother Rooney, and Phillip . . . well, he's named after an old friend of mine."

"Died in the war?" Blasey asks.

Officer Rooney gives her a curious look. "I didn't say he died — but you're right. He died in an accident when he was twelve."

Blasey pretends to write this down, yet I know her ESD is recording it — and her sister is listening as well. I feel dumb for not participating. Shouldn't I be asking questions, too? "Are you from Kansas?" I offer.

Blasey shoots me an I'm-in-charge-here look. She probably doesn't want her sister to suspect she has a "sleuth assistant."

"Yes, from Wichita," the officer says.

"Tell us more about your friend," Blasey urges. "This Phillip . . . what did you say his last name was?"

Officer Rooney opens a tin and takes out a mint. "I didn't say his last name." Popping the mint into his mouth, he studies Blasey, then me. "I don't recognize you two. What school do you go to?"

"We're new to Wichita," she tells him. "Our family just moved here."

She nudges my foot. I assume she wants me to go along with the bit about "our family."

"Where do you live?" he asks, absently twirling a pencil.

Blasey stares at me in earnest. I realize she doesn't know the name of my street. She's waiting for me to answer. "On Parkwood," I say.

Officer Rooney drops the pencil. "Parkwood? The house . . . ? I mean, which house?"

"I think you *know* which house," Blasey says, challenging him with a dead-on stare.

He rises from his chair. "I think it's time for you to leave. This is not a school assignment; it's an interrogation." He strides out of his office so we can't ask further questions.

I'm both amazed and appalled by Blasey's boldness. I

cannot believe she hinted that *we* knew *he* knew what happened in the house on Parkwood.

We find ourselves outside on the hot sidewalk faster than you can say, "The plot thickens." I still have chill bumps from the air-conditioning, so it takes a minute to heat back to the melting point.

"Can we get a lemonade? There's a Spangles on the way back."

"Sure," Blasey says, then checks her watch. "Oh, wait, I gotta leave." Her head whips one way, then the other. "I gotta leave *now*."

"What's up?" I ask, bugged about the way she keeps me in a constant state of confusion.

"I'll be back tomorrow," she says in a rush. "Be ready to take off on the bikes at noon."

"But aren't you — ?"

"I *really* have to leave, Kit. See you tomorrow."

With that, she dashes *back* into the police station — which totally confuses me. Curious, I follow. The reception area is empty. Maybe she ducked into the restroom. I wait until a female officer comes out. "Excuse me, is there a girl in there?"

"No. Can I help you find someone?"

My dread of running into Officer Rooney is stronger than my desire to search for Blasey. "No, thanks."

I hurry outside, somehow knowing Blasey is long gone. But to where, I have no idea.

* * *

UNEXPECTED

WALKING TWO BIKES HOME IS AWKWARD. I PUT TROY'S AWAY, then ride to a nearby library. Inside, it's wonderfully cool. I research old newspapers until I find the article I'm looking for:

Boy Dies from Accidental Fall

I skim the article from April 1975, surprised at how moved I am over the demise of Phillip Hutte — especially when I see his picture. Longish dark hair. Plaid shirt. Looks a little like Troy. I have to remind myself that, had he lived, he'd be in his forties.

AT NOON THE NEXT DAY, I'M WAITING IN THE DRIVEWAY WITH both bikes. The gray sky is misting, so it's not as hot, but twice as muggy. Precisely at twelve, Blasey steps around the corner of the house.

"We're going to the library," she states without even saying, "Hello."

I remember the cool room I lingered in yesterday. "Fine, let's go."

We take off. I have a list of questions, but right now, I'm too curious to know what Blasey's next move will be. At the library, we lock our bikes and go inside. "I know where the reference department is," I tell her.

"Don't want reference. I want the children's department."

I blink, letting my eyes adjust to indoor light. "You want to look at books?"

She smirks as if she loves keeping me in the dark. "No, I want to look at the librarian."

I follow, noticing today's clothes: raggedy bell-bottoms and tie-dyed tee. This girl's got a weird sense of fashion.

We trudge to the children's books section. Tagging along behind Blasey is starting to annoy me. If she doesn't fill me in soon, I'll refuse to play her stupid game. But, for now, I'm hooked — for Phillip's sake.

We hunker down near the periodicals to watch a librarian at the checkout desk. She's younger than my parents, with reddish hair in a long braid. I have no idea why we are watching her.

"Okay," I begin. "Why are we here? What are we looking for? And while I'm at it, why did you have to leave yesterday, like Cinderella fleeing the ball? Why isn't your sister sleuthing with you instead of me? And where did you buy this stupid game?"

She's flipping through *Seventeen* magazine, snickering at the fashions — as if she, Miss Fashion-Impaired, has anything to snicker about. Sighing, she puts the magazine back in the rack.

"Okay, I was hoping we could do this without me saying too much — which is one of the rules. If they find out I've mingled with one of you, I won't be allowed to play anymore."

"Mingled with one of us? What are you — an alien?" Now it's my turn to snicker.

She doesn't laugh at my joke. "You have to promise you won't tell anybody."

I shrug.

"I mean it, Kit. You have to promise you won't tell a soul."

"I've lived in Kansas for three days. You're the only soul I know."

I could tell by her smirk she liked my answer.

"I'll fill you in later, but all I can tell you right now is that we're here because the librarian, Kate Rooney, is Officer Rooney's little sister. The clues for the game suggest she might have been in the room when the accident happened. I thought maybe we could ask her some questions."

"Then let's do it," I say, fully confident Blasey will do all the talking.

Before I can move, a hand grasps my shoulder. I look up at the bear in blue — Officer Rooney. His other hand is grasping Blasey's shoulder.

"I had a funny feeling you two might be dropping into the library."

Uh-oh. He knows why we're asking questions. We could be in big trouble. If he's covering up a crime and thinks we're on his trail, who knows what he might do?

Releasing my shoulder, the officer points at a poster

of a sleeping walrus. SHHHHHH, it says. "Let's go outside to talk."

The librarian notices us. Waving, she hurries over. "Hey, Will, what are you doing here? Arresting patrons for reading above their age level?" She laughs. Must be a librarian joke.

"Hi, Sis," he answers. "Just want to talk to these two. I'll visit with you later."

She cocks her head in curiosity, then returns to the desk.

The officer herds us out of the library. I'm embarrassed because people are staring — probably wondering if we're criminals. My heart is skittering in fear because I don't know how far Officer Rooney will go to protect his secret — if he *has* a secret. And we can't run to the police for safety because . . . well, he *is* the police.

Outside, we sit on a bench in a flower garden. "Want to tell me what this is all about?" he asks.

I glance at Blasey, waiting for her to speak for both of us. She's twirling her hair in a nervous sort of way. "I'll just come right out and say it," she begins.

Her voice is wavering. I can tell she's as scared as I am.

Blasey lifts her chin and meets his gaze. "You were in the room with Phillip minutes before he fell to his death."

A shadow glides across the officer's face. I glance

up. The mist has cleared and clouds are breaking, but somehow I think *this* shadow springs from an inner storm.

"What are you implying?"

Blasey takes her time answering. She probably hoped to win the game by hiding behind trees and taking notes, not by coming face-to-face with an alleged killer.

"Back in 1975, police decided Phillip's fall was an accident. But you were *there*. You know what really happened." Turning her eyes away, she adds, "And maybe you're hiding something."

"Why would I hide anything? Phillip was my best friend."

"Because . . . because . . ."

I hate the way the officer is leaning into Blasey's face, trying to intimidate her. I leap to her defense. "Because it might *not* have been an accident," I tell him. "You might be hiding the fact that Phillip fell because of *you*."

Now Officer Rooney is in *my* face. "All this was written up thirty years ago as an accidental death. Why are you sticking your nose where it doesn't belong? I don't have to prove anything."

"Did you do it?" Blasey blurts. "Did you push him?"

I hear a gasp and think it's the officer. Then I realize it's coming from behind. I whirl around. Kate is there. Her face is pale and both hands cover her mouth in shock.

"Sis, calm down. I didn't tell them anything." Officer Rooney turns on us. "Now look what you've done! How dare you upset my sister?"

"It's okay," she says, sniffling. "Why don't you just tell them the truth? It'd be a relief to get it out after all these years."

"So, it's true!" Blasey gushes. Her eyes spark as if she's figured out the mystery of the Loch Ness Monster.

"Well . . ." Kate begins, standing up tall and brushing tears from her cheeks.

Officer Rooney's hand trembles as he grasps her arm. "Stop. You don't have to tell these kids anything. Go back inside. I'll take care of them."

"It's fine, Will. We did nothing wrong."

"Yeah, right," Blasey says, gloating.

Suddenly I hate the gutsiness I had previously admired in Blasey. She's being mean. Before I can stop her, she barrels on. "Your brother made Phillip fall from the window."

"No, he didn't," Kate shoots back. "I did."

WE ARE SITTING BENEATH THE COTTONWOOD IN MY BACK-yard. Mom has provided lemonade and lemon bars. (She's on a lemon kick and has polished all the doors with lemon oil.) Mom asks Blasey the usual mother-questions: "Where do you live? Where do your parents work?" My strange friend's answers are as murky as a thirty-year-old crime.

After Mom gives up and goes inside, I say, "Congrat-ulations, Sleuth 2500. You've solved the mystery."

"But it wasn't murder, like I thought," Blasey reminds me. "Kate was only four years old. She was playing. Phillip was teasing her with a candy bar."

I try to picture how it happened. The way Kate ex-plained it. She chased Phillip, and he hopped onto the desk to get away. The window was open. He leaned against the screen. Big mistake. The screen popped out and he lost his balance.

"I wonder why they didn't tell the police at the time?" I ask, then remember Officer Rooney's adamancy about protecting his little sister. How he'd told everyone *he*, not Kate, had been the one chasing Phillip.

It reminds me of the time Troy told our grandfather *he'd* thrown the ball that broke the garage window when it really had been me. I never forgot that. Of course, af-terwards, Troy kept reminding me I owed him lots of favors. . . .

I remind Blasey that she promised to fill me in on the rest — why her sister never comes with her, why she suddenly fled yesterday, and where the heck she lives.

She stays quiet, giving me the evil eye.

"I promise not to tell," I groan. "We've been over this already."

Picking up the ESD, she clicks off a switch. "My sister won't like me telling you. Now she can't hear." She

"Before you go, tell me what life is like in 2512?"

She sips lemonade, thinking. "They don't have good stuff like this. I want another glass before I go." Sighing, she takes a third lemon bar. "Life in the future is . . . different. Sometimes, when I visit the past, I wish I'd lived then."

"So stay in 2005."

She looks longingly at the now blue sky and the green yard. "I can't. If you stay behind, you fade."

"Fade? You mean, literally?"

"Literally. Remember, I haven't been born yet. My body can exist in previous centuries, but not longer than a few hours at a time."

"Wow. Why would you want to play such a game?"

"It's fun. Everybody does it. And, since we can't go outside, it's a way to experience the outdoors."

"You can't go outside?"

"No. The entire world lives underground. The environment was pretty much wiped out by the end of the 23rd century, so this is how people survive."

"Sounds awful."

"It's the only life I've known — until they invented the sleuth game. So you see why I keep playing?"

I nod, realizing she's about to leave for the last time now that she's "won" the game, and I'll never see her again. "Can you at least show me how the ESD works?"

"Only if I can have more lemonade."

"Sure."

Handing the device to me, she says, "First, punch in the date you want to travel to. Then put in the present date and hit the key that glows purple. I preprogram all the return dates, so I end up at home in case anything goes wrong."

"How would they *know* if you went back to the year of the crime?"

"They wouldn't. We're on an honor system. Lots of things in my world run on the honor system." She glances again at her watch. "Oh, no! Gotta get more lemonade before it's too late."

I watch her hurry to the patio and go inside. Then I study the ESD, wondering what my house looked like in 1975. Will I ever have another chance to find out?

Blasey is talking with my mom. My heart is about to jump out of my chest. *Do it!* I tell myself.

No! I can't get Blasey into trouble, my conscience answers.

She said *no one would know. She's on the honor system.*

Yeah, but you're not supposed to. . . .

Before I can question myself any further, I punch in 4/12/75 and hit the purple-glowing key. At the same instant, I realize I forgot to program the return date.

I don't have time to worry about it because I'm whirling inside a pink tornado. (Yes, pink!) In seconds, I'm back in my yard, but everything looks different. The cottonwood isn't there. A forest borders the yard instead of homes.

I face the house. It's blue instead of gray. I slide the ESD into my pocket and walk on trembling legs to the patio door. I hear voices above through an open window. My bedroom window. Or rather, Phillip's.

I go inside to the kitchen. The refrigerator is a strange shade of green. Linoleum covers the floor instead of carpet. I am shaking in fear and anticipation, but continue up the stairs.

Three people are in my room. I recognize Phillip from the photo in the paper. The other boy must be Officer Rooney — Will. And the little girl must be Kate. She is sniffling and reaching for something Phillip is holding high above her head.

I cannot believe I'm here, watching a scene described to me thirty years in the future.

Kate chases Phillip toward the window. He hops onto the desk, squatting like he plans to leap off.

"HEY!" I holler, wondering if I'm invisible.

All three freeze and gape at me. They can see me!

"Who are *you*?" Phillip asks. Same thing I'd said to Blasey.

"Did you know that screen isn't locked in?" I say, acting as if I belong here.

Phillip gives me a *So what?* kind of look, then turns to inspect it. He glances back at me. "How'd you know?" Without waiting for an answer, he tosses the candy bar to Kate, then snaps the locks on the screen into place and lowers the window.

As he's doing this, I back down the hall, flabbergasted at what I've just done.

But I'm not stupid — I know I need to get out of here before they start asking questions. I duck into a room that is now my mom's home office, frantically yanking the ESD from my pocket. I hear Will shout, "Hey, where'd he go? Let's find him."

I punch the purple key. The last sounds I hear are footsteps pounding down the hall toward my hiding place.

This time, the tornado is deep red and lasts a lot longer. Before it ends, I realize why. I'm not returning to 2005, I'm traveling on to 2512. . . .

MY EYES GROW ACCUSTOMED TO DIM LIGHT. IS THIS BLASEY'S underground world? I'm standing in a room with bunk beds. Everything is made out of metal. There is no color — all is chrome. A girl is sitting at a desk. She looks up, startled.

"Blasey!" I exclaim. Now she's dressed in pants and a tunic made from a shimmery olive material. "Boy, am I glad to see you. Please don't be mad."

"I'm not Blasey. I'm her sister, BlaseyTwo. Who are you?"

"BlaseyTwo? Did they run out of names in the future?"

Ignoring my attempt at humor, she squints at me. "I have a bad feeling you're the boy my sister blabbed to."

I stare at her. Same face, same mannerisms as Blasey.

"You guys *have* to be twins," I say, remembering that Blasey said they were not.

"No, you idiot. We're birth clones."

Birth clones? And I'm supposed to know this?

BlaseyTwo is glaring at me. *Time to go, Kit,* I warn myself. Lifting the ESD, I tap in 8/25/2005.

"Give me that!" she yelps. "What have you done with my sister? This is against the rules!"

I hold out an arm to keep her from lunging at me. I cannot let her take the ESD from me. "Your sister is fine. She didn't break any rules. This is my fault, and I'm off to make it right. Don't be mad at her. She'll be home in a few minutes."

I hit the purple key and feel the tug that yanks me back inside the tornado — pink again. The ride is shorter this time. I desperately hope that when the whirling clears, I'll be sitting beneath the cottonwood with a very angry Blasey.

My wish comes true.

She snatches the ESD from my hand. "What have you done?"

"Stay calm," I tell her, loving the way the tables are turned and now *I'm* the one who knows what she does not. It's my turn to smirk. "I've gone ahead and smoothed the way. BlaseyTwo is waiting for you."

She gasps — then begins to laugh. "I can't believe you went to my world. I've been wanting to get back at my sister for making me stay too long in San Francisco in 1906. Right up to the start of the earthquake! I think we're even now."

I laugh with her. "So can you come back sometime? Just to talk?"

"Sorry, Kit. Once a case is solved, *no one* can return to this time."

I lift the plate of lemon bars. "Well, then, take a couple of these to remember me by."

"I don't think my sister will ever let me forget you."

Regardless, she takes *all* the lemon bars.

This time, I get to see her vanish into thin air just as she's saying, "Thank you."

"You're welcome," I tell the empty patch of grass. She'll never know how much I really *did* help. Helped Phillip, I mean.

I carry the empty plate inside.

"Where's Blasey?" Mom asks.

"She had to go home." I chuckle over my simplified explanation.

Opening the phone book, I hold my breath as I flip through the "H" pages until I find: *Hutte, Phillip. 321 Winterberry.*

I locate the street on an Internet map, then take off on my bike. Don't know what I expect to see when I ride slowly past the house. I don't expect Phillip himself to be sitting on the front steps — and he isn't.

But there *is* a toddler on a blanket on the lawn. The

mother is kneeling, picking weeds. I just *know* it's Phillip's child and that he lives here. At least I hope it is. Still, it would be nice to know for sure — which I never will.

Turning my bike around, I start home just as the mother stands and walks to the blanket to lift the toddler. "Hey, little Will," she coos. I look at her face. It's Kate from the library. Phillip's best friend's little sister. Now Mrs. Phillip Hutte?

I grin all the way home.

Author's Note

While moving into my own "new, old home" in Wichita, I began to find bits and pieces of the lives of people who had lived there before — stickers, game pieces, and even a tiny shoe on the top shelf of a closet.

I began to wonder about the six families who previously resided in my house. Who were they? What were their stories? Soon after, I found a five-dollar bill on which someone had scribbled: "In loving memory of Phillip."

A story idea was born: What if Kit found a cryptic clue, left behind by a boy his age? What if it led him to discover something awful had happened in his room? Something sad, scary, and mysterious?

What if . . . ?

DIAN CURTIS REGAN is the author of many books for young readers, including *Princess Nevermore* and the Monster of the Month Club quartet. Her stories appear in many anthologies, such as *Shattered*, *Dirty Laundry*, *Period Pieces*, and *First Crossing*. Originally from Colorado, Dian has also lived in Texas, Oklahoma, and Venezuela. At present, she lives in Kansas in a house mysteriously similar to the one in the story, complete with a built-in desk beneath the window in her office.

R.L. STINE
Goosebumps®

Hey, kid. Wanna read somethin' scary?

CAMP TELLYJAM

IT CAME FROM BENEATH THE SINK!

GHOST CAMP

ATTACK OF THE MUTANT

THE CUCKOO CLOCK OF DOOM

More than Forty Titles Available—Dare to Read Them All!

◪ SCHOLASTIC

GBT

As Night Falls, a Dark and Deadly Force Comes to Life

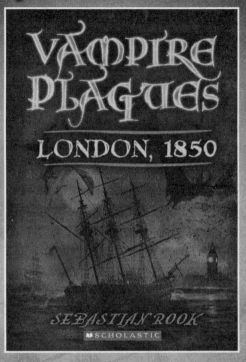

Jack Harkett thinks he is the only one who has witnessed a ghost ship sail into the harbor and release its deadly cargo: a black cloud of bats. Until he meets a boy— the ship's sole survivor—who tells Jack about the vampire plague that killed the ship's crew... and is about to attack London.

SCHOLASTIC

SCHOLASTIC and associated logos are trademarks and/or registered trademarks of Scholastic Inc.

VPT